A.E.G.I.S. TALES

A Retro Pulp Anthology

FIRST EDITION
ISBN: 979-8-9861181-8-5
Copyright © 2017 Todd Downing & Deep7 Press
All Rights Reserved Worldwide
Additional Editing by Raechelle Downing
Cover art & design by Todd Downing

Based on the *Airship Daedalus / AEGIS Tales* setting and characters by Todd Downing and published in various media by Deep7 Press. *Airship Daedalus™* and *AEGIS Tales™* are trademarks of Deep7 Press.
WWW.AIRSHIPDAEDALUS.COM

Deep7 Press is a subsidiary of Despot Media, LLC
1214 Woods Rd SE Port Orchard, WA 98366 USA
WWW.DEEP7.COM

To my fellow authors and creatives—
Thanks for coming to play in the sandbox!

The AEGISverse is a better,
more immersive setting because of it.

- Todd Downing
Spring, 2018

CONTENTS

Introduction
by Dan Heinrich
7

Where the Red Ghoul Grows
by Trish Heinrich
12

The Spirit Was Willing
by Todd Downing
45

The Pugilist
by Ron Dugdale
81

Long Live the Tsar
by Dave Clelland
115

Last Call for a Ghost
by James Stubbs
151

The Shanghai Incident
by R.L. Pace
191

Mind Mists
by Dan Heinrich
225

A Valkyrie in Repose
by Colin Fisk
259

The Veiled Lady
by Trish Heinrich
293

Ukungu
by Todd Downing
326

Introduction
by Dan Heinrich

As long as I have known Todd Downing, which is a couple of years more than a double handful by now, he has had an idea for a retro pulp adventure saga with airships and evil mystics and two-fisted heroics. He called the idea *Airship Daedalus*. It was born out of his love for old pulp stories and his belief that with a few updates, they were perfect for modern audiences.

Why did he think that? Because at its essence, pulp isn't a genre but more of a style that can be applied across genres. The core points for pulp are that the stories are "vivid, swift with no words wasted" according to master story teller Lester Dent. (And Lester Dent, as the preeminent pulp writer of the '30s, knew of which he spoke.)

Looking at how genre-savvy modern audiences have become, Todd figured he could combine genres and, as long as he kept true to pulp's key points, readers would gladly come along for the ride. So he created a world of super science, mysticism, lost civilizations and powerful artifacts. A setting where the crew of the most technologically advanced airship on the planet would have to face off against rocket-pack-wearing-proto-Nazi zombies.

He turned *Airship Daedalus* into a comic, with great artwork by Brian Beardsley. (You can still read the original comics at *www.airshipdaedalus.com*.) Action, suspense and large doses of derring-do all wrapped up in a classic four-color strip.

It was a true labor of love, so when Beardsley's school schedule and interstate move halted production of the comic (sadly before the proto-Nazi-rocket-zombies made their appearance), Todd went looking for another way to tell his story. He found many. First were the throwback radio dramas. Then came the role-playing game. Then came the novels. There is even a TV series pitch ready to go. (Not to be too shameless, but if you happen to know anyone who spends money to make television shows, Todd will absolutely take that call.)

I've been pleased to have played smaller and larger roles in all of the iterations after the comic in part because the stories are ridiculously fun, and in part because Todd is a great collaborator.

Which brings us to the cool thing about Todd Downing. Well, one cool thing. There are, in fact, many cool things about Todd. But for our purposes, we'll focus on only one. He loves collaborating. He *loves* seeing what other artists can do with his stories. He loves it almost as much as creating stories himself. So here was this artist with a desire to collaborate, and he happened to have a great big sandbox. It was time to invite other kids to come over and play. And let me tell you we had a great time, because Todd made a damn cool sandbox.

In the aftermath of the Great War, the sinister mystic Alistair Crowley accumulates power for his own diabolical ends. He creates a globe spanning group to carry out his dark desires. He calls them the *Astrum Argentum*—the Silver Star. A group of heroes sees the rising threat and moves to counter it. Using the means and know-how of founders Thomas Edison, Henry Ford, and Harvey Firestone, they form a shield to protect the innocent and call it *AEGIS*—the Allied Enterprise Group for

International Security. Like the Silver Star, AEGIS needs a world-wide presence of agents, informants, and the occasional helper. So while the *Airship Daedalus* novels follow Dorothy Starr and Jack McGraw and their adventures aboard the eponymous airship, these short stories get to explore that wider world.

Todd's challenge to us was to write 6,000-word stories using Lester Dent's master outline as a guide. (In short, start the protagonist at a disadvantage, by 1500 words in they should be in deep trouble, by 3000 words the trouble should be even worse, by 4500 it should be dire then the last 1500 words resolve it all. Authors in this volume followed it to greater and lesser degrees, so you're not reading formulaic stories.) He told us we could use settings and characters already established or create new ones but they had to fit the larger parameters of the *Daedalus* world.

The results? Well, in this volume you will travel from the bustling streets of Shanghai to the remote slopes of Mount Rainier, to the catacombs of Paris, to the underworld fight clubs of Cairo, to a land time forgot in the Congo, as well as the mean streets of New York, Chicago, San Francisco, and Los Angeles. You will meet spectral vigilantes, psychokinetic detectives, Osiris death cults, bootleggers, the bogeyman, spies, kids with nothing left to lose, ghouls, and rampaging dinosaurs. You'll see heroes battle villains over stolen blueprints, drugs, illegal hooch, the souls of the living, the secret to immortality, and the simple need to survive.

And you're going to have a blast doing it, too.

After you're done, share it with your friends and then pester Todd for more. Because I can speak for all the authors in this volume in saying we want another invitation to the sandbox.

Where the Red Ghoul Grows

by Trish Heinrich

Wanda "Wings" Jensen loved night flying. The feeling of being all alone in an ebony sky filled with stars, the air around her face, the hum of the Allison V-12 engine.

She looked down at the quaint plots of orange groves and avocado trees, and small homes on straight, new streets that characterized Riverside, California. The sight of the new farms, so neat and loved, made her a little homesick for the Midwest farm she'd grown up on. When it had come time to find a place to settle down, Hollywood would've been the most convenient, but Wings hated the noise and constant press of people. So, when a friend told her about Riverside, she flew right over and was mesmerized by its simple beauty. In a few days, she found out that one of the larger orange farms in the area was looking for a crop duster. When she showed up, the Donaldson brothers almost hadn't let her fly, but she convinced them otherwise and they hired her on the spot. It wasn't a demanding job by any means, and it still allowed her to keep her stunt flying job in Hollywood. Wings loved that she got the best of both worlds: farms and daring acts of flying.

Her stomach gave a loud, hungry gurgle and Wings wondered if she should've taken Doug Fairbanks up on his offer of dinner after all, and then shook her head. He was far too handsy with her.

"Now if Mary had been around, that would've been different," she said.

Her mind immediately wandered from the large eyes and creamy skin of Ms. Pickford to someone less polished, but no less beautiful.

"Maybe more so," she murmured, feeling a blush rise to her wind-buffeted skin as she thought of the woman she'd fly through lightning to see.

Tall and curvy, with smooth brown skin and wide brown eyes. Short, dark, wavy hair that showed a hint of red in the hot California sunshine. The curl of full lips when she smiled. A silvery laugh.

Last time Wings had seen Gloria, her square face had been patched with grease from the engine she'd been repairing, a dirty bandanna around her head. And with all that, not one of the starlets Wings knew from Hollywood could hold a candle to Gloria.

She'd shown up three months ago and somehow convinced the Donaldson brothers to hire her as the mechanic for their farm equipment and two small planes. From the moment Wings laid eyes on Gloria, she knew there had been a connection, but of what kind Wings couldn't be sure. She'd tried to feel Gloria out, see how she felt. But Gloria had been elusive as hell, and, in spite of the attention she paid to Wings, there was no clear indication of how she really felt.

Wings swallowed the ball of nerves in her throat. She was excited to see Gloria tomorrow, and not a little hopeful that maybe, just maybe this time she'd somehow find out the answer to her question.

As the small farm came into view, Wings frowned. It wasn't late, yet there were no lights on in the large house and around the barn. Two quick flashes came from the orange groves and worry gripped her empty stomach.

Gunfire.

Wings banked the one-of-a-kind Douglas XA-2 and descended for a landing, but instead of using the well worn strip just outside the orange groves, she managed a bumpy landing at the other end of the farm next to the dirt road that led to the main house. She discarded her jacket and goggles, and grabbed a nickel-finish .45 automatic from the storage compartment. Taking a quick moment to make sure she had her brothers' trusty lighter in her pocket, Wings took a deep breath and stepped out into the dark.

Usually the sound of belching and angry voices punctuated the night as the Donaldson brothers ate their dinner and smoked their pipes. But tonight there was nothing but the chirp of crickets and hoarse song of frogs. The hair on Wings' arm stood up, sweat tickled her back in spite of the cold air she'd just flown in.

Crouching low, Wings walked with silent feet around the front of her plane and looked for whoever that gunfire had been for. She had a moment of worry for Gloria and then remembered the day when the middle Donaldson brother had tried to grab Gloria's rear. The sound of his yelps as Gloria broke his nose was still fresh in her mind. Gloria could take care of herself.

After a few minutes of intent looking and listening, Wings realized no one was near the farmhouse. She walked from behind the plane, body still ready for the slightest sign of trouble. As she neared the huge, red barn where Gloria worked on the engines, Wings saw four large, metal barrels. She walked closer and stopped a few feet away. All of them were tipped over, the remnants of some kind of red liquid on the dirt. It didn't look like any fluid she'd ever seen used for an engine, and though the Donaldson brothers were grouchy, foul mouthed men, they were far from slovenly.

Wings stood up and looked around, straining for the smallest sound. She was about to inspect the dark farm house when the sharp clack of more gunfire reached her ears. In the thick darkness she could see the flash of the gun.

Her short legs were powerful and it didn't take long at full speed to reach the orange grove. The moon was half full, casting its pearly light on the tall trees set in neat rows. The tang of earth mixed with the sweetness of the blossoms on the trees, and the air was gentle against her skin. It was the perfect kind of night for a walk in the moonlight. Unless something dangerous was happening, of course.

Wings jumped as a guttural moan pierced the calm night. Her heart was hammering in her chest, and instinct told her to get the hell out of there. But that simply wouldn't do.

So she walked in the direction of the moan, sweaty palm tight around the gun she held up and ready. Another moan sounded to her right, closely followed by one straight ahead and then to the left. It wasn't like anything she'd ever heard before, and Wings thought she'd heard enough animals to know most of them. Whatever it was, it was big and in some kind of pain.

"Or very angry," she said as the moans began to have a bit of a growl to them.

The trees rustled like someone was barreling through them. A dark figure came straight at her and Wings leveled her gun-

"Gloria?" Wings said as the mechanic came into view, a gun in her hand as well. "What the hell—?"

"Run!" Gloria cried, turning behind her to shoot at another hulking shadow right on her heels.

Gloria grabbed Wings as she ran past, pulling on the sleeve of her shirt. "Run!"

If the usually calm Gloria was fleeing like the Devil himself was pursuing, that was good enough for Wings. She felt fingers graze the back of her shirt as she took off at a dead run and made the mistake of glancing back.

By the light of the moon she could clearly see the older Donaldson brother, Truman, covered in red, his eyes milky and his skin the texture of peeling leather.

Wings yelped and shot the pistol at Truman's chest. The impact sent him to the ground. Then, out of the corner of her eye, Wings could see another man, this one the middle brother Ban. He was running as fast as his paunch would let him, meaty face almost exactly like his brothers'.

This time it was Gloria who raised the gun and fired, but she missed.

"Aim for the head!" she shouted.

Wings didn't know why Gloria would want that, a head shot was the toughest of all, but she did it anyway. Her shot was low and hit

Ban in the shoulder. It stopped him for a moment, and then he was after them again as if he hadn't been hit at all.

"What the hell—?" Wings wondered again.

Kenny Donaldson appeared out of nowhere, snarling like an animal caught in trap and heading straight for Gloria.

Wings raised her gun and fired.

This time she didn't miss.

Kenny's head exploded like a rotten melon and it took every ounce of self control Wings had not to vomit right there.

A movement to her right caught Wings' eye and before she could move completely out of the way, another man ran toward her. She didn't know who the hell this one was, but he had the same red, peeling skin as the Donaldson brothers. He managed to collide with her hip, knocking her to the ground.

"Damn it!" Wings said, as the gun flew from her hand.

She rolled as the man grabbed for her and leaped to her feet. Gloria was on the steps of the farmhouse and reached down for her. Wings took her hand and jumped just as Gloria pulled with all her strength. Wings vaulted over the steps, just out of the reach of whoever the newest red man was.

Gloria pulled the door open, slamming it behind Wings. The gun cabinet was by the kitchen, and Gloria didn't hesitate to break the glass to get to the firepower.

She handed Wings two Winchester shotguns and a box of ammo, a hiss of pain escaping her lips.

"What's wrong?" Wing's asked as she looked down at Gloria's shoulder.

Where Brett's blood had splattered on the shirt, there were now holes, as if someone had burned it away. The flesh underneath looked as if it had received the same treatment and was seeping blood.

"What can do that?" Wings asked, shoving a handful of shells into her pants pocket.

"It's a long story," Gloria said, the sound of heavy boots on the porch cutting off anything else she might have said.

Gloria grabbed one of the shotguns and backed down the hall to the stairs. She crouched down under them, Wings following her lead.

"Does it have anything to do with those barrels?" Wings whispered.

"Yes," Gloria loaded her shotgun. "Look, this is going to sound crazy, but I'm an agent for a group called AEGIS. They monitor a dangerous organization called the Silver Star—"

"Wait, the Silver Star?"

"Yes, and I know about your father. It's one of the reasons I'm here. We thought the Silver Star might come after you as well. I was sent to make sure you weren't attacked and also see if the Silver Star was recruiting out here."

Wings stared at Gloria, the words making clear why Gloria had paid so much attention to her all these months.

And I thought... Just goes to show, never assume anything. Especially something like this.

"I'm sorry I didn't tell you," Gloria's large brown eyes softened. "I wanted to but...it was always safer not to."

Wings swallowed. "No I, uh, I understand. I'm just shocked, I guess."

"There's something else," Gloria said, as the front door suddenly shook. "I might be infected now with whatever did this to them."

"We have to get you to a doctor!"

"Only the doctors at the AEGIS facility in San Diego can do anything for me. But if we don't get out of here in time, you have to shoot me in the head."

Wings' mouth fell open and her heart felt as if it had stopped beating. "Are you crazy? No, I'm not doing—"

Gloria grabbed Wings' shoulders and looked her in the eye. Her face was so close, Wings could feel her breath on her face and in spite of the danger about to bust in, Wings' eyes fell, just for a moment, to Gloria's lips.

"Listen to me! Whatever this is, it's contagious by bite or blood. I have to be able to rely on you to stop it from spreading. Please? Can I rely on you?"

Wings held Gloria's gaze. "Yeah, you can count on me."

Gloria's shoulders collapsed, a quick sigh escaping.

"So are they dead or...?" Wings asked, loading the Winchester.

"Essentially, yes. But something is animating them, something...well, you wouldn't believe me if I told you."

"Try me."

Before Gloria could respond, the door broke off its hinges, the hulking, red faced figure of Ban Donaldson coming through.

"Try to get out the back," Gloria stood. "I'll cover you."

Wings grit her teeth. "I can help, you know!"

Gloria fired the Winchester, jerking back just a little, the wounds on her shoulder opening. She yelped as she fired two more times, her shots hitting Ben in the chest and arm.

Wings heard the windows in the kitchen break to her right and ran toward the kitchen door just as Truman barreled through it. He snarled, large hands grabbing onto her arm. She raised the gun to fire and something hit her from behind.

It was Gloria. She fell against the wall, the sleeve of her injured shoulder covered in blood. Immediately, Ban came into view, a vicious snarl on his face.

"Nice to see their personality hasn't changed," Wings said.

Gloria was about to fire when Ban hit the rifle out of her hand.

Wings tried to pull her rifle free from Truman's grasp but the dead man had an iron grip on the gun.

Well, he's still a man right?

She brought her knee straight up into Truman's groin. He howled, hands releasing the rifle. Wings brought the barrel up and was about to pull the trigger when Gloria shouted for her stop.

"The blood!" Gloria shouted, punching Ban across the jaw

"Damn it!"

Instead she hit Truman square in the face with butt of the rifle. It stunned him enough that Wings was able to adjust her grip and, holding the rifle like a club, hit Ban on the head. He fell to the ground with a grunt.

"Go!" Gloria ordered, grabbing her Winchester from the floor.

They ran into the kitchen and out the door, which was hanging by its hinges.

Outside they were completely exposed and Wings turned in a quick circle, her pulse hammering against her chest.

"We—we have to get inside!" Wings said.

"The barn," Gloria pointed.

They slammed the barn door behind them just as the sounds of growling moans pierced the night. The barn was used less for animals than it was for spare engine parts, farm equipment and, of course, the Donaldson brothers' home-brewed liquor, stacked in a wood pallet tower of brown bottles. Engines in various stages of repair sat in the middle of the barn, the walls lined with shelves where tools and various parts were stored. For the things that Wings could only assume were part of the illegal still the brothers operated, there were dozens of boxes piled in the farthest corners. Old ropes and rigging had been left tied to the ceiling and against the walls where they wouldn't get in the way. On sunny days the barn was open and pleasant, the wide doors open and the sunshine streaming in through the windows.

Gloria yanked on Wings' arm and pointed up at the hay loft where the brothers stored their still with extra bottles of home brew and sundry bits of equipment.

Wings shook her head, they'd be sitting ducks.

Gloria nodded more emphatically and shoved Wings toward a ladder. As she climbed, Wings could hear Gloria's labored breaths behind her, and wondered how much of that was the blood starting to kill her.

She's not gonna die! I won't allow it!

Gloria fell onto the wood planks, her eyes pinched tight and her jaw clenched to keep from screaming in pain.

"Let me see it," Wings whispered.

Gloria shifted and sat up, a quiet sob escaping her full lips as Wings pulled the blood-soaked fabric away. The first thing Wings noticed was the smell, like rotten meat. What had looked like burns before were now actual holes in Gloria's skin, as if someone had taken a spoon and dug out chunks of flesh. But that wasn't all. The skin around the wounds were becoming scaly and peeling, just like the Donaldson brothers.

"I'll be fine," Gloria whispered.

Wings looked into her warm brown eyes, so close to hers. "I'll make sure of it."

"I'm not leaving until we know they're neutralized."

"Alright, so what's the plan?"

"They'll know we came in here," Gloria pointed to the lower level. "And when they come into sight—"

Wings smiled. "We can shoot their heads off without getting their blood on us."

Gloria grinned. "Exactly."

Wings looked down into the shadows cast by the equipment, trying to see where anything flammable was so she could avoid setting the whole place on fire. That's when she saw something that made her stomach leap to her throat.

"You've got to be kidding me."

"What?" Gloria whispered.

Wings pointed to the dozen silver barrels that looked identical to the ones she'd spotted earlier, tipped over outside the barn. These were upright, but the longer she stared at them, the more Wings could swear she could see them move.

"*Mierda!*" Gloria said, moving to get a better look at the barrels. "They have someone in them. What was the Silver Star planning with this?"

"An epidemic? Maybe an army of mindless...things?"

"Maybe. But they'd need someone able to control them. And so far I don't think that's possible."

The doors of the barn shook, moans punctuating the groan of the hinges.

Wings met Gloria's eyes. They were fever bright, her face shining with sweat. Wings could tell that the smallest move of her arm must be causing Gloria immense pain. But she grit her teeth, readied a shell in the Winchester and sat up on her knees.

"If I'm gonna die," Gloria said. "I'm going out with a smoking rifle in my hands."

"You're pretty magnificent, you know," Wings said before she could stop herself.

Gloria smiled, just a little. "You're not so bad yourself."

"You got extra shells?"

"I did, but I think they're in the house."

Wings gave a handful of her meager stash to Gloria, hoping they'd have enough for the new red people that were about to hatch from the silver barrels.

They pointed the rifles in the direction of the doors as the wood began to splinter under the unusual strength of the two remaining Donaldson brothers and the random stranger that was with them.

A clatter to Wings' right made her look over in time to see a woman climb out of one of the barrels. She was covered in red, scaly skin, a familiar groaning growl coming from her lips.

"I'll take the door," Gloria said. "You cover those barrels."

Wings shifted, took aim, and fired.

The woman's head shattered, splattering blood, bone and flesh all around her. She staggered for a moment and then fell to the ground like a marionette relieved of its strings.

Wings smiled. "This might not be so bad."

"What is wrong with you?" Gloria hissed. "You don't say things like that!"

"But—"

One of the barn doors finally gave way and the Donaldson brothers came through. If they hadn't been so red from whatever had turned them, Wings would swear their faces would be flushed anyway with the fury that blazed in their dead eyes. Wings was about to shoot when the clatter of falling metal made her look to the right, where three more red people were coming out of barrels.

Wings shot one, but it was too low and hit the man in the chest, knocking him back into a woman who was crawling out of the barrel. The impact sent the woman back in and Wings couldn't help a chuckle. She lined up her next shot and this time hit the man in the head.

Wings glanced over at the barn door and saw what she assumed was Ban Donaldson's headless body lying a few feet from it. A shot rang out and the stranger fell to his knees, stopped for only a moment. Gloria tried again, this shot also missing the mark.

She's in too much pain, and we can't waste the ammo.

But before she could tell Gloria to stop, the loud *clank* of the rest of the barrels falling over as their victims climbed out distracted her. Wings swung her Winchester to take quick aim. She was able to take the heads off two red people before needing to reload.

By now all of the red people and Truman Donaldson knew where the shots were coming from. The element of surprise was lost and they were now making their way to the ladder.

"Have they gotten quicker or is it just me?" Wings said.

"It's... They...yes," Gloria said.

Gloria tried to shoot one Truman just before his foot touched the lowest rung, but her shot lodged into the barn wall instead.

"Damn it!" Gloria said, taking another shot, which hit Truman Donaldson in the shoulder, knocking him back just a little.

Standing to her feet, Wings aimed the Winchester at Truman's head. "Nothing personal, Truman."

The loud squish his exploding head made was enough to make Wings very glad she'd skipped dinner with Buster.

"I've...only got three...shells left," Gloria gasped, her breathing ragged. "And... I—I..."

Wings looked down to Gloria's wound and her stomach dropped. Scaly patches were starting to work their way over Gloria's arm and up on her collarbone. For a moment, a low moan came out of Gloria but then she shook her head to clear it.

"I don't think... I've got much time left," she said.

"Then we better hurry," Wings said, shooting a man who was climbing over Truman's body.

Gloria glanced over her shoulder at Wings. "Do you have a plan?"

Wings dug the remaining shells out of her pocket and knew she didn't have nearly enough to take out all the red people, even if she made every shell count.

And Gloria's almost useless with her shoulder... Think, Wings!

"Better... hurry!" Gloria said, shooting a woman who had started climbing the ladder.

Wings looked around to see if maybe the Donaldsons had stashed any guns up in the loft. But all she saw was some old rags, a box of rusted parts and...

"Liquor..."

Digging her brothers lucky lighter out of her pocket, Wings laughed.

"What—?"

"Here," Wings handed Gloria her loaded Winchester and the four remaining shells. "Keep them from getting out."

Gloria frowned. "Getting out?"

"You'll see. Just keep them from coming up here or getting out the door."

Gloria nodded, taking the Winchester and the ammo.

Wings hurriedly ripped up a couple of rags into six fuses and stuffed them into the bottles she opened. She looked down and saw that most of the red people had gotten to the bottom of the ladder. Taking quick stock of how the barn was laid out, Wings lit the first bottle and threw it at the bottom of the ladder.

Gloria jumped back. "What the hell—?"

The red people howled in fear and pain. The one closest to the fire collapsed and didn't move. Wings lit the next two and hurled them down, one at the door and the other in the very center of the barn.

"Wait—!" Gloria shouted.

But Wings had already lit the fourth and threw it so that the red people were completely hemmed in by the fire. Not trusting that to be enough, she lit a fifth and threw it with everything she had so that it hit the shelf and papers on the other side of the barn.

Smoke was filling the barn fast. The smell of liquor, machine oil and roasted flesh made it feel thick in Wings' nostrils. The fire was spreading below them faster than Wings would have anticipated. But what was more worrisome was the fact that the ladder had carried the fire quickly to the loft itself. Now the wood was being consumed with alarming speed.

It was then that she realized why Gloria might have wanted her to stop and why she was now rushing toward her with a look of pure murder on her face.

"Oh crap," Wings moaned.

"Are you crazy?" Gloria demanded.

Wings ran to the other end of the loft as Gloria followed her. There was no ladder on this end, just the old ropes hanging beyond the edge. She looked down and saw a window that was low enough to make falling onto the ground outside not a deadly endeavor, but high enough that they might be able to launch themselves into it from this height.

If we're lucky.

Her fingers rubbed against the lighter in her pocket.

Here's hoping my brother was right about this lighter and it really is lucky. Or this is going to hurt. A lot.

Grabbing the Winchester from Gloria, Wings reached out and tried to hook one of the ropes around the barrel of the gun. It was just out of reach. Wings let her toes hang over the edge of the loft just a little more and felt her body pitch forward as she lost her balance.

Gloria's calloused hands grabbed Wings' hips and pulled her back. They fell onto the hard wood of the loft, Gloria crying out in pain.

Wings looked around, her heart sinking. The smoke was now so thick that it was getting hard to breath, and the flames raged in garish yellow and orange all around them. In minutes, the barn would be consumed, and them with it.

"I'm...taller..." Gloria said, grabbing the Winchester.

After two tries, Gloria had one of the ropes.

"Can you hang on?" Wings asked as she grabbed on.

"I—I hope so."

Wings put her arm around Gloria's waist and, with a small running start, they sailed out of the loft and into the window across from them.

The impact was harder than Wings had anticipated, and she felt shards of glass cut into her face and arms. She fell onto the warm earth with a force that knocked the breath from her lungs.

She lay back, the sky spinning above her, the smell of flames nearby. For a moment, she couldn't move or speak. Instead she took huge, gulping breaths and tried to shove away the nausea that was creeping up her gut.

A moan to her right caused Wings to startle, expecting a red person to come barreling at her. Instead she saw Gloria, and smiled in relief as she moved.

Then Gloria groaned again.

And Wings' chest tightened.

"No," she whispered. "No."

Wings hesitated before stumbling to Gloria and turning her on her back. Gloria's jaw was clenched tight, her eyes rolling back into her skull. As Wings watched in horror, Gloria's body arched as if racked with pain, and a growl came from the back of her throat. The scaly skin was now all over her throat, chin and jaw. It had also spread over both collarbones, and Wings bet her entire chest, too.

"Gloria?" Wings soothed, brushing thick curls away from her face. "C'mon. It can't end this way."

Wings looked up, desperate for any idea of how to help Gloria when she saw her plane. It was a one seater, but she was desperate and make it work somehow. As Wings tried to calculate if they'd have enough fuel to make it to San Diego, she heard a strange shuffling sound behind her.

Looking behind her, she came face to face with the man that was in the fourth barrel with the Donaldson brothers.

He lunged for her, and Wings rolled to the side but not far enough to be safe. He grabbed for her again and Wings half stumbled, half crawled in an attempt to get some distance. It was no use. She was wounded and exhausted, and whatever this man was he had enough speed and determination to get her.

Scooting back on her butt in the dirt, tears starting to sting her blue eyes, Wings felt the dread of impending death in her gut. As the man lunged for her again, Wings' fingertips brushed against something hard and cold. It was the side arm she'd lost earlier that evening.

With one quick motion, Wings snatched it up and fired point blank into the chest of the red man, barely remembering that his blood was toxic.

The man stopped, shuffling back a few steps.

Wings stood as quickly as her shaking legs would let her, and fired again, this time at his head.

The blood splattered all around, hitting her boots with a hiss. She half fell in an attempt to get away from the corpse, hitting her head on the hard packed dirt. Nauseating waves of pain shot through her for a moment, her vision sparkly.

Once the pain had faded enough to think, Wings felt cool air on her feet and saw that holes were already showing where the blood had hit the boots. As quick as possible, Wings shucked her boots as the sound of cars coming up the dirt drive reached her ears.

"I hope those are the good guys," she said, the headlights blinding her.

Wings stood, the cuts stinging on her face and arms, her head pounding. A man and a woman jumped out of the first car before it had stopped all the way. Wings recognized the man as Gloria's father, Mr. Sanchez but the woman wasn't familiar at all. The driver was next, a man in his forties with gray wings of hair at his temples and a lean body.

"Oh my God!" Mr. Sanchez said, running to where Gloria still lay on the dirt.

"Wait!" Wings grabbed him by the arm. "You can't, not until—"

"Let me go!"

"You don't understand—"

"It's alright Miss Jensen," the driver said. "Mr. Sanchez is one of our best researchers. He'll be alright."

"But she's infected with whatever turned these people into red monsters!"

That brought everyone up short and for a moment Wings thought she saw the woman draw a sidearm.

She better not try it.

"The red dust?" Mr. Sanchez said.

"Yes," the driver said. "It appears they've found a use for it."

"The antidote may or may not work, I...I haven't really tested it yet."

"You have an antidote?" Wings asked, jerking on Mr. Sanchez's arm. "She needs one, fast! Where is it?"

Mr. Sanchez jerked his arm free and ran to Gloria, who was starting to make more growling moans.

Another vehicle came careening down the drive, this time a truck. Half a dozen men and women jumped out of the bed, rifles at the ready.

"Stand down," the driver said. "It seems that Miss Jensen and Miss Sanchez have done our work for us. Though I would like a sweep of the perimeter, just to make sure there's no one else around."

"Shoot them in the head," Wings said, wincing as her arm began to throb. "It's the only thing that'll stop them."

"You heard her. When you're finished report back here."

"And don't let the blood touch you!" Wings yelled at them.

The driver stared at Wings, the hint of a smile on his lips. "You seem very comfortable giving commands."

Wings snorted. "When I know what I'm talking about, sure."

"I assume Miss Sanchez told you about us?"

"Yeah," Wings looked at Gloria, a deep frown on her face. "Is she going to be alright?"

"I don't know, but her father is going to do everything he can to save her," he held out his hand. "I'm Dominic Granger, tactical advisor for the San Diego office. I've heard a lot about you Miss Jensen."

"I bet. Spying on me all this time."

"Surveillance. I hope you understand that all of this must be kept confidential."

"Yeah, yeah sure," Wings put her hands on her hips. "I want in."

Dominic blinked. "I'm sorry?"

"I want to be a part of this."

"If it's revenge you're after—"

"A little sure. But..." she glanced at Gloria, who was now being tended by the mysterious woman as well as Mr. Sanchez. "It's a good fight, maybe the most important one if I trust what my gut's telling me. And I'm tired of *pretending* to fight good fights, I want to actually do something. So, I want in."

Dominic studied her. "You are quite determined."

"Yes."

"And this has nothing to do with Miss Sanchez?"

Wings felt heat rise to her face that had nothing to do with the barn still blazing nearby. "She's impressive and brave. Of course she has something to do with it. But not all, no."

"Alright," he said. "I'll put in a word for you."

"We have to get her on the truck," Mr. Sanchez said. "I injected her but we won't know anything for a few hours and if it doesn't work..."

Dominic nodded. "Miss Jensen, you may accompany us and receive medical attention as soon as we arrive."

Wings nodded, grateful to finally sit down and have someone else take over.

☙

It was two weeks of paperwork, interviews and training before Wings was officially taken on as an AEGIS operative. By that time, the incident at the Donaldson farm was covered up as a fatal fire due to the improper use of a homemade still. Wings had to laugh at how mad the Donaldsons would've been about that, they always took great pride in knowing everything about everything.

Dominic's recommendation had helped push her through the process quickly, but that meant her days were filled to bursting every minute. It was just what Wings needed, a good distraction from thinking too much about Gloria, who had slipped into a coma. Every night, Wings went to the private room they'd given Gloria and read to her or talked about what was happening. The scaly skin had disappeared but in its place was pink and wrinkled patches, as if she had been burned. Wings wondered if she'd have to live with those scars.

Not that it matters, Wings said to herself as she ran a brush through her blond hair. *She's still gorgeous.*

"Miss Jensen?" Dominic knocked on her open door. "I have some good news for you. You've been cleared for your first assignment."

Wings' stomach flipped and then plummeted. She wanted this, very much. But she'd very much wanted to see Gloria wake up, to tell her...

"Thanks," she said, taking the plain envelope he held out.

"You don't seem happy."

"No, I am, I'm very excited and grateful that you pushed me through so quickly, it's just... I wanted to see if Gloria was going to make it."

Dominic grinned. "Open the envelope Miss Jensen."

She frowned at the command but did it anyway. Her blue eyes scanned the first page of the dossier and she smiled.

"Well?" Dominic said. "She's waiting for you."

Wings bolted from the room and ran to the western corner of the complex where Gloria's private room was. Without knocking, she burst in and felt tears leap to her eyes.

Gloria was sitting up, her hair braided to the side. A tray of barely touched food was sitting near the bed and a manila folder was open across her lap.

She looked up at Wings, brown eyes sparkling as she smiled.

"Hi, partner."

The Spirit Was Willing
by Todd Downing

It was New Year's Day, 1927, and the last thing Detective Sergeant Peterson expected to find at the grave site of Meredith Langston was... Meredith Langston. The recently-buried corpse lay slumped against the marble headstone, eyes shut, makeup as fresh as when they'd put her in the ground four days previous. The gown she'd been buried in was undamaged, sentimental jewelry still present and accounted for.

Two questions Sergeant Peterson had was how she'd come to be there, and why? The grave site was otherwise pristine; not an ounce of dirt had been moved. The unmolested state of the corpse seemed to indicate this was not a grave robbery. If it was a prank, it was in poor taste, but extremely well-executed. And why did the body of a noted San Francisco philanthropist decide to show up above ground the very morning her grandson—recently home from Stanford for the funeral—had disappeared from his bed?

It took Peterson the rest of the day to get the court order to exhume Meredith Langston's casket. The evening shift had just come on duty and Peterson knew it would be another all-nighter for him. He didn't know what he was expecting to find in what should have been an empty coffin, but it sure wasn't the dead body of Charles Langston, the missing college boy.

Times like these are usually when I get a phone call.

My name is Jim Holland, and if you saw me on the street, you probably wouldn't look twice. I'm the kind of guy who can disappear in a crowd. "Nondescript," as Peterson is fond of saying. Five-foot-nine, pale complected from living nocturnally, hair and eyes the color of mud, and usually a day behind on my shave. I wear the same gray suit every day, and the tie usually hangs loose. I smoke too much.

My partner, Mandy Hart, is my opposite in most every way. A tall, slim Creole gal from New Orleans with skin of deep cocoa, keen fashion sense and discerning amber eyes that can scan a person's soul and peer deep into the spirit world. In all my years of exposing frauds and charlatans, Mandy's the only true psychic I've ever encountered. And her legitimate skills have come in extremely handy.

"Happy New Year," Peterson greeted through the phone. I could already tell he wasn't too pleased with it. Then he explained the part about someone who should have been buried not being buried and someone who should be alive being buried where the first person wasn't buried, and before I'd even lit a cigarette, Mandy was standing by the office door with my coat and hat.

By the time we got to Laurel Hill, the cops had already wrapped both Langstons and packed them in an ambulance for their trip to the morgue for an autopsy. Peterson was pacing up and down in front of a row of headstones, lit cigarette wobbling in his lips as he muttered to himself.

"Nice night for a stroll through a graveyard," I greeted.

Peterson shook my hand, then Mandy's. I could tell she was already picking up a scent off the place.

"Show me the Langston grave?" she requested.

Sergeant Kenneth Peterson of the SFPD was close to six-foot-five with a chest like a bootlegger's barrel. He was impossible to miss, silhouetted against the encroaching fog—even on such a dark, moonless night. The orange falloff from his cigarette gave his face a vaguely nefarious look. He led us to a plot where several uniformed officers and cemetery workers stood around a now-dormant steam shovel. The whole place was a criss-crossed tartan of flashlight beams.

Mandy immediately wandered over to examine the coffin and the hole it had recently been liberated from.

"So let me see if I've got your story straight," I said to Peterson. "Mrs. Langston passed away... the 28th, was it?"

"The 28th. Tuesday," he confirmed.

"And the funeral was yesterday, on the 31st?"

"That's right."

"And when was Charles Langston reported missing?"

"This morning. Missing from his bed. No signs of forced entry or struggle."

"And also this morning..." I pointed at the open grave.

"Mrs. Langston was discovered next to the headstone. Six feet of earth, undisturbed." Peterson scratched his receding hairline and probably contemplated taking the vacation he never seemed to get. "We dug up her casket and found Charles Langston's body inside."

"So it's the ol' corpse switcheroo," I said, lighting my own cigarette.

"Except Chuck wasn't a corpse when he was put in the coffin," Mandy said matter-of-factly as she rejoined us away from the grave site.

"Chuck?" I asked.

"That was what he went by," she said casually.

"Actually, that's true," Peterson confirmed. "From what the family told us."

A lot of supposed "psychics" are earnest in their demeanor, needing constant validation that their statements are correct. Mandy isn't earnest. She just smiles and goes on her way, confident in her certitude.

"So what are we looking at, Holland?" Peterson squinted and the soft, orange light on his face went out as he dropped his cigarette to the ground and stepped on it.

I honestly didn't know what to say. It's not like this stuff is in the encyclopedia. We spend so much of our time debunking fake psychics and paranormal events, when the real stuff pops up, we often haven't a clue how to react.

"Well, I could take some shots with one of our special cameras, see if they pick up anything, but I'm more inclined to hear what Mandy has to say."

And boy, did Mandy have something to say.

"This is a new kind of entity I've not encountered before," she said. And that meant something, given her childhood steeped in the haunted past of New Orleans. "It has the ability to move matter through the astral plane."

Peterson shook his head. "How do you figure?"

"You've seen the result with your own eyes," she answered with a cryptic smile. "The entity feeds on the psychic energy of the victim, which is heightened at the moment of death. Add terror to the mix and you have an exponential release of such energy—it's a feast for this...thing."

I followed Peterson's lead and stomped out my cigarette on the ground. "So there's something... some kinda psychic vampire... taking living people and blinking them into graves, then removing the previous occupant, just for kicks?"

"Not for kicks," Mandy corrected, quite serious. "For food."

"I..." Peterson began, trailing off as he shook his head.

I nudged him back to the case at hand. "Sarge. This isn't your first dance. You helped us with the Noe Valley portal and solved the Jade Demon murders in Chinatown with Danny Long."

"That doesn't exactly make any of this *normal*."

"Fellas," Mandy said gently, stepping between us. "We will need to keep a wary eye on the local cemeteries in the coming days. This may not be a spirit of human origin, but it has a taste for fear, and I think we will see more of these 'displacements'."

"Okay, Mandy," I nodded. "Let's play this smart. You consult with Oscar, see if you can't figure out a way to fight it. I'll check with the coroner and make sure this is what we think it is."

"And the P.D.?" Peterson asked, rubbing his jaw.

"Keep a detail stationed at every cemetery in town. The moment a corpse shows up out of the ground, you dig up that grave, pronto. Chances are good you could save a life."

Early the next day, we called on the city coroner, who had examined both Langston corpses. Mandy had called our licensed mage consultant, Oscar Morgan, but there was no answer, so she decided to tag along with me and we could both see Morgan later.

The morgue was in the basement of an old brick building which had somehow survived the '06 quake and subsequent fire. It smelled like formaldehyde and a peculiar kind of body odor—the kind that shows up after weeks of not taking a bath. The kind one might try to mask with rose oil or fresh-cut flowers.

Doc Sawyer—his real name, I kid you not—was a short, bald man of 55 with spectacles and a bushy mustache. He had already done his examination of the two bodies, which had been shut away into two of the new refrigerated drawers where they could be kept indefinitely.

"Meredith Langston, female, age 79," Sawyer said, reading from his written reports. "Nothing different about her body, save for a few days' worth of decay."

"The body was not messed with in any other way?" I asked.

"No sir," Sawyer answered with firm assuredness before continuing. "Charles Langston, male, age 23. Definitely died of suffocation, but the condition of his hands and fingers, corresponding to the damaged interior of the casket, indicates he was alive at the time of...placement...and tried to claw his way out."

"Horrible," Mandy shuddered, and we all silently agreed.

I jotted down some notes and pointed at Sawyer's clipboard. "Was there anything else?"

"Just the residue," he said, walking to a counter and grabbing a glass vial with a cork stopper. "Found around the young man's eyes, nose and ears. It's not nasal discharge, nor any human bodily fluid."

Sawyer handed me the vial and had me sign for it. Mandy knew instantly what it was.

"Ectoplasm," she announced.

Sawyer almost rolled his eyes, but then he remembered all the weirdness that had descended upon San Francisco in the past year and corrected himself.

We thanked the good doctor and left with a vial of spirit tissue and confirmation of the entity's M.O. At the phone booth outside Edie's on Market, I spent the nickel for a call in to Peterson's precinct downtown.

Peterson wasn't in, and he'd left no message.

Another nickel bought me confirmation that Oscar Morgan was home, and would see us.

I got lost in my head as the trolley whisked us down Market to the Mission District. Mandy, too, seemed miles away. This was a different kind of case—the kind that becomes personal, whether you want it to or not. I was glad we were getting some help. Morgan was a well-traveled and "financially-secure" occultist and author, renowned for his expertise in ancient magics. He owned a Victorian townhouse a couple blocks away from the actual Spanish mission that was the neighborhood's namesake.

He met us at the door in a black and gold satin smoking jacket, hair slicked back with Murray's pomade. He was tan, his pencil-thin mustache was flawlessly trimmed, and he reeked of aftershave and exotic travel.

"James! Amanda! Do come in!" he greeted in a baritone so buttery smooth it even made *my* temperature spike.

"Oscar," Mandy replied, allowing him to kiss her hand. "It's been too long. When did you get back from Paris?" She was gracious, but clearly immune to whatever sex appeal Morgan had on display. I remember thinking that was just as well.

"Why, Amanda, I wasn't in Paris," Oscar protested. "I just returned from Shanghai on business."

"Oh, so the gentleman was a passenger on the ship?"

Now I was intrigued.

Oscar raised an eyebrow. "Why I'm sure I don't know what you—"

"I've encountered enough Parisian gentlemen in New Orleans to be able to pick up that particular scent anywhere in the world. My dear Oscar, he's all over your smoking jacket."

There was a tense silence, then Morgan cracked a wide smile. "Fair play, Amanda! You got me!" He waved us into the parlor and set out a tea service. "His name was Jacques and he was lovely. Would you like tea? I just made it. It's oolong."

We sat and drank Oscar's tea and I gave him the rundown: a corpse which should have been in the ground had been swapped with a live person who *shouldn't* have been in the ground, who had *become* a corpse. Then, I let Mandy run with the ball. She knew how to talk to Morgan. They spoke different dialects of a common language. They went on about various types of inter-dimensional entities, lobbing options back and forth like they were playing tennis. I counted the word "entity" spoken at least thirty times. They might have actually mentioned "ley lines" as well. Finally, given the M.O., they settled on an entity of non-human origin—that is to say, something that didn't originate on our plane of existence, and which had *never been* human. It wasn't a ghost or a lost soul; it was a malevolent psychic vampire with the ability to pop through dimensions as easy as hopping on the cable car.

And we all agreed it had to be stopped.

We realized we'd talked well past sunset and into the night. It was already 10 o'clock and I was famished. Morgan said he needed a bit of time to locate a certain component that he could turn into a helpful tool in our kit. We took our leave and headed back to the office—which was also our apartment—stopping for takeout at Chu's on the way.

We feasted on chow mein and Mandarin chicken and talked some more over a couple bottles of near beer. I fell asleep on the sofa, and Mandy in the armchair.

I dreamed I was searching through an enormous, empty mansion, in the dark. I knew Mandy was in danger, but everywhere I looked, I couldn't find her. I suddenly turned the corner and saw her at the end of a long hall—she was bound by tendrils of ethereal light, struggling to move, unable to cry out. I began to run toward her down the hall, keeping her in the beam of my flashlight.

And then the face appeared—vaguely human but definitely not of this world—with blurred features, skull-like, and a mouth full of dagger teeth. It popped up over her shoulder, grinning its terrible grin, and I could tell the tendrils of light belonged to the thing. It would feed on Mandy's psychic energy, and feed well. I yelled her name, running down the hall at an agonizingly slow pace. The entity grinned and leered at me, then my flashlight flickered and died.

At 5 a.m. the phone rang, sending a jolt through my body. I sat upright and grabbed the receiver from the candlestick. It was Peterson. They had another displaced corpse, and another victim. At another cemetery.

We called a cab and headed back downtown.

Calvary Cemetery lay southeast across Geary from Laurel Hill, and due east across Masonic from Ewing Field—where just last November I'd seen the Oakland Oaks football team crush my San Francisco Tigers 3-0.

Along Geary, from Arguello Boulevard to Baker Street, it was pretty much "Cemetery Central", with the Oddfellows, Masons, Calvary and Laurel Hill graveyards surrounding a multi-purpose sports arena. Hooray for the home team, but if you get slaughtered, we have you covered.

There had been a lot of talk about shutting down the graveyards within the city limits and moving the bodies out to increase the local property values, but so far the voters had said no. Even so, the new burials in the area were usually restricted to family crypts, or plots that'd been paid for years ago. The Jewish cemetery had already put a moratorium on new burials, so most of the newly deceased were sent to Colma or South City. This made the recent interments something a bit special.

It was a few minutes shy of dawn by the time our cab pulled up. A surly beat cop named Stubbs was on the lookout for us, and led us deep into the cemetery. Another crowd of uniformed officers and funeral home employees stood gabbing around another steam shovel, and we were treated to the sight of a dapper old gent in a black pinstriped suit splayed out unceremoniously next to an open hole. The casket had been dug up and lay open nearby, and the recently dead body of a young woman lay inside, staring up into eternity.

Peterson stalked toward us, orange light from his cigarette making his face into a gargoyle again. "Where you been? Sleeping?" he demanded.

"Happy to bill you overtime," I answered, unflinching. "Who are the stiffs?"

"The swell in the suit is Antonio Feri. Age 67 when he died last week."

"Why does that name ring a bell?"

"His nephew, Jerry, is a bootlegger." Peterson flashed a look that, even in the dark, I could tell was frustration at his failure to bring the entire criminal element in San Francisco to justice.

"Jerry Feri," I chuckled. "You can't write this stuff." Funny names aside, I was glad the Italian mafia hadn't infiltrated my beloved city. Yet.

Mandy was already standing over the open casket nearby. "Anita," she whispered. Her cocoa-brown fingers flitted over the corpse's face, closing the poor woman's eyes and collecting some greasy residue from inside the coffin lid. She scraped it into a glass vial much like the coroner's and stopped it with a cork, dropping it back into her handbag.

Peterson nodded, ambling over to the coffin. "Anita Scariso. Antonio's daughter. Age 35. Married to Alfredo Scariso. Also a—"

Before Peterson could finish saying "bootlegger", a well-dressed man in pinstripes, spats and a Longley bowler hat came pushing through the small crowd of police officers. He was clearly distraught and, upon seeing the woman in the casket, paced back and forth next to the open grave and shook with tears of anger and regret.

"Anita! What happened? What has happened here?"

Peterson was all business. Clapping one large hand on the man's shoulder, he offered a cigarette with the other. "Alfredo Scariso. Can you tell me where you and your wife were last evening?"

The bootlegger composed himself and finally stood still, taking the cigarette and nodding. "Anita and I had just returned from a gala luncheon at the Orpheum, but it was just champagne and hors d'oeuvres, so we decided to have an early supper in the kitchen."

"When was this?" Peterson asked, scribbling in his notebook.

"About 4:30 in the afternoon."

"When did Anita disappear?" Mandy asked quietly, eliciting a shocked look from Scariso.

"I—I'm not sure," he stammered. "No later than 5. I went to the cellar to bring up a bottle of wine, and when I arrived, she was gone. I searched the house and walked the neighborhood... I returned after an hour and took the car out in a wider search. After scouring the city, I returned home and have been waiting by the telephone since then."

I could tell Scariso was a tough guy by nature, so it was oddly endearing to see him tear up over his late wife.

"And we called you just before 5 a.m.?" Peterson noted, checking his watch.

"Yes," Scariso nodded, transforming suddenly into a mass of conflicting emotions. "How could this happen? And what are the police doing to find her killer? What are *you* doing, Sergeant?" Although he was shorter than Peterson by nearly a foot, Scariso puffed up on his toes and got within three inches of his face, cheeks dark red with fury. We could see the spittle fly.

I knew I'd regret it, but Peterson and I went way back, so I intervened. "Look, Mr. Scariso. We're dealing with a supernatural entity here. There's nothing the police—"

"You're the ghost hunters I heard about on the radio, eh?" he turned his attention on me, face red and eyes ablaze. "I got a lot of friends in this city, Mister Ghost Hunter. You find whatever did this to my Anita, maybe you get to call yourself my friend, *capiche*?" He made a show of straightening my tie just a bit too tightly, inferring what would happen should we be unsuccessful. So much for the city being mob-free.

Peterson was a statue. "Stubbs," he said in a clipped tone, "come take Mr. Scariso's detailed statement and make arrangements for the autopsy." As the surly cop approached to take care of the bereaved bootlegger, Peterson added, "Condolences, Mr. Scariso."

"Yeah, thanks," Scariso muttered as he walked away, turning back briefly to point at me. "I'll be keeping an eye on you, Mister Ghost Hunter."

"So we have a slightly better timeline to work from," I said to Peterson as Stubbs escorted Scariso away. "The wife disappeared sometime before 5 p.m. When was Mr. Feri's body found displaced?"

Peterson flipped a page in his notes and fished his pocket for another cigarette. I pulled one from my own jacket and lit both with a wooden match.

"About 3 a.m., a night watchman was making his rounds and apparently got the bejeezus scared out of him."

"So if our psychic vampire abducted Anita at about 5..."

Mandy knew where I was going and completed my thought. "The average person can survive five and a half hours inside a sealed casket."

Peterson swallowed. "And how do you know... Nah. Never mind."

"That means we're looking at a time of death before midnight," I said.

The Sergeant took a deep drag on his cigarette and looked right at me. "Time of death is only relevant in the matter of 'how fast can we dig up the grave after the corpse appears?' What's interesting to me is that the new victims are linked by blood."

"Not with each other," I argued.

"No, not with each other. With the previous occupant."

Mandy's eyes went wide. "It's using the family bloodline to find the location. Most entities we know of that shift between dimensions need to have seen or visited a location before. But it can't have seen the inside of these graves. So it's using the victim's ancestry as a map."

"Hey Mandy," I said, "my Uncle Mike is buried at Laurel Hill. I want you to know that in case I go missing."

Mandy smiled. "Your Uncle Mike has been dead for ten years. This entity needs a closer connection to point the way. Both Langston and Feri were buried within the past week."

"Yeah," I nodded. "Just the same…"

"I'll dig you up with my bare hands if I have to," she promised with a wink.

Peterson gestured at Mandy with his cigarette. "What does your, uh, *juju* tell you about this thing's limitations, if any?"

"Well, the cemeteries are close together," she began. "Where was Chuck abducted?"

Peterson consulted his notepad. "The Langston family home is in Pacific Heights. The Scarisos live in North Mission."

"Those are just a few city blocks away from each cemetery," I offered. "Maybe this thing doesn't have an unlimited range."

"It's found a convenient food source," said Mandy, making Peterson shudder. "As long as it can find new victims, it won't be letting up any time soon."

"We should get back to Oscar Morgan," I said. "See what he's come up with to help us catch this thing."

Peterson nodded. "You do that."

"Hey, Sarge," I added, "Post some uniforms around all four cemeteries and have those steam shovels ready to burn. That way we'll have a better chance of finding a displacement soon enough to save the buried victim."

"Yeah. And we'll have the precincts keep an ear on the switchboards for any missing person alerts."

Mandy touched Peterson's shoulder as we began to head back to the street. "The displacements will be recently interred, in plots purchased before the 1901 moratorium," she said. "And the victims will be adult blood relatives."

"Stop the presses," Peterson put up a hand and halted Mandy in mid-stride. "Why adult?"

A gentle look washed over Mandy's face as she explained. "Why, because this entity requires absolute terror when it feeds. And while a child might experience terror of the unknown, an adult will feel terror from *knowing* what is happening."

We left Sergeant Peterson alone in the graveyard, as a cold morning breeze blew in off the Bay. We hailed another cab and headed back to the Mission District, to Oscar Morgan's town home once again. As anticipated, he met us in that same gold smoking jacket and offered us freshly-brewed oolong tea. The man was only unstructured in his carnal proclivities; everything else, it seemed, was by-the-book. This visit, however, held a gift in store. As we were comfortably ensconced in Oscar's front nook, sipping proper tea from China, he disappeared into an office and returned with a small wooden box. Several phrases and symbols—what I figured to be arcane spells—had been burned into the wood, which was beautifully finished with walnut oil.

As he approached, Oscar gave us each a parental look of warning, before opening the box and allowing us to see the contents in the morning sunlight. Inside the box, on a bed of dark green velvet, was a curious transparent object. It resembled a stone or crystal, yet it was artificially round, as if it had been crafted, like a warped marble with a convex side and a concave side. About four inches in diameter, it drew the sunlight into it and seemed to glow on its velvet seat. Mandy reached for it, but began to swoon. Oscar closed the box and I reached over to hold Mandy upright.

"Whoa there," I said. "What's that all about, Morgan?"

Oscar grinned a broad, white grin. "It's a psychic lens," he explained. "The crystal absorbs psychic energy from the convex side, while the user remains behind the concave side."

Mandy nodded. "So we can trap the entity."

"Precisely," Oscar kept smiling. "It also allows the user to see through the lens into the astral plane."

"It's beautiful," I said. "So how do we use it?"

"I'll do it," Mandy jumped in. "I can draw the entity to me."

"Are you sure?" I hesitated. "That thing almost toppled you here at the table."

Oscar chuckled. "As long as she stays behind the concave side, it should be fine. And she's right—her psychic ability can summon the entity to her."

"Where did this come from?" I wondered aloud.

"I found it on an expedition in Arabia," he explained. "It took some time and a fair bit of training to be able to figure out its properties and how to control it. It's been sitting in my collection for the past six years. Glad it can be of some use to you and Sergeant Peterson in the meantime."

We offered Oscar Morgan some money for his psychic lens, which he refused. Then we said our goodbyes and headed home to the office.

With a belly full of roast beef on rye and a root beer or two, I passed out on the Murphy bed in the side office—shoes, hat and all. Mandy meditated, sitting quiet and still in the overstuffed armchair in the corner. The psychic lens lay on its velvet bed, box open.

I awoke to darkness. I tried to sit up but bumped my head and had to lay back down. Drawing my lighter from the inside breast pocket of my jacket, I flicked the lever, creating the small, amber flame which presently illuminated my surroundings. The silk bunting was a dead giveaway, no pun intended. I was in a casket, and when I called out, I could tell by the dull acoustics that the casket was underground. As much as I tried to maintain my cool, the truth is I've never been keen on tight spaces. I gave myself the privilege of a few punches to the lid's interior and a second shout, before deciding to conserve my air and hoping aid arrived soon. But then a face—that horrible, blurry skull—thrust itself through the casket lid above my own, glaring down on me with evil intent. I cried out in surprise, and the thing began to smile. It was more a grimace, or an approximation of a smile performed by someone with no emotional reference. The thrum of a beehive on high alert erupted within my head. The buzz became a ringing, and I became dizzy. I watched the face as it smiled its practiced smile, and the casket began to rattle and shake apart. I braced for the imminent cave-in. Then Mandy's face replaced the entity's cruel visage, and I realized I'd been dreaming.

"What's the scoop?" I asked, trying to be casual.

"You were dreaming of it, weren't you?"

"What do you mean?"

"Well, to be clear, you were out of your body. You were traveling."

I struggled to a sitting position, reached for my pack of cigarettes on the side table, and fished one out. "Yeah, so I was dreaming. So what?"

"Jimmy. Psychic energy is a two-way street. Your astral body was roaming while you slept, and that is where this spirit travels. You didn't just dream the encounter. You were there—just not in your physical body."

"Lucky me."

Mandy looked into my eyes. "It now has your scent. We're not safe. Neither of us."

"Yeah," I agreed. "So we need to end it." I rubbed my temple, head still buzzing. "Did I hear the phone?"

Mandy sighed and gave my neck a therapeutic squeeze. "It was Peterson," she said. "There's been a new displacement. Masonic Cemetery."

It wasn't until we exited onto the street that I realized how late it was. We hailed a cab and headed back to Cemetery Central. Mandy clutched the carved wooden box tightly to her.

We arrived to find six uniforms and three detectives, a steam shovel work crew and the cemetery night watchman, all standing around a corner plot. The Masonic cemetery had sat unused for twenty years, as there were no vacant plots and most Masonic families were already using the funerary facilities in Colma. Nobody had been interred in the last week, month or even year. It was just dumb luck that the watchman had discovered the skeletal remains of a George Lamont—dead since 1897—splayed out like a Halloween decoration next to his own headstone.

"This is a new activity," Mandy worried.

"Well it sure ain't the M.O. you suggested early this morning," Peterson agreed. "What's it doing dragging thirty-year-old bones out of the ground?"

"Maybe its feeding has been making it stronger, able to trace bloodlines back farther," Mandy suggested. "Or something else."

I had a hunch, but I wasn't sharing it just yet. It occurred to me that sometimes objects, and not genetics, could carry a psychic impression over a long period of time. It could be that an item which had once belonged to the displaced—a Masonic ring, perhaps—might be the ticket. If they dug up the victim and he or she was in possession of such an object, my hunch would be proved.

Mandy paced nearby, shaking her head in frustration. She even peered through the lens a few times, scanning our surroundings. Every now and again, she'd catch my eye and say, "nothing" under her breath. The steam shovel went to work, and within fifteen minutes, the casket lid was visible. A team of cops in shirt-sleeves surrounded the casket in the hole and Paterson ordered it opened.

Mandy and I stood at the top of the grave, peering down over the cops as they pried the pine lid away from the box to reveal its contents. It was empty. Mandy walked away, disgusted. "It knows."

A shudder ran down my spine as I realized the implication. "It pranked us!" I spat.

Mandy stopped in her tracks, her jaw set like stone. "It knows. It knows *us*. It knows we're onto it, and now it's strong enough..."

"To throw us a curve ball," I finished. "Just great."

Now I was mad. We had to find this thing. Find it and dispose of it. It had become a personal affront to my honor and reputation as a ghost hunter.

Peterson was already flagging one of the plainclothes detectives. "See if we can track down the family that belongs to Mr. Lamont here. Make sure there's been no abductions or disappearances. At the very least, maybe this thing's playing a game of round-robin— might've stashed a potential victim in a different grave or something."

I tapped the sergeant on his massive shoulder. "Hey, Sarge, we're gonna see if Mandy can pick up the scent. If you find a home address, leave a message for me at the precinct. I'll keep checking in."

"Alrighty," was his gruff reply. "Go to it. I've had enough of this thing, and I'm counting on you two to kick its behind back to whatever dimension it came from."

We headed out from the cemetery gate and hailed a cab. Mandy held the lens to her forehead and scanned the city with her intuition open and her eyes closed.

"Balboa," she said softly. "1625."

"1625 Balboa Street," I instructed the driver, and when I looked back at Mandy—she was gone.

The psychic lens sat undisturbed on the seat next to me. The cab door was closed. There was no way she could have fallen out without someone noticing, least of all, me.

"Driver! Stop!" I barked.

The cabbie hit the brakes and the hack screeched to a halt. I opened the back door, panicked. "Mandy!" I called out, but no reply came.

In a fit of desperation, I removed my fedora, grabbed the lens from the back seat of the cab and held it up to my forehead, clamping my eyes shut.

Nothing.

Turning slowly from west to east, I began to see impressions, shadows, like peering through an aquarium at a face on the far side. If this thing could see the spirit realm, it made sense that sweeping it along Cemetery Central would have yielded some ghosts. And boy did it ever. They mostly roamed back and forth on their hallowed ground, content to replay old conversations or messages to their loved ones. None paid any attention to me, and I continued my sweep south and east, back toward—*there!* Suddenly my mind filled with a picture so vivid it could have been a new Douglas Fairbanks movie.

I could see the lights of the city against the night sky. The view panned down and I could see Mandy's dress and new patent leather flats. It was as if I were her. Or rather, she was sending me the images and I was picking them up through the lens. I knew she was trying to give me all she could so I could get to her fast. At her feet lay a small, gold signet ring of some kind. Was that the Masonic symbol? The view tilted to the left: the silhouette of a giant bell. Then to the right: a Spanish adobe arch overlooking... Market Street? Only one location in the city with that particular view: Mission San Francisco de Asís—or "Mission Dolores", as it was commonly known. Specifically the bell tower of the new basilica.

I ducked back into the cab and slammed the door. "Mission Dolores," I ordered, "and step on it!"

The cab took off like a sprinter with a hotfoot, screaming down Geary and Arguello, down Stanyon through Golden Gate park. I kept the lens to my forehead, angled toward Mandy at all times. Occasionally the cab would have to swerve or hit the odd pothole, which disrupted my connection, and that separation filled me with a dread I'd never known. I couldn't lose her. Not now. Not like this. As we weaved down street after street toward the Mission District, I kept getting glimpses of Mandy's situation—moving from arch to arch, looking for any egress, chased from the hatch and passage by a frenetic crackle of blue-white energy. She was trapped in the belfry, her only escape from the entity a fifty-foot drop to the pavement below.

And there it was.

The spirit from my nightmares, billowing like a sheet on a clothes line, snapping savage tendrils of ectoplasm. And the face. The sneering face of evil, an impish skull grinning blade-like teeth, eye sockets empty but for two tiny, glowing sparks—just inches from her own face. I could hear its thoughts, through Mandy and the lens. It had sensed her after the first killing, and as we came closer to discovering its true nature, it had used Mandy's psychic sensitivity like a convenient cable car, hitching a ride right to her physical body. The displacement of Lamont, the old Mason, was indeed a ruse. This dimension-hopping entity saw her not as a predator, but as a competitor. Of course either one meant it must be rid of her.

Glowing ember eyes burned into her psyche. Mandy tried to look away, to keep it from maintaining psychic contact with her, all the while trying to keep me connected, and that effort was exhausting her. It wouldn't be long before simply resisting the entity would prove too much, and she would plummet to her death, and it would feed.

I tossed a five into the front seat of the cab. It screeched to a stop in front of the basilica, but I was already out and sprinting across the sidewalk and up the front steps.

The entry was locked from the inside.

I jogged to the north side of the bell tower and called up to Mandy. All I could see was a strange, flickering blue light and a buzzing sound like a playing card stuck in an electric fan—just like the sound from my nightmare. I held up the lens and could see flashes of light and that sneering, snarling face. Then it looked at me—not at Mandy, but *through* her and straight into my head.

And then I was wrapped in tendrils of blue-white spectral energy, and my ears popped as we blinked away into nothingness, and reappeared in midair at the top of the bell tower. Mandy screamed from the arch facing me as I seemed to hover weightless for a split-second. Immediately aware of what was in store for me, I tossed the lens toward her, and she caught it. Then I felt gravity take over, and the ground rushed up at me. As I began to plummet toward the pavement, I caught the quickest glimpse of Mandy holding the lens to her forehead, eyes closed in the use of her power.

I heard an unholy scream from above, and my shoulder exploded in agony as my left hand snapped out and caught the wrought iron balcony railing of the first level. The pain dimmed for a moment as shock started to kick in, then it washed over me with a vengeance.

And there I dangled, thirty feet above the street, as a small crowd began to gather on the sidewalk. I knew I could survive a ten, maybe twenty-foot fall onto cement, but survival at thirty wasn't guaranteed, especially if I impacted the wrong way—ribs could puncture lungs, skull could crack open like a coconut. It felt like I was hanging there for hours, but was probably only a couple minutes at most. The fire in my arm radiated from my neck to the tips of my fingers, and I began to lose my grip as those same fingers began to go numb.

And I let go.

The next thing I knew, I was being hauled into the alcove by Mandy and a chubby priest with glasses who said his name was Father Paul. Mandy clutched me tightly and kept repeating, "we did it."

We did it, she said. *We did it.*

My arm stopped burning and everything went numb, and I passed out hard.

When I awoke at French Hospital two days later, my left shoulder and arm were in a cast and Mandy was sitting in a chair next to the bed.

"Morning, Jimmy," she smiled.

"You okay, doll?" All I could think of was the peril I'd last seen her in, and how much she meant to me.

My concern was met with a shy smile and the wave of a hand. "I'm fine."

I tried to piece together the fragments in my head, but finally had to ask what happened.

"You threw the lens to me," Mandy explained, "and I summoned the entity. It was so intent on killing me that it didn't hesitate, and I drew it in through the front of the crystal."

She adjusted my blanket and added, "I took it to Oscar and he's locked it away for safe keeping."

That didn't surprise me at all. Of anyone in the city, Oscar Morgan was probably the most reasonable choice to make sure that thing never got loose. And as long as Sergeant Peterson didn't have to deal with it anymore, I knew he'd be okay with that. Although I wasn't sure how he'd end up reporting this case. Then again, that was Peterson's job, not mine.

I noticed a large bouquet of flowers in a crystal vase in the corner, and immediately wondered if I was in the right room. "Nice flowers," I observed.

Mandy noticed my quizzical look. "They're from that fella, Scariso," she said. "Apparently we have a new friend."

Oh good, I thought. *Now we have the attention of a Sicilian family of bootleggers.* At least the attention, for now, was favorable. I hoped it would remain that way.

I tried to sit up, but the stabbing pain in my shoulder had other ideas.

"Uh uh," Mandy scolded, arranging the blanket around my chest. "You tore your pectoral muscle, dislocated your shoulder and fractured your collarbone."

"That's quite the laundry list," I said.

"They've got you on morphine for the pain, and you'll be in the cast for six weeks. So you might as well relax until they let me take you home."

Let me take you home, I thought. I liked the sound of that.

For what it was worth, 1927 was off to a great start.

The Pugilist
by Ron Dugdale

The fighter flung the wetness from his brow with one swipe of a gigantic green-stained fist. He barely noticed it wasn't blood, but mere sweat; no matter how many blows his opponents landed, he never seemed to bleed anymore.

He grunted, standing to his full height of seven feet and shook more sweat from a head that looked as if it had come shipped in a tin can: a barrel-shaped skull covered in leathery flesh, fringed in a salt-and-pepper crew cut, and punctuated by the straight line of a mouth and a Roman nose broken more times than he could remember. Deep-set blue eyes peered out from under a thick, chiseled brow, a sharp contrast to his suntanned skin which rivaled the pigment of any native Egyptian. He wore olive corduroy trousers with a black leather belt, leaving his upper body unclothed.

His hands and feet were wrapped in a gauzy linen.

He gazed down briefly at the sawdust floor. The details of his environment blurred away at the edges—the chipped plaster walls of the less-than-strictly-legal boxing establishment, the musty stench of sweat, hookah and money, and the reddened, shouting faces of local men trying to stretch their poverty by gambling at the cockpit. He focused intently on the giant Kenyan boxer in the opposite corner. Somewhere behind him, a bell clanged twice. By instinct, his meaty, green hands came up to their defensive position, huge fingers curling into fists of stone...

Those hands.

A flash of memory returned to him. He'd been a contender for the title, once upon a time, before his last manager ripped him off after an exhibition fight in London and he ended up taking a job as the bodyguard for Lord James Stewart-Murray. A guy had to eat, after all. And, all things considered, protecting the 9th Duke of Atholl was a pretty okay gig.

John Mabry recalled the invitation sent to Lord Stewart-Murray from Howard Carter to explore the tombs uncovered in '22 in the Valley of the Kings. Only Carter's close friends and select members of the press received such a privilege.

The Kenyan slammed a fist into the big man's ribs, and the crowd cheered.

John remembered the tomb. His curiosity had casually forced him to turn down a side passage as the rest of his party continued to the main chamber. After a few minutes, he'd found a particularly attractive wall relief tucked away in an unadorned alcove. He had marveled at the carving of a beautiful woman attending an ornately-decorated sarcophagus. John leaned closer, so vexed was he by the image that he took a clumsy step on the uneven walkway. He fell forward toward the relief, but rather than being allowed to catch himself against the carving, the façade gave way completely and, with a soft grinding, the wall formed a steep ramp that deposited him into the musty darkness.

Another punch, this time a left to the gut. The mob was becoming ravenous.

John remembered lying in on a stone altar, bound and drugged. Then he remembered being awash in fear, and a voice ringing in his head like a battering ram.

SERVE OR DIE, it had demanded.

SERVE OR DIE.

The Fighter shifted his weight and remembered answering the voice with the single word: "Serve."

The Kenyan ducked away from a punch that never came, landing a right cross on the fighter's jaw. The crowd roared in anticipation.

John recalled the sensation of blood draining from his body, replaced by otherworldly power. He remembered watching as his hands began to turn an oxidized blue-green in hue.

And he remembered changing his mind.

Green fists suddenly flew like a broadside of cannon-fire. The Kenyan, surprised at first, rocked back on his heels, curling into a defensive stance. The pugilist landed a left on the Kenyan's torso, then another left, then a right. The cracking of ribs echoed through the ring.

A left cross, then two lighting-fast right jabs. The linen wraps on his hands began to stain dark red with the Kenyan's blood. The opponent staggered back, clearly straining to remain upright.

Serve or die.

The uppercut started deep within the Fighter's seemingly molten core, erupting out of his right arm, through his fist and into the Kenyan's jaw. There was a sickening *crunch* as the Kenyan's head whipped backward, his skull disconnected from his spinal column. The huge man sailed through the air to land shoulder first in the sawdust on the floor, backside up, a huge ebony rag doll.

The fighter didn't hear the irate shouts of the local men who had just lost their money; their anger and hatred were just a background hum as he turned away from the limp corpse of his former opponent. He might have heard the bell ringing again, signifying the end of the match, but it ultimately didn't matter. He'd won. John ducked between the ropes and hopped down out of the ring.

The Frenchman's name was DeBeque and he had a handful of cash waiting for John in the alcove by the exit. Mabry towered over the smaller man, grabbing the cash in one green fist. Even stained with the Kenyan's blood from his hand wraps, the money would still spend the same.

"*Sacre bleu, monsieur,*" the Frenchman remarked, lighting a Turkish cigarette, "did he even touch you?"

"He got a few good hits," Mabry answered in a deep bass.

"Even so, you're not supposed to kill them."

A few of the local gamblers decided to take their losses out on John Mabry, but the Frenchman's bodyguards stepped in and ushered them back to the bar in the corner. DeBeque nodded at them and returned his attention to Mabry.

"I have another challenger if you are interested. But you cannot fight here anymore. The odds against you are already dropping to nothing."

John flipped through the handful of bloody, wrinkled bills. "Gezira Club? Always wanted to fight there."

DeBeque stifled a surprised laugh. "You're kidding, *non?* You would never be allowed on the island, much less fight at the Gezira Sports Club. No, this is a warehouse used by the local dock workers for various 'events'."

"I'll find it."

"Tomorrow night," DeBeque reminded, as Mabry stepped into a pair of black boots, shrugged into a long gray trench coat and stalked out of the club.

When the night breeze off the Nile hit his face, John finally relaxed. He fished a cigarette out of the half pack of Helmars in his coat pocket, striking a match along the stucco wall of the building as he turned and ambled in the direction of the boarding house on Sharia Abbas, near Ismailia Canal. Inhaling smoke from the Turkish tobacco sent his mind wandering back, as it so often did on nights like this, and he added more vignettes to the mental scrapbook of who John Mabry was.

He remembered being a young man, working as a stevedore on the docks in San Francisco, moonlighting as an amateur prizefighter for drinks and the occasional trip to the red light district. By the time the war came along, he'd gone legit—with a manager and everything—and was starting to make a name for himself in professional boxing.

Unfortunately, the managers always got greedy, and John had been ripped off by a string of them. John's fights became fewer and farther between. The money disappeared and so did the women, and soon he was just another former somebody. Then Lord Stewart-Murray came along.

John Mabry liked being a rich man's hired muscle. The hours weren't so good, but the money was much steadier, and he didn't have to do much actual fighting. He just scowled and most adversaries backed down.

Two locals reeking of hashish stumbled from the club and immediately noticed the huge man striding away into the night. They began hurling insults in Arabic and John ignored them, pulling his trench coat a bit tighter around his chest as he continued on his way. The men were intoxicated and definitely angry. Probably lost money on the fight, John presumed.

They followed him for six long blocks, down Sharia El Madabegh, before John finally turned to face them.

"Look," he warned in his gravel pit voice, flicking his cigarette butt on the ground and stepping on it, "I don't want no trouble. I'm just trying to get home and get some sleep. *Comprende?*"

The hash heads glanced at each other and shrugged, and a third man emerged from the shadows of the alley. John suddenly felt the sharp point of a stiletto pressing into his kidney. Another hand rifled through his coat pockets.

John sighed. "Come on, fellas. Is it really worth all this trouble for a few pound notes?"

The man with the knife to his back continued to go through his pockets, finding the wad of bills John had earned at the fights. Mabry frowned. The language barrier was one thing, but he didn't figure they'd be talked out of their score even if he did speak the language. And that money was his—he'd earned it. A huge green hand clamped around the smaller man's arm and he immediately dropped the cash. John hauled the surprised man around in front of him with the other two. The cutpurse just stared for a moment, shocked at the enormity and brute strength on display. Then he remembered the stiletto in his hand and instinctively slashed with the light blade, opening a deep cut on John's left cheek.

John gazed down at the knife while searching his face for the damage. The wound ran from the corner of his mouth almost to his left earlobe. "Aww hell."

Maintaining his grip on the man's arm, John hoisted him up into the air, flinging him into the alley whence he came. He felt a *pop* as he let the man go, indicating a dislocated shoulder at the least. The other two men paused for a moment, reexamining their life choices. Then they fled into the night.

A thin film of mucous streaked with blood oozed down his cheek, but no further bleeding would occur. He bent down, picked up his winnings and the dropped knife, quietly folded the blade into its handle and dropped it into his left pants pocket.

Nice knife, he thought. *Think I'll keep it.*

ଔ

John got back to his flop and paused before going in. He pulled out the tattered note his manager, Thomas Worthington, Lord Stewart-Murray's traveling secretary, had left for him at the Mena House hotel on the main strip. According to the manager, John had been missing for nearly a month, and, after two weeks of waiting and searching, Stewart-Murray had taken leave of Cairo. He'd left

Mabry a ticket back to London at the hotel purser's office, but Mabry needed traveling money and the Frenchman's off-the-books fight club was his quickest option.

He dropped the note in the gutter and walked into the boarding house. The owner gave him a curt 24-hour notice to vacate the room as he walked past the desk.

Fine. He couldn't afford to stay here any longer. It was time to go. Tomorrow, anyway. Right now, he just needed a belt of whiskey and some shut-eye.

Mabry trudged up the makeshift flop house's creaking central staircase to the third floor. He paused for a moment in front of the long mirror at the end of the hall. John had always prided himself in his physique as a prizefighter. Now it was as if every physical attribute had been amplified. His chest was truly barrel-shaped with more muscles than any strongman he had ever seen. His arms and legs were huge knots of twisted anchor cable more at home on the bow of a destroyer than wound around a man's limbs. His jaw was square and solid, like a stack of bricks hidden under sun-baked burlap. Blue eyes stared back at him, the only part of him that he truly recognized.

He ran a huge, shovel sized hand through short hair, and tipped his head toward the flickering gaslight. The cut he had received earlier had all but disappeared. Only weathered sandstone skin remained, stained with red. He stared for a moment longer at his hands. His hands were tinged in green, like aged copper. He rubbed them together, trying his best to scrape off the unnatural hue but nothing changed. He let out a deep sigh, then stuffed his hands back into his over-sized trench coat to find his key as he headed down the hallway to his room. Exhaustion was creeping in, and all he could think of was bed and sleep.

It was moderately-sized apartment—which an establishment of this grade would call a "suite"—with a double bed and a couch on the facing wall. There was a warm breeze blowing in off the alley behind the hotel. Soft street sounds echoed into the room mixed with the scent of cinnamon and freshly-ground *dukkah* coming from the cafe down the block.

Funny. He didn't remember leaving his balcony doors open.

Out of the blackness to his left shot a club aimed for the back of his head. It made a hollow thump as it hit him squarely, then splintered in two as if impacting a cement post. John came around with a blind left that sent his attacker flying back through the open door to the third floor landing. The robed man landed in a crumpled heap in the hallway, knocked senseless by the almost casual slap.

Before John could turn around, two more men came out of the shadows. One held a cudgel similar to the first assailant's, while the other had decided a long-bladed knife would do better to persuade John to relent.

The American was in no mood to relent. He came in low, his stance automatically setting up the for the next attack. The fighter parried the club with his huge left forearm. The wood slid down his massive limb without leaving a mark, his skin the texture of sandpaper and as hard as the tree the club had been carved from.

The knife found its target though, and pushed deep into Mabry's left side just below his ribs. The knife man smiled wickedly, twisting the blade as he pressed up close.

Mabry should have felt something. He should have felt the knife pierce his skin and enter his guts as his blood spilled over the ancient hardwood floor and worn rug upon which he stood. He should have doubled over in pain and shock.

He should have died.

But he didn't.

He barely felt anything. The wound held the knife like a butcher's block, his blood resisting the effort of physics and biology to drain from his body. He grabbed the knife man, picking him up by the back of his neck like he were a puppy in need of correction from a disappointed master. Both he and the knife man looked down at the blade as it remained stuck in the hulking boxer's side.

The fighter smiled.

He threw the knife man out the door, landing him on top of the first assailant who was just getting up from the floor to rejoin the fray. They crashed together and lay motionless.

The club man stepped back, mumbling something incoherent and arcane as he dropped the cudgel and fumbled through his robe for something. He pulled out a medallion, palm sized and made of gold. It glittered in the bright moonlight that poured in from the open balcony, illuminating the room in stark blacks and whites. John turned to the man, his green stained right fist cocked and ready to knock him into the hallway with the rest of the trash.

"Serve!" The smaller man pushed the intricately carved circle into Mabry's face.

The boxer stopped dead in his tracks. He glanced down at the floor of his room. Faintly glowing symbols had been drawn on the worn wood. They began to pulse and surge with a green light as the robed man continued to chant his high pitched, strangely familiar words. This wasn't the Arabic of modern

Cairo. These were ancient words of power, uttered in the very tongue of the earliest pharaohs.

He could feel his strength slip away like water draining from a punctured bota bag. He stumbled backward, his legs weakening, buckling under him. He felt like he had just gone fifteen rounds with Dempsey. His vision blurred as he stumbled toward the moonlit night outside.

Mabry grabbed for the edge of the balcony doorway but he was too weak. He stumbled, then tumbled forward, over the iron railing, arms and legs flailing.

He fell, and fell, and fell...

◌

Falling.

Ancient, desiccated sandstone slid past John at an angle too steep for him to arrest his descent. He tumbled down, down into the darkness, until, finally, he came to rest at the bottom of the chute. Voices, guttering torchlight and the smell of pitch and incense led him to the only exit. John crawled to the opening, and was immediately grabbed by multiple hands. Scraped and bruised, Mabry was pulled from his hole into the middle of a larger room. Men and women dressed in robes of white stood in a circle around a hulking form lying on a stone altar. Looming above them stood a colossal statue wrapped in ivory and gold, its green, jeweled eyes sparkling in the guttering torchlight.

Too dazed to fight the multitude, his arms and legs were bound with coarse cloth wrappings. He cried out, but something was stuffed in his mouth—honeysuckle sweet and bitter at the back of his throat. He felt lightheaded as his muscles relaxed and he ceased struggling. The multitude of hands lifted him high into the stifling air for a few moments before he felt the cool flatness of stone beneath him.

Only moments earlier he had been part of Professor Carter's tour.

Now, he lay helpless, bound and drugged.

☙

John fell nearly three stories to the alley below. He'd lost consciousness for a few moments—long enough for his assailants to load him into the back of the canvas-covered bed of an old Peugeot delivery truck.

The truck bounced and clattered through the back streets of Cairo, its horn blaring at a merchant's cart which had the nerve to cross its path. They were driving fast, forcing the lazy, late night traffic to match pace.

"He's not bleeding. No broken bones. Marvelous! We must hurry before he comes around." The small man's voice nearly sang as he surveyed Mabry's form in the poorly lit darkness of the truck bed. He had not meant for their quarry to fall, but it had saved them all the trouble of carrying the huge American out of the boarding house.

"The High Priestess will be pleased. Very pleased." The man smiled and pulled a cloth and a jar from a bag. He smeared some paste from the jar onto the rag and began to stuff it into John's mouth. Once again, Mabry tasted the bitter sweetness as his muscles softened and his mind began to float away.

Without notice, the truck's worn out brakes screeched and clawed to bring it to a halt. Automatic gunfire erupted from the shadows, round after round piercing the truck's hood before it walked up through the windshield, killing both driver and passenger. The battered truck rolled to stop just as two more machine guns opened up on the left. The guns were aiming high on purpose—wood splintered and canvas tore, causing the two men at the rear to duck low while the cultist dove for the front of the truck bed as he fumbled for his pistol.

Before the suppressing fire came to its deafening end, the rear flap of canvas parted just enough to allow two matching Mauser C-96 automatics to do their work. The knife man and his partner died without firing a shot. The cultist raised his barely functioning Webley in time receive two matching bullet holes to the head from the Mauser twins.

The man climbed into the back of the truck and looked down at Mabry. He was dressed in a black, tailored uniform complete with riding boots and cap adorned with a bright, four-pointed Star. He had already holstered one of the Mausers, the other carefully covering the huge man who lay on the floor. His pencil thin mustache twitched with disgust as he pushed aside the body of the knife man so that he could have the dead man's seat and contemplate his prize.

"So, this is the parcel I was to acquire. Excellent! Now, be a good chap and don't resist. I would hate have to deliver you in less-than-living condition."

◌

John was an unwilling participant in his own demise. He felt lethargic, heavy and unable to lift himself off the stone alter he had been deposited on. At some point they had cut his wrists, small, shallow wounds meant to leak away his life's essence, not drain him too quickly. Warm blood trickled slowly from him, pooled around his hands, then ran into bowls of jade carved with symbols unknown. Hands pried open his mouth and poured a strange, copper-tasting mixture down his throat. Fire and pain mixed in him as he swallowed. This went on for hours, then days—that was John's perception, anyway. He hovered on the edge of death as unknown voices chanted in a language both known and unknown. More drugs, more blood, more pain and, always, the chant, pressing upon his mind like fists to the side of his head.

"SERVE OR DIE." The words slowly emerged from the dark, unceasing voices that smothered him without end. It was all he heard, all he could understand as his life ebbed toward nothingness.

"SERVE OR DIE."

Slowly, like climbing a from the bottom of a long forgotten well, John began to become aware of himself and his surroundings. The walls were covered in hieroglyphs, carvings and images of the gods of Egypt. Slowly the story came to him like a dream; the death of a king at the hands of his own brother, his body dismembered and scattered, then, brought back together by his loving wife and queen. Finally, he saw the end—his end—as a warden, a guard that watched over the king as he ruled for all eternity.

"SERVE OR DIE."

The priestess looked down at John as she raised a jade chalice to the great statue he'd barely noticed before now. The statue looked familiar. He has seen it at the Egyptian Antiquities Museum days earlier with Lord Stewart-Murray. "Osiris..." The name leaked out of his lungs in a horse whisper.

"Yes, Osiris!" The priestess looked down on him and a smile spread across her shadowed face. She renewed her chanting, her speech remaining unknown to him but for the three words that now pressed on him like the weight of the Great Pyramid itself.

"SERVE OR DIE."

John's eyes focused for a moment, gaining clarity. The priestess noticed the change, and spoke to him in English.

"Will you serve my god on this side of the river, protecting him against all who would attempt to breach the Underworld? Or will you die, and forever be bound to the West, the land of the dead. It is your choice..." The woman looked down at him, the chalice poised to punctuate his final answer.

"SERVE OR DIE."

"Serve." It was all he could say. He was tired of fighting the pain, the constant pressure in his head. This was the end, the end of him and the pain and constant pressure that pushed at his mind and body. He relaxed and let the momentary respite wash over him.

The priestess smiled. With a final look to her god, she began to pour the liquid, first onto each of John's hands, then into his mouth. John could feel his life, his will, slipping away. His skin began to dry out, taking on the coarseness of the very sandstone walls that trapped him. His hands and wrists soaked up the potion the priestess poured on them, taking on a pale green tint. Each drop of the liquid felt like a punch to the face. He felt like he was sinking into the stone altar, or rather the stone was being drawn up into him, eating away at his flesh until only stone remained. Like sinking in a pit of blood-black quicksand, John let the liquid wash over him as the pain was replaced with a mindless nothingness; the blackness of eternal servitude to a foreign god.

NO

NO

NO

I will NOT. I am John Mabry! I will not serve. I will not SERVE! No no NO!!!!

With a flurry of motion unexpected by any-one in the crypt, John sat bolt upright. Sand-soaked wrappings layered with partially-dried tar cracked, and priests at his hands suddenly began to gasp and shake. John had each of them by their throats, his dripping hands spasming with mindless anger. He could feel the strength in his body spike as their necks snapped. With a dull thud, he dropped the two bodies on the floor, then swung his legs around as he jumped off the altar. A back-handed swing crushed the chest of one priest as he pushed another into the far wall with such violence the man's head cracked like an egg. Over his shoulder, he heard the priestess scream and then pull out an amulet.

Strange words searched for him and for a moment, they found him.

"Take your place Guardian! SER—!" The last sound, the sound that would have com-pleted that word, drowned in a deep, gurgling sigh as John's hand found her mouth and ripped the lower jaw from her face. Her eyes rolled back in her head as she collapsed dead in his arms.

John felt nothing. He stumbled blindly, unthinkingly through a maze of passageways, lost in an Egyptian underworld made for dead kings. He didn't know what he'd become—had no clue as to the transformation he'd undergone. A transformation halted prematurely, but executed enough to have made him into something...not fully human. The Cult of Osiris had tried to transform him into an eternal guardian, a servitor for the God of the Dead. Yet he wasn't fully under their sway. Not yet, anyway. He had to get away. Run. Voices followed him. Torches and flashlights searched for him. Echoes chased him from dead end to staircase to burial chamber until finally, he found a shaft the released the faintest of breezes. His animal brain smelled fresh air. He began to climb.

Finally, John Mabry, pugilist, bodyguard, and most recently Guardian of Osiris, found a passageway back to the Land of the Living.

☙

A multitude of hands hauled John out of the back of the truck as he slowly came to. The night air felt cool on his coarse skin, and the sudden change seemed to jar him out of his stupor. He tried to catch his balance and began to stumble, but resisted the direction of the multitude.

"*Effendi*, he is coming around." One of his captors tied a stout piece of rope around his right wrist, hauling on it as another man pulled his left arm behind him.

"Hold him still. Nothing personal, old chap, but we can't have you thrashing about—at least not yet." The man in the black uniform tapped a large syringe with a gloved forefinger as he pressed the air out of the hypo. He jammed the needle into the side of John's neck, but, rather than watching the needle pierce the man's skin, the needle bent, then broke off.

"Not a good idea, pal." Mabry shook off his handlers with unnatural ease and stood on unsure legs. Multiple guns came to bear, bolts pulled back and bullets chambered, but no one fired. They circled him on all sides, a dozen or more men, locals mostly. Then the man with the needle dropped the broken implement to the ground and raised his hands in mock supplication.

"Mr. Mabry. I apologize, where are my manners? Captain William Tallridge. I represent a very important person who very much wishes to meet you. No need to make this any more difficult than it already is...." The tall man pulled out a strangely-shaped pistol from a hidden pocket in his long coat. It was made of a shiny bluish material with translucent coils that encircled the back portion of the barrel.

Without warning, a small contingent of armed men came marching noisily around the corner of the shadowed alley. Four of the uniformed men knelt while the remaining five stood behind, rifles raised.

"Everyone, put down your weapons—you are all under arrest!" This voice rose above the sound of bolts being pulled back.

The officer stepped into the moon-silvered light while the rifle squad's guns were trained on the big American and his current minders. He was young, his British Army uniform worn and dusty, but his attitude was strong and cocksure. His men were locals, dressed in white suits and black fezzes, armed with the ubiquitous Enfield rifle. Lieutenant George Somerset pointed an old Webley service revolver at John and waved the rest away, as if the throng standing before him were a mere nuisance.

"I have a warrant to detain and question Mr. John Quincy Mabry concerning the death of Duke James Stewart-Murray, Duke of Atholl. You will come with me, if you please...." Two of Lt. Somerset's men stepped up, one holding a pair of bright silver handcuffs. John, for life of him, could not fathom what he had done to attract so much attention, but he certainly didn't want to go along with either Tallridge or the young army officer.

Tension filled the air between the two factions. Rifles and pistols, clubs and knives all began to level off in the hands of the opposing armies in miniature, as each sized up the other, waiting for the first shot to signal the start of the war. Rage and sweat soaked the street in tension, and John stood at the center of it all. He wasn't much of a sweet talker, opting for a swift right hook rather than a cutting comment.

Moving faster than a man his size had any right to, John shifted to his left and grabbed the rifle that been poking him in the small of his back. When the man decided to fight John for the weapon, the huge fighter simply lifted the man and his gun into the air and tossed him into the middle of his mates, like a kid tossing aside a bag of half-eaten peanuts. His momentum continued to the left, and he elbowed the soldier holding the handcuffs in the side of the head. The shocked militiaman crumpled to the ground, his head lolling atop his shoulders like an egg rolling on his mother's kitchen counter.

"Don't fire, we need him alive!" Captain Tallridge ordered his men, stopping most of their trigger fingers from closing. A few did fire, their nerves already thread-thin. No one was hit, but the starting bell had been rung. Saps and daggers were pulled from sheath and holster on one side, while on the other, well-drilled soldiers brought up their rifles to firing position, as their officer stood stock-s-traight with pistol raised.

"Aim to wound, lads. Steady. *Fire!*" A fusillade issued from the hastily configured firing squad. A hive of angry metal bees skipped and stung through the throng, taking down a few of Tallridge's men, which only enraged and encouraged the rest. Tallridge's unruly mercenaries charged the line of fire, eyes wild, mouths frothing in zealous anger and bloodlust. Club and dagger met rifle and bayonet as the forces clashed. Somerset's men were well-trained and stood their ground, but the ferocity of the charge broke their line and carnage ensued.

The melee spread to encompass the entire street. Somerset put down one, then another foe with his Webley before he was overrun and taken to the ground by a trio of robed attackers.

For a moment, John and Captain Tallridge were left standing, looking at each other in disbelief as the melee momentarily passed them by. Tallridge was the first react.

"If you want something done..." Tallridge muttered to himself as he leveled his odd-looking pistol at Mabry and fired. Consecutive circles of force issued from the alien weapon. The energy of the blast hit John square in the chest. He felt sick to his stomach as nausea and blackness threatened to overwhelm him. The huge man went down to one knee, holding his head in both hands as if he were trying to keep it from falling off his shoulders. A moment later, the darkness subsided and he returned to his feet.

John shook his head to clear away the cobwebs. He looked at Tallridge and smiled. "That all you got, pal?"

The fighter stalked his opponent as if he were coming out of his corner after the bell. Pale green fists came up and feet squared as he circled the backpedaling Tallridge. The black-clad man fumbled at a knob at the top rear of the pistol, but he couldn't seem to get the control to reset.

So focused was John on closing with his prey that he failed to see one of the Captain's men come around and slash at him—with a sword of all things! The man was good. His blade spun and circled in a display of skill and control that John both admired and feared.

Gleaming silver slivers of death cut the air all around John as he faded and juked, giving the swordsman his most difficult target. The first blow deflected off his right shoulder but the follow-up cut a sandy red gash into his back from hip to shoulder blade.

The pugilist barely felt the wound. Blood oozed from the slash but did little to slow down the boxer's retaliation. He wheeled on his attacker, and with one punch caved in the man's chest like a stone through a wicker basket. Breastbone and ribs curved inward, and John could almost feel the man's spine as he pulled back his fist. He looked at his green paw for a second—slaked with crimson—as the swordsman slumped lifeless to the ground. The fighter's blood was up now and he turned on Tallridge with a fury he had never known.

Tallridge saw what had happened to his man. His teeth clenched as he finally got his pistol set and brought it back in line with his quarry.

Bugger this. Captain William Tallridge was not about to be killed by a monster, a beast, a mistake such as Mabry. He was too dangerous to be transported—it was clear he needed to be put down. The pistol had a disintegration setting and he wasn't afraid to use it.

He fired again. This time the gun whined, its crystal glowing a reddish-black before it released a beam of energy focused at the hulking man coming toward him. The blackened energy bolt hit John in upper-left chest. Alien power punched a gaping hole into his body, and the impact spun the giant man around and down to his knees. Pain, darkness, and a growing emptiness filled John's mind as his heart struggled to keep him alive. Trauma and shock overwhelmed him as he looked at the open, blackened wound.

He had been shot before, but nothing in his entire life compared to this. His left arm hung useless at his side, the destructive power of the weapon's disintegration ray cascading damage to his sundered shoulder and nearly severed limb. Blood flowed like a crimson river from the wound, coating his entire left side as his life poured out of him. His breathing slowed. A deep rattled sigh escaped from his lungs as his head slumped and came to rest on his bleeding and blackened chest.

Tallridge walked around to face his prize, triumphant. One more trophy for his wall. He had hunted many monsters in the bush of Africa, even America, but this brute was among the most dangerous, most primordial beasts he had ever bagged. He would not mount the man's head on the wall, of course, but he would always remember this day. Yes, he would have to answer for his failure to bring John in alive, but at least they would have a body to probe and cut and study. He used the blackened barrel of his raygun to tip John's head up so he could look into his eyes as he breathed his final breath.

What he saw would be something Captain William Tallridge would never forget.

Green fire burned behind the monster's eyes. Death had not taken him. His breath came back heavy and sharp. Tallridge could see the wound had already begun to soften and turn from blackened, dead flesh to brown, sandstone skin. The brute's smile came back wickedly as his huge, powder-green right hand reached up, engulfing both the pistol and Tallridge's hand.

Bones and plastic and crystal popped and cracked and fractured. John stood, twisting and squeezing, as he regained his full seven-foot height.

The smaller man's face had gone white with surprise, then anger, then unendurable pain as his bones snapped like dry twigs. Tallridge's eyes went wide, then rolled back into his skull. John continued to turn his hand over until the Captain's elbow simply parted ways with the rest of his arm. Blood erupted from the stump as John took a step back and dropped the offending limb to the ground. It slid from the Captain's black sleeve and landed on the dirty street with a soft, wet sound, like a leftover T-bone being scraped from a plate to land on the ground below for the family pet to devour.

Now, it was Tallridge's turn to slump to his knees. He clutched his sundered stump against his chest as blood pumped out invisibly into his black uniform. The captain howled in unknown agony. He looked at his empty sleeve as shock overcame him. Darkness crept in, the edges of his vision turning to black, as he looked up at the inhuman thing that stood half-dead before him. Tallridge wasn't afraid to die, and raised his head, ready for the killing blow that was surely to come.

It never came.

In the moments the Silver Star officer had spent contemplating his own mortality, John Mabry had simply walked away.

☙

The tramp freighter *Kali* labored even in a following sea. John found an idol of Shiva on every deck and wondered if this was what kept this creaking, wallowing tub on top of the water. The old diesel had been belching black smoke into the cloudless sky for nearly a week as they'd traversed the Red Sea and made a hard hook around the Arabian peninsula, and he could feel the crew's eagerness to make the last sprint for Bombay and home. Most of them spoke English, yet few had the courage to talk to the strange American with green hands. Only Captain Rajiv was unimpressed by his size or his oddly-stained mitts. He did seem to appreciate a man over seven feet tall, who could load a pallet into his hold faster than five of his own men. They were shipping machine parts back to India, and John was more efficient than any block and tackle rig.

John had decided going back to England, even the USA, would not be safe. He had no idea what had happened to Lord Murray. Murder? Worthington's message hadn't mentioned anything about that, and John had never bothered to pick up a newspaper while in Cairo. He had no intention of spending any amount of time in a foreign prison. Then there was Tallridge. He didn't recognize the uniform, but the emblem on his cap meant something and might be a clue to what the man wanted with him. Not to mention what the strange ritual had changed him into. No, he had to find a new path, a path that no one would expect him to walk. He had so many questions and he needed time to figure things out, hence his job as a laborer on a tramp freighter heading for India.

After eight days at sea, he was surprised when the Captain invited him to dine in his cabin.

The food was simple but much better than the fare he had suffered in the crew galley. Rice and curry had worn out its welcome days ago, and John had reduced his menu to flatbread and water. Captain Rajiv was, surprisingly, a great host, ending the meal with a fine cigar and a glass of even finer brandy. They talked for a while about the sea, the ship, and finally, John felt himself open up. He left most of the details vague, but, when he mentioned Tallridge and the star emblem on his cap, Rajiv stopped and looked at John with renewed concern.

"That is the insignia of the Silver Star. It is an organization that you are lucky to be free of. I can see now why they would be interested in a man such as you." He paused for a moment, then walked back over to his small desk, scribbling something on a small card.

"When we put into Bombay, may I suggest you go see a friend of mine? I think he will be able to help you. Your life has become complicated, John Mabry, and perhaps this will set you on a path to the answers you seek."

John took the card as he let Rajiv's words sink in. His life had certainly "become complicated". From an ex-heavyweight contender to a bodyguard for a duke to a fugitive from the law and who knows what else. He read—in a fine flourish of ink—the name of a Mr. Ravi Sachdeva of the Indian National Congress, and one word that would forever change John Mabry's life:

AEGIS

Long Live the Tsar
by Dave Clelland

Popov House, July 17, 1917

"What? What?"

Gunshots filled the room as Alexei Tsarevich Romanov looked around in panic. His father crumpled to the floor as his mother slumped in her chair. Two of his sisters scrambled into a corner screaming while the other two fell to the floor, their lifeless eyes staring up at him. Two thuds hit his chest and stomach, but the jewels sewn into his underleggings and undershirt kept the bullets at bay.

"Stop shooting, you fools!" One of the soldiers barked. "Bayonets."

The two girls screamed again as the soldiers advanced. Alexei watched in horror, still glued to his chair. His father had been the one to carry him in, so even if his shock-filled brain had registered to run, his legs were in no state to do so. The blades could not penetrate the girls' clothing, the jewels embedded into their undergarments protecting them.

Where had Leonid gone? His playmate had been sleeping with him until they were rudely awakened by the soldiers and separated. The family had been gathered and marched into the small room, being told they were moved because of an approaching army. When they'd arrived, two chairs were provided for him and his mother to sit.

Then, instead of instructions for their next move, Yurovsky read an execution order and the guards opened fire. Alexei shook in terror, helpless to fight or flee. Yurovsky stepped forward, towering over him, and pulled out his revolver. Four shots sounded behind him, and the screams of his sisters ceased.

"Feign death, Alexei." The soldier muttered, raising the gun to his head.

The terrified boy nodded, and Yurovsky pulled the trigger twice. He held his breath as he slumped forward like his mother had done next to him. He sat with his eyes closed as he heard the soldiers filing from the room.

"Retrieve a cart. We must dispose of the bodies as quickly as possible." Yurovsky shouted.

"*Da,*" one of the soldiers slurred. He passed by Alexei, and the boy stifled a gag on the rancid smell of garlic and stale vodka.

Once the soldiers had left the room, Yurvosky pulled him up. "There is no time. I must strip you from your clothes." Another horror, being pulled from his clothing, including the jeweled undergarments, and sitting naked in the cold room.

Two raps followed by a single knock sounded from the door, and Yurovsky hurried to open it. "Bring him in."

"Leonid," Alexei gasped as another soldier carried in the boy. His friend was dead, two bullets to the head. The room was full of the corpses of his entire family, but seeing his young friend murdered made the anger swell in him.

"Silence," hissed Yurovsky. "Your friend died for you. Don't make it in vain."

The soldier hauled the body to the floor in front of Alexei and dressed it in his clothes. Once finished, the man stood and stared at Alexei.

"The Great War is over for Russia, but while you live, the Bolsheviks cannot succeed in their revolution." Yurovsky nodded at Alexei as he addressed the soldier. "Wrap the Tsar in your cloak and get him to the safe house. Quickly Sergei, there is no time. Those drunken idiots will be back any second."

A heavy cloak enveloped Alexei, and the soldier Sergei hefted him onto his shoulder. "Don't move or speak, Tsar Alexei. Let them think I'm carrying one of the corpses."

Alexei's mind whirred as he tried to take in all that had happened to him and those he loved. How could an injured thirteen-year-old, who was a threat to Lenin and his revolution, possibly be useful to his family's executioner?

Sergei carried Alexei for a long way covered in the cloak. He did his best not to shiver in the cold dead of night. He couldn't see where they were going, and his terror grew with each minute.

Finally, the soldier came to a halt, and Alexei heard knocking on wood. Hinges creaked, and a woman's gruff voice burst into the night. "About time, Sergei. Do you have him?"

Sergei's hand patted Alexei's back. "*Da.*"

"Then get inside, you fool."

The strong man moved again, and Alexei was enveloped in warmth. Sergei hefted him from the sturdy shoulder and let the cloak fall away from his face. Finally able to see again, Alexei took in his surroundings and saviors.

Sergei was dressed in a Bolshevik uniform. His long beard reminded Alexei of Rasputin, the now dead mystic his mother had insisted he see. Unlike Rasputin, Sergei's eyes were remarkably clear, blue, and his face had a kind look about it.

The other person hovering behind the soldier was a plump, peasant woman with a round face, cheeks and nose red from too much vodka, and beady eyes that surveyed him with a piercing stare.

"Now what?" she squawked.

"We wait for Yuri."

Alexei finally found his voice. "Why have you brought me here?"

"Yurovsky will explain."

Three hours later, Alexei still sat in the chair Sergei had set him on and clutched the cloak around his naked body. His legs ached from the cold and the injury he'd sustained a few days before. Sergei and the woman Alexei had discovered was called Mina, played cards at a wooden table.

When the door opened, a blast of chill along with the early morning sunshine poured over Alexei and he shivered. "My apologies for keeping you waiting." Yurovsky turned to Sergei. "Those pigs. They tried to molest the tsarina as she lay on the cart naked and dead." He spit on the floor. "The truck got stuck twice, so instead of the mine shaft, we buried the bodies under some planks."

Sergei shook his head. "This has been a disaster, Yuri. The townspeople heard the gunshots, and the soldiers were drunk."

Yurovsky eyed Alexei, making the young man pull the cloak tighter around him. "A good thing in some respects, though. We'd never gotten the prince out if they'd had all their wits about them."

Tired of being talked about instead of to, Alexei jutted his chin forward. "What do you want from me?"

Closing the door behind him, Yurovsky knelt before Alexei. "Do you wish to live forever, my Tsar?"

◌

Mount Rainier Forest, 12 August 1927

Brandeleine Reed ran through a glade of trees on the slopes of Mount Rainier. The document case she clutched in her hand weighted her down, but she knew she couldn't just leave it for her pursuers to reclaim.

Splashing through a frigid, gurgling brook, her now soaked shoes sloshed and squelched as the chill numbed her feet. Dogs barked behind her. Maybe the stream would mask her scent. She stopped for precious moments at the side of a cliff, surveying the scene around her. To the right, a wall of rock covered the path, likely a recent and inconvenient slide. To the left, the hillside covered with ferns and salal sloped down and narrowed to a thin trail along a craggy rock face.

With a deep breath, she summoned her courage, resisting the onslaught of nerves, and sprinted for the trail. Knowing she'd need to inch her way along the ledge, speed was of the essence. Just as she reached the narrow path, a dog broke through the clearing and sniffed the air. With a sharp turn, the German shepherd growled at her, sounded a bark, and charged.

Brandeleine set the case on the ledge and pulled out her service pistol. With a loud, echoing shot, she dispatched the charging hound. If her pursuers didn't know where she was before, they sure as hell did now.

Pebbles clattered around her, and she looked up. The rock face seemed unstable. Scanning the wall above her, she spied an outcropping she figured would come crashing down with a well-aimed shot. Two figures emerged from the forest and settled their eyes on the dead dog.

With a start, Brandeleine recognized the man. Joshua Monaghan, her partner and confidant during her mission on the outskirts of Seattle. Together, they'd managed to steal the plans for the Silver Star's latest weapon, but she was sure he'd been killed trying to steal the prototype. Ava Fofanoff knelt over the dog. She headed the Silver Star cell and had a reputation for double dealing to gain her ends. The cold hatred in her eyes when her gaze locked on Brandeleine sent a cold shiver through her body.

Still holding the gun, Brandeleine grasped the handle of the case and edged along the path. She fired a shot in the couple's direction, and more pebbles showered down on her.

Joshua and Ava crouched for a moment, then Ava handed Joshua a gun. Brandeleine knew the weapon immediately. It was the very prototype they were sent to steal.

With a wave and a smile that would have been friendly had he not been pointing a gun at her, Joshua ran down the hillside toward the narrow ledge with Ava following close behind. Brandeleine increased her speed, hoping to get around a curve in the path and put a rock wall between her and her treacherous former partner.

Joshua arrived at the edge of the cliff and pointed the weapon at her. Energy crackled around Brandeleine as she fought to keep her balance.

"Youth or age, Brandeleine?" Joshua shouted. "It's your choice."

Though her body was on fire with pain, she fought to raise her gun. "Neither," she managed to scream out.

Ava barked a vicious laugh. "You heard her. She wants neither. Maximum setting."

Joshua faltered. "She'll burn."

"Do it!" Ava screamed. "She killed Doctor Riktov."

Seizing her chance, Brandeleine brought her arm up with great effort and squeezed off a shot. The bullet hit the outcropping, and the entire ledge gave way. Joshua and Ava looked up, but couldn't get out of the way as tons of rock crashed down on them.

The energy faded around Brandeleine as the duo were buried under a large chunk of the rock wall. She pressed her back against the rock, grateful to be alive. Holstering her gun, she bought a hand to wipe over her forehead, but froze upon seeing it. The skin, once sporting the age marks she remembered from her grandmother's hands, was stretched smooth over slender and shapely fingers. Careful to maintain her balance on the ledge, she ran her fingers over her cheeks and forehead. Strands of bright orange hair fell around her face, and she gently pulled them into view to examine. No gray.

Pulling herself together, she shoved aside her shock and moved back along the ledge toward the rock slide. Climbing over the rubble but careful not to dislodge any of the stones, she managed to return to the hillside. Sinking to her knees, she breathed deeply.

A gleam of metal brought her attention to her right. She pushed aside a small stand of fern fronds and found the prototype, battered and likely broken, but still intact. Thanking her lucky stars, she rose to her feet and sprinted back toward the trees.

CR

Captain Frederick Grant paced the deck of the aircraft carrier *Buckley*, the heels of his service boots thunking along the wooden beams. He reached the wireless room and pulled open the door. "Any word from Brandeleine?"

Seamus McMurray, the communications officer, shook his head. "No, sir. She and Joshua failed to report in at the designated time. Perhaps the mission took longer than they anticipated."

"Unlikely." Captain Grant sighed. "The operation was planned to the second. It should have been a quick grab. The base at the foot of the volcano was completely mapped, and the route should have been clear."

A series of tapping came through the wireless machine, and Seamus whirled around and lifted the headset. He recorded the message, then tapped out a quick response and turned with a grim expression on his face.

"Please shut the door, sir." Seamus's features darkened.

A foreboding filled Captain Grant as he entered and closed the door behind him. "Who was it?"

"Brandeleine. She's reached the rendezvous point. Alone."

"What about Joshua?" His stomach tightened.

"Dead. He was a Silver Star agent."

"Impossible," Captain Grant hissed. "He was recruited from the cream of the crop at Annapolis. One of the best and the brightest."

"One more thing, sir." The pain in Seamus's eyes was unmistakable.

"Yes?"

"Brandeleine is requesting a medical officer."

Captain Grant's eyes widened. "Is she hurt?"

"She only asked for the officer. No details."

"Thank you, Seamus." He pondered Joshua's betrayal as he opened the door and stepped from the cabin. Striding across the deck to the stairwell, he ascended to the medical wing and stepped into the sickbay.

Doctor Martin Walker stood up straight and saluted. "Captain Grant, sir!"

"Oh, for God's sake, at ease, Walker. You don't need to injure yourself every time I walk into a room." Though Captain Grant liked the protocol on display when they were in port, at sea, he preferred a more casual interaction with his crew. Poor Walker hadn't figured it out yet.

"Sir!" Walker barked as he stood at parade rest.

Rolling his eyes, the captain leveled his gaze on the young doctor. "Brandeleine Reed is requesting a medical officer to accompany the recovery aircraft from the base of Mount Rainier."

A momentary look of panic flitted across Walker's face before he steadied himself and nodded.

Arching an eyebrow, Captain Grant regarded the young man's face with some curiosity. "What is it, doctor?"

"Uh, nothing sir. I'll have my medical kit ready in five minutes and report to the hangar." He made no move from his parade rest.

Captain Grant crossed the room and laid a hand on Walker's shoulder. "Tell me what has you panicked, Martin."

Walker stared at the floor. "I hate flying, sir. That's why I requested and took an assignment on a naval vessel."

"It can't be helped." He gave the man's shoulder an encouraging squeeze. "You'll do fine. Lieutenant Albers is one of the best, and this shouldn't be a dangerous assignment."

A shudder trembled through the doctor. "Shouldn't, sir?"

"Trust me."

With a nod, Walker scurried to the cabinet next to the surgical bay and returned with a small case. "I'm ready, sir."

"I'll accompany you to the hangar." Captain Grant let out a sigh. "And you can dispense with the sirs when we're not in port. Honestly, they make me feel like an old man."

Walker saluted, turned on his heel, and marched out the door like he was on parade at the naval academy. With another roll of his eyes and a shake of his head, Captain Grant followed him.

☙

Brandeleine crouched near the line of trees bordering the broad meadow and waited for the plane to arrive. She'd managed to avoid two patrols of Silver Star agents, but now she felt like a sitting duck. Regardless of Fofanoff and Monaghan's demise, she still was being hunted.

An hour after she'd managed to send the wireless message on the hidden equipment in the forest, she heard the buzz of a small plane. Scanning the sky, she spotted the familiar International CF-10, modified as a three-seater, circling the meadow and making the approach to land.

Another dog barked in the distance, and she realized they'd have to be quick getting out of there. The plane bumped along the field until it rolled to a halt, propellers still spinning as Brandeleine broke cover and ran. Relieved to see Lieutenant Beatrix "Ace" Albers at the controls, she hurried to the lowest of the three wings, hoisting herself up to face Ace.

The pilot's eyes bulged. "B-Brandeleine?"

Brandeleine nodded.

Ace turned to the second seat. "Doctor!"

Facing the startled young man who looked on the verge of vomiting, she noted the ashen face of an otherwise handsome young man.

"He okay?" She addressed Ace.

With a shrug, Ace grinned. "He apparently only has sea legs."

"I can't believe Captain Grant lets you fly this bucket on a rescue mission."

"Bucket?" Ace furrowed her brow and set her mouth in a scowl as she crossed her arms. "I'll have you know this plane is top of the line. Why, her twin is flying in the Dole Air Derby endurance race as we speak."

A loud explosion sounded in the woods, followed by a plume of black smoke.

Ace stood in her seat. "What the hell was that?"

"A little surprise for my pursers," Brandeleine yelled over the buzz of the twin prop engines. She leaped off the wing, the ease of it surprising her, and bolted for the third seat, throwing the case to the doctor as she passed. He caught it with a startled yelp. Flinging herself over the lip of the plane and into the seat, she pulled on a pair of goggles and donned the helmet. She reached across to the doctor and took the case from him.

"Why did you need a medical officer?" He yelled, looking angry and sick at the same time.

"I'm fifty-two years old," she hollered back at him. "You tell me."

The plane's engine roared louder as the doctor's face turned yet whiter, and drowned out the words on his lips. Three Silver Star agents burst from the trees. Brandeleine whipped out her revolver and managed to hit two of them. Their bodies sank to the ground, turning to black goo and smoking. The third agent got off a shot, but missed the three of them. Brandeleine squeezed off another round, hitting the agent in his chest. Smoke rose from the wound, and he crumpled to the grass.

Not sparing another moment for their po-tential killers, Brandeleine faced forward. The triplane lifted off the meadow and rose into the air. She let out a sigh of relief and sat back. For the moment, she was safe and on her way back to the *Buckley.* She thought of Joshua, and what a terrible blow his death will be to Seamus. Not just his death, but his treachery.

Exhausted from her ordeal in the forest and on the ledge, she let her eyes drift closed. She awoke with a start when the plane bumped as its wheels touched down on the aircraft carrier and taxied to the end of the runway. Captain Grant strode forward when the plane came to a halt and Ace shut down the engine.

"Brandeleine, thank goodness you're...my God." His face blanched in sheer disbelief as she deftly swung herself out of the seat and pulled off her helmet. "How is that possible?" He turned to the middle seat. "Martin, pull yourself together and get out of that plane. You've got a patient here."

Ace hopped from the cockpit and tossed her goggles and helmet onto the seat. She joined Brandeleine and Captain Grant, sparing a glance at Walker's white knuckles gripping the fuselage. Plucking a tire pressure gage from her flight jacket, she smacked his knuckles.

"Ouch!" His fingers flew to his mouth. "What was that for?"

"Snap out of it and get out of my plane." She turned to Brandeleine, reaching a hand out to her face, disbelief shining in her eyes. "I can't believe it's you."

"I don't know what's happened. Joshua shot me with some sort of ray gun, but I managed to bury him and Ava Fofanoff under a ton of rock." She covered Ace's hand still pressed against her cheek. "What do I look like?"

"You're younger than I am." Ace removed her hand from Brandeleine's face and pulled a small, square mirror from the front pocket of her flight jacket.

With an uncertain glance at Ace, Brandeleine accepted the mirror. Holding the glass up to her face, she gasped. "How can this be?" She touched the cheek of the woman in the mirror, hardly believing it was her own reflection. She hadn't seen the face staring back at her in thirty years. The scar under her chin from the fall she'd taken at thirty-two was gone, as were the lines and crow's feet around her eyes. The skin along her chin was tight, no longer threatening jowls.

Walker finally slunk from the plane and stood on wobbly feet. He joined the two women and the captain. "Is it true you're fifty-two?"

"What a cheeky question, Doctor Walker," Ace tutted.

"Okay, Ace. Let him do his job before he loses his lunch on the deck." Captain Grant stiffened and swung his head toward the aft of the ship.

Brandeleine tensed and followed his gaze. Fifteen small, dark dots grew larger in the sky.

"Enemy planes off the port bow. All hands to battle stations!" he roared as he took off running.

Walker blanched again, gave a quick glance to Brandeleine, and made to run. She caught his arm. "Wait." Reaching into the plane, she grabbed the Silver Star's gun and the briefcase. "Take these to the captain. Then tell Seamus to contact AEGIS Admin and inform them I found the plans and a prototype. Got that?"

With panicked eyes, he nodded and took off for the nearest hatch.

Ace grinned. "Wanna come with me for a little fun, young lady?"

Handing back the mirror, Brandeleine returned the grin. "I know you like 'em older. Do I still fit the bill?"

"Definitely." His eyes blazed. "Let's go knock the Silver Star out of the air."

As the klaxon sounded around them, Brandeleine and Ace grabbed their helmets and goggles from Ace's CF-10 and pushed the aircraft to the side, tying down the wheels. The heavy winches at the stern of the ship lifted sleek new single prop planes onto the flight deck, and pilots scrambled into the cockpits and gunnery seats.

Ace and Brandeleine ran for the nearest fighter. Ace climbed into the cockpit while Brandeleine familiarized herself with the new machine gun affixed to the tail. The engine roared, and the plane rolled down the runway as the first of the Silver Star fighters strafed the deck. Pockmarks appeared in a line down the runway, barely missing another of the AEGIS planes taking off.

"Get us airborne!" Brandeleine screamed. Far from fear, a surge of exhilaration surged through her body. She relished the return of her youthful recklessness that middle age and a tired body had suppressed.

The plane picked up speed, and Ace pulled on the stick, swinging the nose in the air. As soon as they were off of the deck and gaining altitude, Brandeleine turned the gun onto one of the enemy planes and opened fire. The bullets struck the pilot, and he melted into a pool of sludge and bones. The plane corkscrewed and crashed into the ocean.

Ace gave a thumbs-up as she maneuvered the plane into the dogfight. Another Silver Star fighter dove at the *Buckley*, but Brandeleine plugged the bottom of the plane full of lead, and the pilot melted away. The plane flew close to the bridge of the ship, but missed by mere inches to be swallowed by the frigid water.

Tracers lit up the sky next to them and tore into one of their wings. Ace banked the plane out of the line of fire, then pulled into a severe climb. Brandeleine held on as the plane looped in a high arch and came down level between two of the enemy planes. She opened fire as Ace activated the gun in the nose of the propeller. Both planes fell from the sky as the third dove.

Lyle Thompson's plane burst into flames next to them, but Brandeline was relieved to see him jump out and parachute to the water below. His gunner wasn't so lucky, and disappeared as the plane exploded into a fireball before falling like a stone from the sky.

Shaking her head, she focused on the next plane coming at them fast. It bobbed and weaved, keeping away from the tracers. In frustration, Brandeleine fired in a circular motion, trying to anticipate where pilot would go and managed to sever the wing right wing clean off with the machine gun.

Two fighters remained, and one of them made a wide arch while the other dove toward the *Buckley*. Three of the AEGIS fighters riddled the plane with bullets, but the aircraft kept falling, flames leaping from the cockpit. The enemy pilot rose his fist in a curse before melting away.

Though the *Buckley* was turning to avoid the fiery airplane, Brandeleine was sure the dead pilot would hit his mark. From below the burning fuselage falling toward the ship, Kerry Marcus's plane swung upward and aimed for collision.

"Bail out, damn it!" Ace screamed as the two women watched the AEGIS fighter plow into the flaming hulk. The momentum pushed the burning plane away from the *Buckley*. Moments before impact, the gunner jumped and parachuted onto the *Buckley*'s deck, hitting hard. Brandeleine could see several crew members running toward the prone officer. Kerry Marcus didn't get free and died with his plane.

The final Silver Star fighter lined up with the deck of the *Buckley*, but instead of opening fire, a small plume of black smoke rose from the gunner's seat, and a white flag stiffened into a square from the cockpit. The AEGIS planes buzzed the enemy fighter, but didn't open fire. The Silver Star plane touched down onto the deck of the *Buckley* and rolled to a halt. Ace lined up their plane to land as crewmen rushed to surround the enemy fighter with guns drawn.

After Ace brought them in, Brandeleine jumped from the plane and ran to Captain Grant. He stood tall, staring down at a young man dressed in the familiar black of a Silver Star uniform. The fair, delicate features of the young man made him look about sixteen years of age, but Brandeleine felt he must be older.

The enemy pilot saluted the captain. "I am Alexei Tsarevich Romanov, and I request asylum."

Brandeleine's jaw dropped. "You can't be."

Captain Grant's brow furrowed. "The Russian royal family were all assassinated ten years ago. You can not be the prince."

"A man named Yurovsky saved my life. He killed my playmate Leonid and buried him in my place." Alexei glared at Captain Grant. "I demand asylum."

The stern voice the captain reserved for recalcitrant young officers and disobedient recruits bellowed from his lips. "You don't rule anything here, young man. Whether or not you are the prince, your family was deposed." He whipped his head to stare at Officer Peter Ritchie. "Lock this man in the brig. I'll deal with him later."

Brandeleine watched the young man marched below deck, then turned to Captain Grant. "Captain, there are some pilots in the ocean. These waters are cold and they won't last long."

Three flares shone bright off the port bow, and Captain Grant barked orders to lower the skiffs. Brandeleine made for the nearest, but he caught her arm.

"Not so fast, Brandeleine. Walker needs to give you a full examination. We need to know why you look thirty years younger than you did when you went on your mission. I also need to discuss Joshua with you." Captain Grant leaned in closer. "And you need to discuss Joshua with Seamus."

She only nodded and headed for the sickbay.

CR

Alexei stepped into the cell, and the door slammed shut behind him. It wasn't unlike Popov House where he'd spent the final hours with his family crammed into a small room. There, however, he wasn't able to move.

Alexei.

A wave of intense drowsiness crashed over him, and he stumbled to the bunk hanging from the wall and secured by two chains.

Alexei Romanov.

The ethereal voice echoed through his head. Barely able to keep his eyes open, Alexei lay on the bunk and drifted to sleep. He woke with a start in a graveyard. Sitting up, he shivered at the stone monuments and the mist swirling between them. The mist formed a whirlpool and solidified into a man. Aleister Crowley's ethereal form floated before him, dark eyes blazing with fury as he stared down at the boy Alexei had once been.

What is your game, Alexei? Do you think you can run from me?

"The AEGIS people will protect me once they establish my identity. I am finished with you."

Alexei trembled as Crowley's voice boomed around him. *Insolent princeling. You know nothing of the world. I cured your hemophilia. Saved you from your family's fate. This is how you repay me?*

"You cured me, but Yurovsky was the one who rescued me from the soldiers." Alexei jutted his thirteen-year-old chin out at the apparition, calling on every shred of royalty he could remember from his father.

Don't trifle with me, child. I can burn you from the inside out. Your life essence will become mine. Crowley brought his hand up, and orange flames ignited at the end of each finger-tip. *Prepare yourself to rejoin your family.*

"Touch me if you dare." Alexei steeled himself for the onslaught.

The apparition floated forward, reaching out a fiery hand. At the moment the flames disappeared into Alexei's chest, intense pain wracked his entire body. His head fell back, and he screamed. Fire burned inside his body, but after a moment, the pain dissipated, and an eruption of energy burst from his chest.

The mists forming Crowley shook and shimmered.

What is happening? Crowley flailed, his form catching fire and burning. The ethereal hands yanked free of Alexei's chest, and the boy collapsed to his knees panting.

"You've bitten off more than you can chew with me. Now I will be rid of you." Alexei brought his fingers together, and energy once more crackled around him. Placing palms together and his thumbs against his forehead, Alexei concentrated on the image of Crowley.

The apparition bellowed and screamed as the fire surrounding Crowley intensified. Vapor shot skyward in a geyser of steam. *You will not escape me forever, Alexei Romanov. I will hunt you down and take your essence. Mark my words.*

Alexei intensified his thoughts, purging every trace of Crowley from his psyche. He jolted awake to find himself in the cell. "I'm free," he whispered. He searched his mind for any evidence Crowley still controlled him. He found none, threw back his head, and yelled at the top of his lungs. "I'm free!" He laughed for several minutes like mad lunatic, then brought his relief into check. He still had to convince AEGIS who he was and then had to plot how to overthrow the revolutionary usurpers blocking his right to the Russian throne.

"You Bolshevik bastard," a young man shouted as he stormed down the stairs into the brig. "What did you Silver Star scum do to Joshua?"

Though deeply offended at being called a Bolshevik, Alexei could see the man was distraught. He knew instantly who the young man meant. Joshua Monaghan. The AEGIS agent seduced by immortality.

"Talk!" The dark-haired man with vivid green eyes roared. "Or I'll come in there and beat you to a pulp."

Alexei came to the door and peered through the bars. "I did nothing to your agent. He was captured, but instead of tortured, he was cured by Crowley's latest experiment in exchange for his service and loyalty. He signed the blood contract."

The man stiffened. "Cured from what?"

"A cancerous tumor that had ruptured and filled his body with the disease. The camp doctor said he only had a year, maybe less, before the cancer would consume him."

Silence for a moment as the man took in the information. "Liar!" He roared and reached through the gap in the bars to grab at Alexei's neck.

Jumping back before the fingers could close around his throat, Alexei raised his hands. "Calm yourself. I'm not lying. Joshua Monaghan was seduced by a dark force. I was as well, but I fought back and am free."

The man slumped from view, and Alexei peered out of the cell window. "Why didn't Joshua fight?"

Alexei sat with his back against the door, imagining his frame leaning against the hurting man on the other side. "The blood contract is usually too strong to resist once signed. He didn't realize what he was agreeing to."

The young man yelled as something banged against the door, making Alexei jump away. Sobs echoed off the walls of the cell, and he moved back to the door, placing a hand on the cool metal.

"I'm Alexei. What's your name?"

The young man sighed heavily. "Seamus."

"Do you have family, Seamus?"

Another trembling sigh. "Joshua was all I had."

Alexei was used to being the center of attention. Only son of the Tsar. Heir to the throne of Russia. He'd never consoled another person before. Never even thought about another person's experiences or hurts. Even his sister Anastasia had remarked how much their parents spoiled him, and she was the youngest. But this man needed someone to talk to.

"You are lucky to have had this young man. My family is gone as well. Tell me about your Joshua."

Before Seamus could continue, footsteps sounded through the brig.

Captain Grant's voice echoed through the room. "Seamus, what's going on?"

Seamus stood, and Alexei could see dark curls against the bars of the cell window. "Sorry, sir. I was speaking with Alexei...uh, the prisoner." Seamus glanced behind him and gave Alexei a tentative smile. "He's been kind."

"Come on, son. I need you to get a message through on the wireless."

Seamus moved away from the door, but paused and returned to look through the window again. "Thanks, Alexei. I'll come back later." His face faltered for a moment. "If that's all right with you, sir."

"I don't see why not." Captain Grant peered through the bars, giving Alexei a guarded appraisal. "I'll see about your request for asylum."

Alexei nodded. "Thank you, Captain."

☙

The *Buckley* slowed as the *Daedalus* hovered in the air over the ocean. Captain Grant ordered the anchor dropped, and the airship came alongside and connected to the docking moors specially fitted to the side of the ship. Deck crewmen affixed the gangway from the *Daedalus* to the *Buckley*, and the hatch opened.

Brandeleine whistled at the small but ultramodern dirigible hanging just off the edge of the aircraft carrier. Her outer skin gleamed in the setting sunshine. Ace stood next to her, as did Captain Grant. The Silver Star prisoner claiming to be Alexei Romanov made up the rest of the group waiting to board the airship.

The door opened, and the four of them stepped across the gangplank to the airship, following a dark-haired crewman to the main salon. Brandeleine settled her eyes on a man waiting beside one of the tables.

Her lips curved upward. "Well, Jack Mc-Graw. I thought you'd given up flying."

Jack grinned. "I should. I'm a father. Doc says I shouldn't, though, so here I am." He peered at her closely. "Brandeleine, how did you manage to get younger?"

"Jack, you are a flatterer." She realized fully his confusion, not really understanding what had happened herself.

His grin disappeared. "You've got to be about..." His eyes fell on Ace who narrowed her gaze and scowled at him. "...twenty-nine." He cleared his throat. "But you look more like early twenties."

Captain Grant stepped forward with the battered gun from the hillside and the case full of technical specs and experiment results. "We've known that Aleister Crowley is trying to extend his life by whatever means possible. These documents detail his latest attempts to defy nature."

"What does this have to do with her 'youthening'?" Jack looked from Brandeleine to Captain Grant. He seemed to notice the other member of their party. "Haven't I met you before?"

Brandeleine stared at Alexei, who shook his head. "I don't think so, though you may have seen photographs of my family. I am Prince Alexei Romanov."

Jack's eyes widened. "Yes, of course." He frowned. "But you died ten years ago."

Clearing his throat, Captain Grant moved to one of the tables in the salon and opened the briefcase. "I read through some of the documents after the attack originating from the Silver Star base near Mount Rainier. It seems our friend is telling the truth. An agent infiltrated Yurovsky's circle. It may even have been Yurovsky himself."

"After saving me from death, he asked me if I wanted to live forever." Alexei addressed everyone in the room. "Men came and took me away to some sort of machine far from Russia. They cured the hemophilia I'd been plagued with my entire life. I swore allegiance to the Silver Star and signed the blood contract with Crowley."

Jack nodded at Brandeleine. "What about her?"

Brandeleine looked first to Alexei and then to Captain Grant. "Was the gun the same technology as what Silver Star did to Alexei?"

Lifting a sheet of paper from the case, Captain Grant read from the page. "Initial tests confirm the success of Operation Fountain of Youth. The machine cures disease as in the case of Alexei Romanov. No traces of hemophilia remain after one treatment. Subjects Fofanoff, Kaine, and Spurgeon physically reversed fifteen years of aging from features and gained remarkable improvement in stamina. The machine is ready to be converted into a weapon." Captain Grant looked up and met Brandeleine's gaze. "You're the result of the weapon."

She thought back to Joshua's words. "Monaghan asked me if I wanted youth or age as he fired the weapon at me. It must either age someone to death or 'youthen' their body back to nothing." She shivered. "Horrible either way."

"The AEGIS scientists can analyze the gun and the paperwork," Jack said as he approached Captain Grant. "It seems we need a team to go in and neutralize the machine."

Adrenalin surged through Brandeleine as she stepped forward. "I volunteer."

Ace moved to her side. "You'll need a pilot."

"And I know the terrain. Take me as well." Alexei volunteered.

Captain Grant narrowed his gaze at the three of them. Brandeleine had seen this look a hundred times in her commander's face. Calculating the odds, looking for flaws, re-assessing needs. Finally, he nodded. "You'll need a communications expert and someone to bring back as much of the technology as possible."

Lifting the weapon in his hands, Jack examined the battered metal. "We're being sent off on another mission, so I can't spare anyone."

With a final stare at Alexei, Captain Grant addressed them all. "I believe Seamus will fit the bill perfectly."

Brandeleine rubbed her hands together. "Let's get to work."

Last Call for a Ghost
by James Stubbs

"Dapper" Vincent Colletti was a big fish in a very small pond. That was his delusion and didn't let small things like the real world get in his way.

The stiff wind of an early winter ruffled his expensive suit lapels as he exited Burkhardt's grocery. He tugged his hat down upon his brow, the fat roll of fives and tens in his pocket compensating for the chill in the air. Another fine establishment of the community was now insured for another month against fickle misfortune.

His driver, Joey, looked up from the battered magazine he read as Vincent yanked open the passenger door.

"Everything jake?" the diminutive driver asked.

Vincent merely grunted as shifted his rear in the uncomfortable seat.

Joey's pockmarked face split into a grin.

"Somethin' funny?" Vincent said with a scowl.

The driver handed over his reading material.

"Naw, but ya might want to put the cushion back 'less ya want to get cozy wid a spring."

The protection man snatched the rag.

"Just drive. We've still got six more places to hit."

"I'd say use the mechanical man on the cover. I think it's thicker th—"

"Joey, shut yer trap."

"You's the boss, boss."

❧

Edna Haskell peered from her vantage spot in the alleyway and fished her notebook out from inside her mohair coat. She jotted down the date and time next to a few similar notations. As the society page reporter for the *Ladies Crier*, technically, she was doing her job. It wasn't her fault that she noticed the distinct lack of newer fashions or hairstyles in the wives and daughters of some of the more upwardly mobile families. In her experience, the only cause ever would be the acute lack of money. Only, in this case, instead of the pinch of hard times, she was sure it was the predication of crime. None of the affected families outwardly seemed to be hurting but, to the trained eye of someone looking out for *haute couture*, she noticed. Her normal, boring assignment had now become something for the crime beat and she couldn't have been happier.

This was the first time Edna had seen the Burkhardts pay but she knew personally the Rosenburgs and the Allens were on the hook. It hadn't taken a genius to spy in her compact mirror as a bag was passed over the counter without a word a month ago at the Ottomans' jewelry shop.

This wasn't something she could take to her editor. She well knew the result of something so stupid, she'd be out of a story, her ticket that would get her out of drudge writing. Plus the cops would get called in and be their usual effective self and that's assuming they'd get ones that weren't solidly on the take.

It wasn't until she looked up from her scribbling that she noticed the gray figure dropping from a fire escape to land in front of the car.

Edna's breath caught in her throat. It was *him*.

☙

The newspapers couldn't get enough of the stories of the mysterious gaunt figure in gray that, over the span of a few months, had become the scourge of both the corrupt and the criminal. The amount of ink spilled on his behalf almost equaled the amount of blood he left behind in his crusade against crime. Edna felt like a small girl on Christmas morning because this was a journalistic gift from upon high and her waiting notepad was about to receive the hottest of hot scoops.

Even from her vantage point, she could see the tall gaunt gunman. His sunken cheeks and thin frame were alarming. It looked like a strong wind would knock him over and she very well might have mistaken him for a dead man like the rumors said if it hadn't been for the flashes of anger she saw in very-much-alive pale green eyes almost hidden in the sunken eye sockets, bags underneath each one indicating the man slept rarely, if at all. However, if the vigilante never knew a decent night's rest, the Smith & Wesson M1917 revolvers held steadily in each hand made a mockery of such thought.

The Gunshade was here. Retribution was at hand.

☙

"Holy Mary!" Joey yelled as the man landed in front of their car and raised a gun toward the windscreen.

"Gun it!" Vincent cried as the glass in front of him spider-webbed from the impact of a bullet. "Run him down!"

Joey didn't need to be told twice.

Flattening a guy shooting at you seemed a lot more sporting than running over some defenseless sap.

The heavy sedan sped forward. The man didn't move an inch.

Another bullet hollowly impacted the solid metal body of the car.

Joey braced himself for the meaty thud of the collision as he felt the acceleration pick up and the powerful engine roar in response to his lead foot.

The gray-clad figure, instead of being thrown over and across their hood, passed *through* it. Joey could swear the man, who should be by all rights dead, laughed as he went through the dashboard and between the two of them before going out the back of the car.

"Get us out of here!" Vincent yelled beside him.

The gangster's demands at least kept the driver from dwelling too much on what had just happened. Joey narrowly missed clipping a street lamp as the car fishtailed through the intersection. A man shouldn't go through a car like a... ghost. The only thing Joey was sure of was that he would be devoutly hitting his knees tonight and sleeping with the lights on.

Joey chanced a glance over at Vinny. He was as white as a sheet and gripping at the gun under his coat as if it would do him any good against a man who was already dead.

The Gunshade had somehow sniffed out their operation and the only thing sure now was that Joey wanted out of this mess and as quickly as possible.

❧

Edna watched in amazement as the Gunshade went through the hurtling car like a specter. There had been speculation and eyewitness reports of him being able to do such a feat but nothing ever "solid". Now Edna had no doubt. Her own eyes didn't betray her. Unlike many, she placed no faith in the supernatural bunk being thrown about in regard to the vigilante. A ghost didn't need a gun and the bullets left in his victims were real enough. A rational explanation must exist.

Even as her mind wrestled with this conundrum, her fingers furiously wrote down the license plate number from the back of the retreating coupe.

Edna's phantom-turned-real darted off into an alley just up from her location and she felt herself let out a relieved breath. The excitement of witnessing an attempted assassination would have been nothing compared to coming face to face with the mysterious crime fighter. The questions she would have!

But, for now, the real question was making use of her contacts and finding out who the getaway car was registered to, assuming it wasn't stolen, which was a very real possibility in Chi-town.

CR

Douglas Graves cursed to himself as he ducked into the dim alleyway. His waiting car was nearby. He hadn't expected the two low-rent hoods to try to run him over, which is why he was only using normal bullets, otherwise the two crooks would be as dead as the day is long. His first shot had only been intended to spook the two of them into running or foolishly trying to shoot it out with him. He'd been hoping to take one or both of them alive. In this case, information would be far more useful to him than corpses.

The Gunshade kept his eyes on the criminal elements of the windy city and Alfonso Bianchi had become far too bold and ambitious. These two thugs were his. Thankfully, most of the bystanders sensibly scattered once lead started firing.

Despite being the third person to assume the mantel of the Gunshade, and being the inheritor of over three generations of mystic knowledge and deadly proficiency with firearms, the fanciful tales of his exploits were that—mostly fantasy. He missed, occasionally, and made mistakes. Douglas Graves was still a man, albeit a very extraordinary one.

Turning incorporeal had saved his life but it had also left him tired. Passing his spirit so close to the realm of the dead never became any easier or more pleasant. The shades there knew he didn't belong and eagerly reached out for his life energy. As the Gunshade he always must be certain that he wasn't bringing someone or some*thing* back with him into the world of the living. One day he would join their number but today was not that day.

"Dapper" Colletti was small game but you needed bait to lure in the bigger fish and the small-time racketeer was the Gunshade's ploy. He'd failed this time and Colletti was now on guard. It wouldn't be as easy to get at him next time. That only made things interesting and merely a matter of time, something the Gunshade had plenty of.

ॐ

"Aw c'mon, Donny, be a honey won't you?"

The perpetually rumpled clerk gave Edna a dirty look.

"Do you have any idea how much trouble that'd get me in?"

"Look, all I'm asking for is for you to tell me who owns the car this number belongs to. I'm even doing you a favor by not telling you why I want it," Edna said with a sly grin.

"Oh, hey, yeah, no problem. It's not like I'm breaking the law or anything. Geez Louise, Edna, if you want it that bad, why don't you go and hire a dick like anyone else?"

"One, because that costs money. You of all people sympathize with the pay of us public servants, and two, none of them want anything to do with me."

"Oh, yeah, I forgot about that. When you send one of them to the clink, no matter how crooked, you get smeared by all of 'em don'tcha? It wasn't *me* who wrote that little expose was it?"

"Part of the job," Edna shrugged. "What're you going to do?"

"Cripes. I can't believe I'm going to put my rear on the line for you. Again."

"There's a really nice bottle of the good stuff in it for you."

Donny's eyebrows rose. "How good?"

"Ten year scotch. Only the best for you."

"Deal. But, if this comes back on me, I'm gonna roll over on you and sing like a damn canary."

"I'd expect nothing less. Now, how about that number?"

Donny sighed in resignation. "What was it again?"

❧

Alfonso Bianchi couldn't be having a worse day. Thus far, his operations fell beneath the notice of the vigilante wreaking havoc on his competitors. This "Gunshade" broke up Carmine De Blasi's network of fences less than a month ago and now it appeared to be his turn. Alfie had no plans to allow one man to take apart the business he'd built over years and the bodies of countless upstarts. His pride demanded this thorn in his side must be dealt with.

The mob boss glared at Joey and Dapper, two dimwits who at least had the decency to show up with the protection cabbage they'd been told to get. They'd both been lucky not to end up cooling on a slab downtown like so many others even if he now had to quietly get a shot up sedan repaired. Fortunately, it would only be money, and he had plenty of that to grease the proper palms. Money and plenty of willing gunmen were never in short supply in this town. All he needed was something to lure the Gunshade in with.

"Mister Bianchi."

The mob boss waved his hand dismissively at the better dressed of the two men standing scared and uncomfortable in front of his desk and pasted a smile on his face. He needed two pawns and these two screw-ups would suffice.

"Boys, it's fine. These things happen. All part of the business."

The two thugs visibly relaxed.

He continued. "But I'm going to have to take you two out of sight for a bit until the heat dies down from this lunatic gunning for some of my best men."

Joey glanced questioningly over at Dapper Colletti, his shakedown man partner and the brains of the two. Alfonso wasn't even sure he could be that generous. The mob boss interrupted any words from the two idiots.

"I'm going to send you two to watch over one of my stills. It's small-time bathtub hooch production, stuff beneath the two of you, but, if you can manage this, there might be better work for you in the future."

Alfonso watched his two lackeys expressions light up with greed. Their kind was so predicable.

"Go and see Mike. He'll give you directions and the password so you don't get full of holes walking in there. And boys? Don't let me down. I reward results."

He fished a cigar out of his desk drawer and leaned back in his chair after the two stooges left. It'd be a damn shame to lose one of his stills but it'd be a very small price to pay if he could take the Gunshade out with it.

Yes, indeed, Chicago's own man of mystery wouldn't be any bother to him or anyone else very soon.

Alfonso picked up the receiver of the phone on his desk and waited a moment for the connection to pick up.

"Hi Mike. Yeah, I've got a job for Sally and the boys."

⊗

Douglas Graves sat by his short wave radio set and heard the call that came in to the police at five minutes after four. Prowl cars were being dispatched to an attack on a delivery truck on Crawford Avenue. The gaunt listener sprang into action, grabbing his hat and jacket and running toward the waiting roadster parked downstairs.

For someone who resembled a cadaver, the Gunshade's tailored suit and snappy C&K fedora were the height of fashion. Some might find this an odd choice for a man who looked like he'd spilled out of the nearest grave, but the well-fitted Londontown jacket gave him mobility you would not get from a cheaper off-the-rack one, and the hat? Well, he just enjoyed a really nice hat and Stetsons had been out of favor for at least a year. If there was sin in vanity, it was a small one compared to the pasts he was fated to atone for.

As he sprung into the seat of his automobile, all indications were leading to the conclusion of a mob hit against another family's operations. Had Graves been a betting man, he would have placed heavy odds on the truck's cargo being booze or the take from a gambling house. None of these hoods ever learned that the only thing accomplished by poking your enemy with a stick is that it brought reprisals, continuing the violence and invariably getting innocent people caught in the crossfire.

All the Gunshade could do was show them the error of their folly, leaving them a little more bloodied and with a few less violent men on their payrolls.

The powerful engine roared to life and the gray-clad avenger gripped the steering wheel, speeding toward a confrontation that he relished whether Douglas Graves cared for it or not. Someone would pay today as many had before.

⌘

Bernie Thomson jumped down from the cab of the truck and ran toward the nearest alley, nodding at the men who spilled from two waiting cars with their guns dawn. A mixture of pistols and shotguns barked, riddling the old vehicle with hot lead. Bernie could hear the cheap crates in the back break and the bottles they contained shatter under the volley of fire being pumped into it.

Bernie weaved his way through the alley to a waiting car with the door open.

"Get in," said the brunette he only knew by her first name, Sally. "We've only got three more minutes before the boys in blue are crawling all over this place."

He could already hear the gunfire slowing down and imagined the "hit" already breaking up as the gunmen piled back into their cars and split.

Neither Bernie, and he suspected Sally as well, knew why Mike had asked them to shoot up one of their own trucks but he never asked questions. You lived longer that way.

Still, he couldn't figure it as Sally leisurely drove away from the scene of their crime, why in God's name would you mess up a perfectly good truck?

CR

The Gunshade arrived moments after the police. A bullet-pocked truck blocked the intersection as the local lawmen took notes and shooed curious onlookers away. None of them looked especially happy to see him. Despite his connection with AEGIS, which gave him a wide berth of jurisdiction, he operated outside of the law. They knew he killed. Even if some of them secretly approved of his methods, they couldn't allow vigilante justice, even if their own government condoned it through supporting AEGIS. It was a nasty double standard that left an uncomfortable taste in the Gunshade's mouth as well although he'd be a fool to turn down the connections and benefits of such a partnership.

A burly officer who seemed to be in charge approached him.

"Don't you have some place else to be?" he growled.

"Not unless you want to name one," the Gunshade said.

"Oh sure, I can tell you a place right now..."

"That's enough, Jones," an older man in a tan suit stepped out of a car that pulled up next to them.

"Detective Harris," the Gunshade acknowledged the man.

"You get anything?" the detective asked. "Jones is a good man but he isn't the best in the brains department."

"I just got here myself," the Gunshade admitted.

"Well, let's take a look and see what we've got. Looks like a mob hit to me."

"I was thinking the same thing,"

"Obviously a liquor shipment," Detective Harris remarked, wrinkling his nose. "I can smell the cheap rotgut from here."

"You can see it leaking everywhere too."

"Thanks for pointing that out. I hadn't noticed."

"I wasn't."

"Calm down. I was making a joke, son."

The police detective walked up to the truck, carefully stepping over alcoholic puddles and giving it a good look.

"Kind of waste isn't it?"

"Of booze?" the Gunshade asked.

"Of bullets. This stuff is so poor it's better paint thinner than tonsil varnish."

The Gunshade opened the back door of the wrecked truck and stepped back as a few broken bottles fell to the pavement, followed by more liquor.

"They made a mess at any rate."

"And left a present," Detective Harris noted as he pulled a label off a broken crate. "Looks like the vice squad is going to get in on the fun. Nice of them to leave us the location of their shipping point."

"Isn't that kind of convenient though?"

"If you mean leaving a shipping label for illegal alcohol? Yeah, but I've also learned to never underestimate the stupidity of the common criminal. Heck, that's how most of 'em are caught in the first place, they do something incredibly dumb."

"All the same, if you don't mind, Detective, I'd like to take a look for myself."

"Son, are you asking me to hold off raiding this place because you want to bust up this booze ring by yourself?"

"Something like that. Just give me a few hours, tops. Then you can send in the cavalry."

"On one condition: Try to leave a few of them alive for questioning."

"Trust me, Harris, I want names of the bigger fish myself. I'll only act to defend myself."

"That's what worries me. I'll give you two hours and then I'm not making any promises once the bulls are let loose."

◌

Edna kept her eyes open for anyone nearby as she wormed her way through an opening in the rickety wooden fence that walled off Bilonski's Garage. This was crazy sneaking into a place possibly crawling with hardened gangsters in the bright of day. However, doing this at night could be even worse and at least she could probably make up an excuse for being here while the sun was still out. Donny's help came through again as her license plate number hadn't belonged to a person but to a business. It remained possible that it had been stolen so she had determined to do a bit of snooping to find out if this was a dead end.

She could hear the faint words of an announcer calling a baseball game from the small shack that served as the garage office as she flitted her way from vehicle to vehicle. Edna didn't have much to go on, only a memory of a black car, which was all of these, and the number. She realized this might take a while and hoped Bilonski didn't keep a dog to guard this place.

At the top of the sixth inning and a strongly-hit double, Edna found her car. The passenger side front window was gone and the plate matched. She would swear that, if she looked, she'd find a bullet hole somewhere in the car's body as well.

Edna pulled in a few favors at the local precinct as well as with the courthouse clerk. No reports had been filed for a stolen car matching this description or a report of plates being taken. It wasn't inconceivable for the garage owner to simply be taking a payoff to conveniently look the other way rather than being tied up with the mob. With times like they were, money was money and morality didn't put food on the table.

A conversation, raising in volume, alerted her to someone about to discover her snooping around a car involved in a crime. With nowhere else to hide, Edna eased open the trunk of the car and slipped inside, slowly lowering the lid until it wasn't closed but likely looked like it from the outside. She could only hope nobody bothered to open her hiding place. It would have been difficult enough to explain her presence out in the yard, this would be impossible.

"Well, look, sorry, I can't do anything about the glass or the... hole, at least not for a few days," a loud voice said.

Someone said something but Edna couldn't make out their words and the louder voice continued. "Sure, I got guys to do the work. I ain't got the right parts though. If you need this jalopy that bad, you can take her, but it's gonna at least be next week before I can do anything about it."

The indistinct voice became louder.

"Ain't no call to get sore, mister. I'm bein' straight with you. Take it if you need it that bad but I can't wave no magic wand 'n make things happen."

Edna heard gravel crunch under someone's heavy step and then the driver's side door open and bang shut. The engine started and Edna became aware of both the fear of being discovered and the growing excitement building in her stomach about finding out something important to break the extortion racket wide open. A promotion to covering the crime beat would be amazing, especially if the current reporter, the always smug Dougan, got ousted by his ear!

⊂≀

Mike Sullivan leaned back and the heavy crowbar he wielded splintered the wooden crate. The neatly stacked sticks of dynamite within awaited the proper moment for use. The tall Irishman paused to wipe his brow and glance over the railing to the warehouse floor below.

His men scurried about setting up the calamity to come. Several guys were emptying barrels of rotgut whiskey onto the floor and splashing it over anything even remotely flammable. When things go "boom," this old rat-trap of a building would go up like a dry twig, taking the Gunshade with it.

The gangster held no fear of the "ghost" that petrified the others. The dead didn't need bullets. No, their troublemaker was a man using some kind of clever trick. Ghost or not, he would roast when they got him trapped.

Mike smirked when he saw McAdams, one of their new boys, douse a burlap sheet and drag it around the floor. That one was smart and might even have a future if he could keep his nose clean and his mouth shut.

"All right. All right," Mike called out. "That looks good, real good. Let's go over the plan one more time because I don't want any slip-ups."

Eight pairs of eyes raised to meet his.

"We've left the sky light unlatched in case he tries to come in from there and the front and back doors aren't locked either. The moment I give the signal, give him a few shots to keep his head down. When I give the second, hightail it out of here. The guys outside will lock the doors after you. If everything goes the way it should, we'll have one less crazy man gunning for our hides."

McAdams spoke up.

"You ain't gonna stick around to get blown up are you?"

Mike laughed.

"Naw, I got plenty left to live for still. Don't you worry about that. I got my own way out. Now, anyone see Howard and the car? He should've been back from Bilonski's by now."

The battered sedan arrived a few minutes later and pulled onto the middle of the warehouse floor as Mike descended the steps to meet the driver.

"What took you so long?" Mike demanded.

The horse-faced gangster who climbed out of the car looked annoyed.

"The old coot hadn't done a thing to fix this bucket."

"Doesn't matter, Howard, there's been a change of plans. We don't need it any longer. McAdams, Hodgson, flatten those tires and make sure this thing isn't going anywhere. It's gotten too hot to be seen, but it's gonna get a lot hotter."

❧

Edna tried to make herself smaller against the wheel hump in the trunk of the car she'd hid herself in. Time and distance had become a blur to her. She had no idea where she was but the voices milling around outside the car told her that it would not be smart to leave her hiding place.

The young reporter knew she did not lack courage but Edna began to question her decision to chase this story, or at least how she'd chose to go about it. Hiding in a car trunk like one of those girl detectives in cheap mystery novels was far less glamorous than they'd made it out to be. However, should she get an opportunity to get out of the trunk, she had no doubt she could break this story wide open.

Wherever she was, the pungent odor of alcohol assaulted her nose. Illegal hooch wasn't much of a shock since most mob families kept their dirty hands in any and all vices. It was a short hop and a skip from protection rackets to stills and even more unsavory things.

Edna heard someone approaching her hiding place whistling and she froze as the distinct snap of a knife opening reached her ears. She heard a grunt and then the car leaned to one side and then a little more a moment later. However she was going to get out of here, it wouldn't be riding back out.

It became apparent to her that she'd reached the end of the line.

ର

The Gunshade observed the dingy warehouse from his hiding place across the street. Nobody had gone in since the old car entered ten minutes ago. It was still too early to crash the party yet. He'd sneaked around the building after parking the roadster and the lack of any obvious sentries put his nerves on edge.

Not that you'd want to advertise a moonshine operation even in this section of town, but there wasn't even anyone "loitering" about unsuccessfully trying to not look like a watchman. This whole thing stunk and it wasn't from the wharf either.

As tempting as it would be to go in through the front door guns blazing, it would likely be what they'd expect and he could only remain ghostly for a small amount of time. Graves glanced across at the building next to the warehouse. He judged that it wasn't a jump of more than four feet. There must be a skylight up there for him to get in.

The Gunshade went into a crouch as he landed on the warehouse roof. Again, he had no problem reaching the fire escape of the neighboring building and scaling the ladder to the roof. He looked about, no guards.

"No time for cold feet now," Graves muttered and made his way to the skylight.

It wasn't locked—of course it wasn't. He dropped to the catwalk below and took in the gloomy interior of the warehouse.

The walkway he perched on was cluttered with old boxes and barrels. It overlooked the floor of the warehouse, which was relatively clean outside of large crates lining the outer walls, two large stills, and the car parked in the center of the building. On the other side of the elevated walk from him there was a door. No lights were visible through the dirty pane.

As the Gunshade watched, a man in coveralls came from behind some boxes lugging a large barrel in front of him. He put the barrel in front of one of the stills and began to drain one of the vats into it, faint whistling reached Graves' ears.

Graves felt the cold grip of his pistols under his hands, they had moved there as if of their own volition. He stopped to remind himself that the man below could be a simple worker and not some hardened criminal despite what he was doing. The Gunshade was a killer but he never took the life of an innocent man.

He briefly considered leaping over the edge, using his ability to go spectral to land without injury, to get down. However, he might need to save that as an ace in the hole. Instead, Graves crept his way to the stairs watching where he was placing his feet. The smell of alcohol became incredibly strong as he descended.

◌♋

From his hiding spot, Mike Sullivan's face split into an evil grin and his grip tightened on the bundle of dynamite clutched in his big hands. It would only be a matter of minutes now before he lit the fuse and Chicago would be rid of one more annoyance.

◯৪

"H-hey, now, mister, I don't need any trouble!" The frightened laborer stared at the Gunshade as he advanced upon him with both revolvers drawn. "I gots a family!"

"Then you won't mind stepping aside while I wreck these stills," the vigilante said.

"Sure, sure, you go right ahead." The man stepped back, his hands raised.

"Get me an axe... and stay where I can see you," the Gunshade commanded.

"Sure thing, mister, you just keep that trigger finger still."

The man slowly inched away from the Gunshade and, without warning, dove behind a stack of broken crates.

As Graves raised one of his pistols to shoot, the sound of many hammers being drawn back and the chokes of several scatterguns clacking froze him to the spot.

The Gunshade seethed with anger. It had been another amateur move to not check behind the large crates while he'd been up on the walkway, although he wasn't sure if he would have been able to see the men hidden from up their either. Someone to his left barked at him.

"Drop it and you might live."

Graves wasn't so much a fool as that. After all the chaos he'd sown among the Families, they'd throw a ticker tape parade to the palooka who put him under.

His hand streaked down to his left holster and the second Smith & Wesson cleared leather.

"Let him have it!"

The cry came almost as soon as his fingers wrapped around the butt of his gun and he willed himself to cross over.

The warehouse became indistinct and wispy yet each hood lit up to his eyes like headlights on a dark empty road, living beacons of sin and wickedness. Time slowed and the Gunshade took the liberty of prioritizing who would live and who would die.

Graves felt a load of buckshot pass through his body. It was like a breeze off the river, as inconsequential as the bullets being pumped into his incorporeal body.

The hammers of both pistols dropped. One man fell, never to rise again, the other hood would wake up screaming in the night in his jail cell for years to come. The chambers rotated two fresh bullets into play.

More disconcerting to the Gunshade was the dead beginning to take notice of him. Ordinarily a confused mass of emotions, the presence of the living drew their gaze and focus. Many of those spirits were never at peace with their demise. He was simply "food" to some and a target to others.

The long and short of it was that Graves couldn't stay like this for much longer. Another of his bullets took off a chunk of wood next one man's head and the man ducked back into cover. His second bullet hit another man who burst into blue flame and screamed like all the powers of hell were after him.

The Gunshade took advantage of the shock this display caused and moved. He couldn't stay and absorb their bullets all day and standing in the middle of the floor would be suicide. The gaunt avenger leaped and rolled towards the parked car letting his ghostly form dissipate.

Gunfire followed him and Graves came up behind the sturdy metal body of the vehicle.

He squeezed off several shots that accomplished nothing other than to lessen the amount of lead flying his way. As good as he was, Graves knew that eventually numbers or a lucky shot would overwhelm him. Besides, his supply of bullets was dropping quickly. He'd never intended this to become a prolonged battle. The Gunshade quickly snapped another four half-moon clips into his guns, and all but emptied the cylinders at his perceived targets.

That was when he heard the screaming and a loud voice call out.

☙

Edna was terrified inside the trunk of the car as the roar of gunfire continued, but she kept herself put until a bullet punched through and missed her head by inches. She wasn't sure if someone had discovered her or not but she was being shot at! Edna wondered if, when she looked back upon this later, she would be amazed at how well she kept her poise. However, her unflappability drew a line at being filled with lead. She screamed and grabbed for the handle before her world was flipped onto its side.

CR

Graves caught something falling from the walkway out of the corner of his eye before the screaming from the car he was hiding behind distracted him. The trunk was swinging open before he caught sight of the bundle of dynamite bounce against the alcohol-soaked floor. He turned quickly to see the gunmen beating a hasty retreat. That this had all been a trap from the beginning became a certainty in his mind.

The Gunshade had no choice. He became a specter again in time to see the bomb explode. Even in his position straddling two worlds, he could feel the blast and watched in fascination as the heavy sedan toppled over on its side and a young woman fall out of the trunk.

More of a concern was the blaze that erupted from the soaked floor. Graves glanced at the doors leading out and noted they were shut. Surely locked too, he thought mirthlessly. The whole place was on the verge of becoming a firebug deathtrap with one crime-buster really becoming dead and an innocent along for the trip.

The woman staggered to her feet, swaying from her blast-addled state, seemingly oblivious to the growing fire that surrounded them.

A gnarled hand grabbed his ankle and the Gunshade looked down to see a smoky desiccated face glaring back up at him. As he went to shake free, he felt another grasp on his shoulder and bony hands clutch at the back of his jacket. A chill even deeper than the afterlife began to seep into his bones. He had gone back to the well once too many times and now it threatened to drown him.

Earthly oxygen flooded his heaving lungs as he bailed out of the spirit realm, air tinted with acrid smoke. Only a superhuman effort kept his exhausted frame from collapsing. His now-human ears could almost swear they heard a parting wail of lament from the dead as the iron-hard grips that had held him vanished.

Heat lashed at his body as he grabbed the confused woman and dragged her across the floor to temporary safety. A laugh from above drew his attention.

"Are you still alive down there, Gunshade?"

The laugh grew more menacing.

"Well, are you?"

Graves looked up and saw a burly man with a Tommy gun step from the shadows. The man pulled the bolt on the gun with a loud *clack*.

"Or do you plan on roasting down there like a dead duck?"

The Gunshade snapped off a shot that missed completely and ducked back behind the diminishing bulk of the sedan as an answering staccato of heavy slugs forced him to seek cover. This was even worse than the Great War. At least there he had a rifle as the Huns tried to machine-gun him. Even then, he had more than three bullets left on him.

"He's right," the woman spoke her first words to him. She seemed to getting over her shock.

"I know he's right. I'm just kind of stuck at the moment."

"Can't you, you know, turn into a ghost or something?"

"Not unless I want to make it permanent."

"Oh."

The Gunshade glanced back up at the catwalk. He didn't see the gunman. He'd either left them to bake or was waiting to ambush them again if they tried to escape.

"What about the doors?" The woman asked.

"Undoubtedly locked. This whole thing was a trap for me."

She laughed grimly.

"And here I thought I was going to get the story of the year." Graves paused. The day kept getting better and better.

"You still might, but that's going to depend upon us getting off this floor and up there. How fast are you?"

"Are you out of your mind?" she yelled.

"I'll cover you. It's either run or burn."

He watched her purse her lips.

"I'll take my chances. Just don't you spare the bullets."

"Sure."

Graves didn't have the heart to tell her he only had two left, one in a gun and the other on his belt that he solemnly loaded in his other empty pistol as she bolted for the stairs.

There was no shooting, only silence as she reached the foot of the stairs and flashed him a hopeful grin over her shoulder.

The Gunshade made his way toward the stairs as the woman ran up lightly before him.

Suddenly Graves caught a glimpse of movement in the shadows up on the walk and he fired a shot in the direction of the movement, watching hopelessly as it deflected off of a metal support. The only benefit of his action was that whatever was moving up there retreated back into the darkness. He watched as the woman took off running into the gloom and he gave chase. She might be a meddlesome reporter but he'd be damned if he was going to let her get killed because he sent her up there.

He still had his last bullet.

As Graves made the walkway, he caught the reporter's frightened eyes, followed by the large gangster with his arm across her neck and the huge maw of his machine gun pointing straight at him.

"Stop right there, Gunshade. *You* might not be able to be shot but I'll splatter her pretty little head everywhere if you take one more step."

The Gunshade bluffed for time until he could come up with a plan. He pointed his pistol at the man's head. "What makes you think I care?"

The hood laughed. "You're too much of a boy scout. Everyone knows you only kill people like me. That'll be the death of you one of these days." He laughed again at his own joke.

Inspiration struck.

"What makes you think that? Who's to say I won't just shoot her and deprive you of a shield?"

Graves shifted his aim between the woman's eyes, which widened with fear.

"You maniac!" she cried. "You wouldn't!"

The Gunshade shrugged. "If it's between you or me... Sorry. That's the way things are."

"Why, you!"

The woman's heel came crashing down on the gangster's foot as he yelped in sudden pain and released her. As the diminutive reporter charged toward him, Graves leaped completely over her and landed a hard right hook to the gangster's jaw. The hoodlum went over the railing with a cry of surprise that cut short at the end.

Graves laughed in spite of the situation. He hadn't expected her to be such a firebrand.

"Are you coming, miss? It appears the way is clear."

He watched her huff and shoot him a dirty look.

"You dope!"

"I've been called worse."

They climbed to the open skylight in silence, as smoke and flames consumed the warehouse. Bianchi wouldn't sweat the loss of the building, but he was now short a dozen or so goons, and would have to hire more. Edna's nerves were frayed and her mind was a jumble of questions. She knew better than to waste this opportunity interviewing the Gunshade. Finally, as they found their way to the rooftop fire escape, sirens distant, she blurted out her first question.

"Would you have really shot me?" she demanded.

"Yes."

He didn't bother to tell her that it only hurt the first time.

The Shanghai Incident

by R.L. Pace

Wednesday afternoon.

It seemed routine enough, a confidential communique from AEGIS headquarters directed to Felix Fogarty, their resident technical genius in British China. Make a trip to the Club Lusitano, part of the scene for wealthy Portuguese ex pats, to meet the mysterious Bruxo Cardoso. Reputed to be a dealer in antiquities of dubious authenticity and state secrets of impeccable pedigree. Governments tended to be less forgiving than individuals if they got phony goods. From there he merely had to inspect and transport the blueprints he was to receive to a prearranged location for what he presumed was a trip back to the United States to Thomas Edison's lab for analysis.

In addition to being a whiz at all things electrical and most things mechanical, he was about as Irish as an American kid could be, commanded seven languages like a native, and a dozen more sufficient to get around nearly anywhere in the civilized world. Which, in part at least, was why he had been personally recruited by Thomas Edison himself to join the Allied Enterprise Group for International Security, despite Fogarty's tutelage under Nikola Tesla.

"*Bruxo Cardoso?* Who names their kid 'Wizard Thistles'?" Felix was looking at the instructions printed before him, memorizing before burning them.

"His mother, apparently. Have you got it?" Joe Frankels was the bureau chief. A squat man, powerfully built with no visible hair save his eyebrows. Felix wasn't sure if he was denuded with a razor or by nature. Either way his brown eyes showed a resolute attitude and his tone was strictly business.

"Yup, I've got it. How will I know this guy?" Frankels handed him a glossy black and white 8" x 10" photo. It was a little grainy and slightly out of focus, like it was taken with a telephoto lens from some distance, but adequate to the task. "Good enough. If I change now I can take a pedicab and make it with time to spare."

"Are you sure you can verify authenticity of the blueprints?" Joe asked.

"Well, no, not really. I can make a guess as to whether or not it's a genuine device that will do *something* when built, but beyond that is a stretch. I mean gosh, a rocket ship is pretty simple, really, but an anti-gravity machine on the other hand..." He let the sentence hang unfinished.

"Yeah, it seemed a dubious claim to me," Joe observed, "but Menlo Park said they wanted it, so here we are."

"I don't understand why this request wasn't marked Top Secret." Felix wondered aloud.

"Probably because the higher you classify something the more interesting it becomes to others. Bad others."

"I suppose. Well, time to shove off. I should be back in about three hours." Tossing the communique in the fireplace Felix headed for the office door.

"You watch your back out there, son. I know you know how to get around in this town, but you are an important part of the team here. Come back alive."

"Always my first priority, Chief." As he departed he had no idea just how difficult the task would turn out to be.

ↃↃ

Since its civil war two years earlier life in China had been a balancing act for foreigners. If you stayed in the International Region you were relatively safe, but only a few months into 1927 Chiang Kai-shek had docked a gunboat at the Bund wharf and general strikes by workers had turned violent, so moving about had become a more hazardous proposition. In an effort to maintain a low profile AEGIS had moved their regional HQ into one of the mansions in the genteel French Concession and had hired more local Chinese. There were risks associated with such a move, but Joe Frankels had made substantial modifications to the site, turning it into a virtual fortress before deeming them acceptable. Now Felix Fogarty was settled into a pedicab heading toward the posh Club Lusitano with one eye on the runner and another on the surroundings.

Situated a few blocks north of Soochow Creek and barely a mile to the Bund, the center of British Shanghai's clubs, commerce and cabals, the building gloried in neo-classic architecture echoing its Hong Kong sister. Lush palm trees guarded the entrance and two doormen flanked the doors. Felix stepped from the cab, which quickly found another fare, and took a moment to survey the territory.

Single entrance, but there must be a back or side door somewhere. Maybe both. Possibly a courtyard behind the main facade. There were at least a dozen places someone could hide if fleeing the scene became necessary. But each of those spots could also hide someone watching him. He peered intently at a few of the obvious sites then adjusted the tie on his tux and walked inside the club.

Inside, the atmosphere was elegant with Art Deco styling. Oil rubbed mahogany paneling glowed, reflecting on the polished marble steps. In the main lounge, a quintet and a torch singer were covering the stateside Ethel Waters hit "Sugar Baby O' Mine". Felix surveyed the scene looking for his contact. A few tables had couples alternately engaged in conversation or listening to the band. At the bar maybe half a dozen men sat alone with their drinks. Nowhere could he see Bruxo Cardoso. Although he had never been here Fogarty knew that the main action was in the billiard rooms so he strolled to the bar looking for directions.

"Mary Pickford," he ordered.

"Si" the bartender replied. A few moments later he set down the sweet, grenadine laced drink and Felix tossed down a large denomination bank note.

"*Estou procurando alguma acao.*" Fogarty said in flawless Portuguese.

"*Meninas?*" The barkeep studied Fogarty then added, "Pardon me, Señor, your Portuguese is excellent but it is not, I think, your native tongue. The action you seek, it is female companionship?"

"No, Portuguese isn't. Ladies aren't what I had in mind. I'm more interested in an import-export situation. Perhaps I could speak to Señor Bruxos" Felix wasn't sure whether it was the import-export or the Mr. Bruxos that did it but the bartender backed away and nodded slightly to a door just beyond the end of the bar.

Felix nodded and said "*Obrigado, mantenha a dinheiro restante.*"

"Sure, I'll keep the change, you won't need it where you're headed," the bartender responded in English.

Beyond the door was a store room with cases of liquor of all descriptions stacked nearly to the ceiling along each wall. There was no Prohibition in Shanghai, of course, so this was palatable stuff, not the paint stripping hooch being peddled in the United States. A hallway illuminated by a single bulb hanging from a dangerous-looking fixture lay ahead. There were three doors, one on either side of the hall and a wider one with brackets for hunks of lumber to barricade access at the back.

Felix, with the bartender's words resonating in his head, grabbed a couple of bottles of vodka and quietly made his way toward the hall. Carefully he poured about half a bottle to douse the floor and a few stacked boxes on either side down the length then, using the dangling bulb wire, tied the second bottle just above the light. He found the wooden barricades and set them just outside the last door, confirming it led to an alley behind the club. He yanked his tie loose and spilled a little vodka on his shirt. With his escape route prepared—should he need it—he knocked on the door to the left.

"*O que?*" rumbled a sullen voice from the other side.

"Señor Cardoso?"

"*Si. O que?*" the voice repeated.

"*Eu sou Felix Fogarty. Posso entrar?*"

"Please, yes, Mr. Fogarty. Do come in."

The office was claustrophobic. Cluttered with file cabinets with paperwork overflowing. Invoices and receipts stacked on the desk and crammed into empty liquor crates. Behind the desk sat the only occupant of the room. A man in his fifties, Felix guessed, who had clearly had a few Sidecars too many in his life. His olive skin had the sallow cast of dissolution to it and his generous nose was covered with a network of broken capillaries. His eyes revealed a jaundice that hinted at a failing liver. In the ash tray next to him smoldered the sodden remains of a Cubano Perfecto cigar.

"I believe you have something for me to look at," Felix began.

"Indeed, and glad to be rid of it I will be."

"Let's get started then, shall we?"

⋅⋅⋅

The previous Monday afternoon.

"What do you mean, 'it's missing'?" There was an ominous rumble to Ernst Hummel's voice.

"Well, *Mein Kapitan*, the technicians secured the blueprints in the safe Saturday evening and when they returned on Monday they seemed to be gone."

The Captain rose to his full height, which at five foot ten still towered over the slight Chinese man before him. His piercing blue eyes seemed to bore holes through the skull, so the lesser man shrank back from the rage emanating from his superior.

"They are either missing or they are not," he intoned. "Why wasn't I informed immediately?"

"Song Li was in Hong Kong and you had not yet docked. We know how sensitive the project is, and thought it wise to wait until a personal report could be conveyed." Wong Lu sneaked a peak at the Silver Star officer to judge his reaction.

"I will presume a thorough search was initiated and interrogations conducted."

"Yes, of course. In fact the last interrogation is underway now. Would you care to join in?"

The Black Dog nodded and followed his laboratory chief to the warehouse. Two hours of screaming and bloodletting later, he had the information he wanted and was driven back to the river, where his sleek gunboat was taking on supplies.

❧

Wednesday evening.

"Surround the building. No one enters or leaves until we have made our recovery." Captain Hummel's voice crackled over the radio. He wanted no excuses, and no mistakes. The blueprints had to be recovered and twenty of his crack marines were heavily armed and spread out, choking off traffic from the neighboring streets and taking up positions overlooking every angle of the Club Lusitano. A couple exiting the club were grabbed roughly and searched then hustled off down the esplanade. One of the doorman offered resistance and was cudgeled into submission with a rifle butt. Looking at the dots on the screen in front of him the captain was satisfied with the disposition of his men and he signaled them to proceed.

Inside the tiny office, one of the dozen or so blueprints was spread out on the desk. A jar of Maraschino cherries held down one corner, Senor Cardoso another while Felix had his left hand sliding along the lines depicting circuitry. He was mentally calculating the effect of a machine built based on these specifications. Suddenly a wall-mounted red light bulb blinked on and Cardoso blanched.

"Trouble out front, best you should go." He slid open a desk drawer and hauled out a 9 mm Luger. "Georg gave this to me himself."

Gunfire erupted in what Felix judged to be the foyer so he rolled up the blueprint and stuffed it back into the round leather tube with the others. Cardoso flung the office door open and stepped into the hallway and was instantly cut down in a hail of machine gun fire. An errant round shattered both the vodka bottle and the light bulb plunging the hall into flaming semi-darkness, lit only by the eerie blue glow of burning alcohol quickly building to a conflagration.

Seizing the opportunity, Fogarty darted into the hallway, tossing the remaining vodka bottle behind him. He crashed through the exit so hard that he sent the two Silver Star marines sprawling, their rifles skittering away. Sprinting down the alley, he spotted an automobile. He threw the blueprint case in the seat, made a quick spark adjustment, and pushed the starter button. The engine sprang to life, and Felix was speeding down the alley as the first fusillade of gunfire whizzed by his head. Rounding the corner, he rammed a marine who flopped lifeless to the ground. He couldn't be sure, but it seemed as though the man was dissolving with a puff of smoke. *Gotta get my eyes checked, that can't be real,* he thought.

Slashing down The Bund at breakneck speed, Fogarty was really beginning to appreciate the 1926 Bentley Super Sport Boattail under him. Sedan chairs and rickshaws scattered haphazardly like dry leaves in the wind. They were dodging each other with passengers and runners disappearing to whatever safe haven they could find. It made it unlikely he would achieve it's one hundred mile per hour top speed, but the bullets chattering from an MP-18 submachine gun behind him were creating a cascade of stone chips from the as-yet-unfinished Palace Hotel. With grim determination he mashed the throttle to the floor.

Colorful, brightly-lit buildings along the Shanghai waterfront of the Wangpoo River to his left flashed by as bullets pocked holes in the windscreen, coach and tuxedo jacket he was wearing. *Whoa! That's much too close for comfort!* Thankfully, the colloidal coating prevented the glass from exploding in a shower of shards, but the AEGIS boy wonder noticed with alarm he had a much bigger problem at hand: the back of the car was on fire. *They must have tracer rounds in the magazine!* Searching the waterfront ahead he spotted something that gave him an idea. Half a block later, he yanked on the brake lever, slowing enough to leap and roll away. Jumping to his feet, he galloped to a nearby motorcycle, noting with approval that it was a British made ABC, and kicked it to life. Felix sped away from the river down Avenue Edward VII. Glancing back, he could see the Bentley fully engulfed in flames and wondered briefly if AEGIS would foot the bill for a stolen car. And motorcycle. And possibly the Shanghai Club at the end of the pier that was now aflame.

For a moment, he thought he had lost his pursuers, and he slowed to maneuver a pair of goggles dangling from the handlebars onto his head, wrestling the blueprint case rescued from the car into a manageable position. As one eye got protection and the other had a lens across half an eyeball, a streak like fireworks crossed in front of him and exploded on the tarmac—then another.

Damn, speed seekers! This must be Astrum Argentum.

He wheeled the bike down a side street before they could get him bracketed and made for Chinese City. If he could make it there, he could disappear in the tangle of streets and alleys and try to figure out what was going on.

☙

"Let him go. We have ten thousand eyes in there. We will know his every move."

Smoothing his black uniform in the livery of a captain of the Silver Star, with its distinctive four point insignia, the speaker sat back from the screen of the tracking device. He was aboard the *Pistris Argentum,* tied to Pootung dock on the opposite side of the river. His given name was Ernst Hummel, but among the Silver Star rank and file, he was known as *Schwarzhund,* the Black Dog.

☙

Felix throttled back the motorcycle and threaded his way through a maze of winding paths and alleys. At six foot three, wearing a tuxedo with a bullet hole, an unruly mop of shocking coppery hair and emerald eyes, he knew he had to get off the streets fast. Melting into the crowd was clearly not an option. After a dozen or so twists and turns, he stopped the bike and leaned it against a hut. He walked another couple of what passed for blocks, drawing curious stares from nearly everyone. *The only way to hide a sore thumb is in a bunch of other sore thumbs.*

Finally, he spotted what he was looking for and ducked inside a ramshackle three story building in the characteristic ornate style of the Chinese. Red and black lacquer peeled from the facade. Once inside, he was enveloped in thick clouds of smoke. Opium, he judged. In the den, all were equal: Asian, European, African, man or woman. Money was the equalizer here. He worked his way through several rooms, barely noted by most of the drug hazed occupants. One set of eyes did take notice, though. When he leaned over and whispered into the ear of an ancient Chinese man, a hidden door in the wall behind slid silently open, just enough to let him slip through. Down a narrow staircase, Fogarty descended several switchback flights, until finally he reached a tunnel stretching out of sight in the distance. Electric bulbs glowed dimly about every hundred feet as far as he could see. *Boy, I hope nobody turns out the lights.*

The staircase and the first fifty feet of the tunnel were contemporary to the building above, but beyond that it got lower and more ancient, carved by and for people nearly two feet shorter than he. Increasingly hunched in his passage, his back was beginning to ache mercilessly as he clutched the blueprints. Finally, after what seemed like hours, he reached a fork, and after a short stop to read the characters on a scrap of wood pointing down one shaft, he continued about a hundred feet, where another staircase led him back up toward street level.

Just beyond the sight line, another shadowy figure glided silently behind.

Fogarty peered through the peephole, and so far as he could tell, the coast was clear. He gingerly turned the handle and winced as the hinges squeaked while he opened the door. He stepped through and quickly closed the door behind him, strode across the room, and stepped into the main lobby of the Ecole Militaire de Shanghai. No longer a military school, it was mostly short-term boarding, and was used by AEGIS as a safe-house for agents in transit, seeking to maintain a low profile. Felix knew he had a few minutes before he expected all hell to break loose, so he ducked into the wardrobe locker to change from his tuxedo into something less conspicuous. And easier to run in. After that, he planned a short stop at the armory. He was at least going to be able to shoot back.

◌

His pursuer had stopped at the fork in the tunnel, well aware of where it led, and equally aware that she couldn't follow him. Instead the ebon-haired woman drifted down the tunnel and up a set of stairs that opened to an alley two blocks away. Stepping out with confidence, the lissome figure strode down the alley to the main boulevard. She was three blocks now from the edge of the Chinese City and, hailing a rickshaw, she ordered the runner to head as fast as possible to the dockside nearest the *Pistris Argentum.*

◌

Slightly surprised that the building hadn't been overrun by Silver Star agents, Felix had taken a moment to grab a sandwich from the mess hall, and was now clad in tropical-weight khaki slacks, a lightweight white shirt, and sporting a brand new pair of Superga Cotu 2750s, the newest Italian footwear fad on the local tennis courts. Perfect for running at top speed should the need arise. Topping off this ensemble was a Montecristi Panama hat. And while he hoped these changes made it less likely to attract attention in the evening, there wasn't anything he could do about his height or hair color. Taking a huge bite out his ham and cheese, he slung the blueprint case over his shoulder, and checked the reassuring holster in the small of his back and headed out the main entrance of the Ecolé into the Shanghai night.

☙

This seems too easy, Felix thought, but the AEGIS boy wonder hailed a pedicab nonetheless and settled into the seat. He gave the runner his destination, resting uneasily as he scrutinized every moving thing along the path. *It is too easy! He's going the wrong way.* It had taken a few blocks to be certain, but he knew for sure it was not the direction he had called for. He yelled at the runner, but instead of changing course, he sped up, turning a corner and suddenly dropping the cab. He tumbled away in a crab-crawl toward the walkway. Fogarty sprang from the seat and grabbed his gun, whipping it into position to fire from a crouch. From the corner of his eye, he detected movement to his left and swung that way, slipping the safety off in the process. He saw a young Chinese boy with some sort of tube up to his mouth. It was the last thing he remembered before he blacked out.

❧

Wherever he was, Felix wished the room would quit spinning. His mouth felt like it was full of cotton bolls, complete with the razor-like seed coatings and the weevils. That he seemed to have no control of his muscles was also worrisome.

"It's Martian Red. We added a paralytic."

Hmmm, female voice.

"Pretty potent drug. It will pass this time. After a second and third time…well, you won't really care."

A bucket of cold water was dumped on his head, which served to at least inform him of which way was up, and that he seemed to be bound to a chair. *How cliché. I think I saw this in a Charlie Chan picture. The Chinese Parrot, maybe.* Trying to speak resulted in an inarticulate grunt followed by a moan and then another blackout.

"He's not ready. We'll need to give him another hour or so before we try again."

The Black Dog scowled, brushing away an imaginary crumb from his uniform tunic. He pulled it down, smoothing away any slight wrinkle that may have appeared. "Mr. Crowley is not a patient man. Nor is he forgiving of failure. This had better work, Song Li, and it better work soon."

"No one has ever resisted this treatment successfully, Captain. It will work, I assure you."

The officer deepened his scowl, turned and left the room. *Well, Mr. Fogarty. It's your head or mine, and I rather like mine right where it is.*

❦

"I trust you are feeling better, Mr. Fogarty. Oh yes, we know your name. And your mission." Song Li's voice was silky smooth, with hint of sensuality.

"Where am I?" Felix had a fair idea of where that might be, but he was playing for time while his vision cleared and his throbbing headache subsided.

"That really isn't relevant, but I offer a trade. I will tell you where you are. In exchange, you tell me where you hid the blueprints you stole."

"I didn't steal anything. Nor did I hide anything."

"Mr. Fogarty..."

"Please, call me Felix."

"Very well, Felix. I am sure you realize by now that your situation is perilous, and that your life hangs in the balance."

Slowly Felix lifted his head, flexing his neck side to side, and brought his focus to the woman before him. She was black-haired, slight of figure, but alluring in a shimmering yellow cheongsam sheath dress with a lotus flower motif, which was slit down the left leg. In a word, she was a dish. Two burly guards flanked a door behind her. They wore the same uniforms and carried the same MP-18 machine guns he had seen on his assailants at the Club Lusitano, and up close he confirmed they were definitely Silver Star. She was right, his position was indeed dire.

"I'm afraid you have me at a disadvantage, Miss..."

"So sorry, I am Song Li. Major Song Li, most recently of the disastrous campaign of Comrade Mao Zedung. But I am a survivor, and now I serve the Silver Star. And that service requires that I recover what you...appropriated."

"That is a lovely uniform you are wearing."

Instantly a leather riding crop slashed across his face, drawing blood. She stepped closer and used the butt of the crop to lift his chin.

"Don't be fooled. I can and will do what is necessary. Now, I will ask again politely. Where are the blueprints?"

Felix deliberately licked the trickle of blood from the corner of his mouth and did his best to look dejected and defeated. He took a moment to make a full assessment of his situation. He was seated about eight feet from the door. Song Li was directly in front of him within arms reach, and the guards flanked the door, which meant the guy on the hinge side of the door was out of position. Crucially, though he was tied to the chair, his legs were free.

"The blueprints are lost," he replied.

"Lost? What do you mean?"

"Burned. I burned them."

"You *what?!*" She had a look of incredulity on her face. "That is ridiculous. Why would you do such a thing?"

"Simple enough. If I can't have them, no one can." This was a calculated risk, because if she believed him they would have no reason to keep him alive. She leaned over, placing her face inches from his own, staring intently into his eyes.

"I don't believe you," she concluded. "You think we don't know you work with AEGIS? You think we are stupid? That we are weak?" She turned to one of the guards: "Go get the kit." The guard opened the door and left. "He is going for more of the Martian Red we used before. Two more doses and we will know what we want, and you will be dead." She stepped back and turned away.

Suddenly, the lights dimmed dramatically, and from somewhere deep below him a thrum of vibration shook the floor. Fogarty jumped up and, lowering his shoulder, he drove himself into Song Li's back and into the door. He swung the chair violently to his right, catching the remaining guard solidly in the midsection, breaking the chair, and, he hoped, a few ribs in the process. Snatching the gun away, he left the two moaning on the floor as he threw open the door and charged into the hallway, sending the surprised second guard and himself tumbling. The guard grabbed for the weapon, but had the wrong end, and Felix pulled the trigger. Three rounds hammered into the surprised man, and as he let go, his body shimmered and hissed then seemed to melt away leaving only a wisp of smoke and empty uniform behind.

Nope, I guess I wasn't seeing things. Cripes, this is pretty weird stuff. Gathering himself, he got to his feet and fired off a few rounds into the door from which he had just exited to discourage pursuit, and as an afterthought, snatched up the uniform jacket. *He won't be needing it.* By now, as he dashed down the corridor, he could hear the shouts and footsteps of pursuers alerted by the gunfire.

"Take him alive!" Song Li was shouting orders as troops began flooding into the area. "He went down the hall. It goes to the vault. And don't spray bullets everywhere—that equipment is irreplaceable!" *Particularly if the blueprints really have been destroyed,* she thought.

Felix crashed through another door and skidded to a stop just inches away from the edge of a catwalk encircling a cavernous space. Looking down could induce vertigo, as the excavation was at least two hundred feet deep, with a faint blue glow emanating from the center. The glow was synchronized with the hum, and also seemed to be coming from the bottom of the pit. It was by his estimation at least one hundred fifty feet wide. The surrounding walkway was dotted with ladders leading to more catwalks above and below the one upon which he was standing, and gave access to a bewildering array of plumbing and wiring. Vacuum tubes glowed orange in a multitude of circuits, providing half of the dim light available. Looking upward, it was another sixty feet to what he judged to be the ceiling. Centered above was what looked like a gigantic camera shutter. Here and there were a few lab-coated technicians peering at meters and gauges. One was tapping a tube with a pencil, smiling when it glowed to life. Slipping into the jacket, which was way too short on Fogarty, he noticed troopers beginning to appear on various catwalks. He imagined they couldn't be far behind at this level, so he strode purposefully to the nearest ladder and began climbing.

Song Li arched her back, rubbing at the ache and marching down the stairs to the control room, silently cursing her own carelessness. Fogarty was still at large, and she wasn't looking forward to notifying the Black Dog that the plans may have been destroyed. While she was confident the prisoner would be recaptured, she was less certain about wringing information out of him—with or without drugs—and was fearful the project might suffer a significant setback. She knew one thing for certain though: she would not underestimate Mr. Fogarty again.

Stepping onto the catwalk, Felix turned away from the nearest troopers and walked forward. Using this process, he managed to climb half a dozen levels and work his way almost completely opposite of where he had initially entered. He nodded perfunctorily to technicians as he passed, and they either ignored him or responded similarly. Guards, however, were working their way toward him relentlessly, systematically cutting off access to ladders and catwalks below him. They worked with implacability but no apparent urgency. He could understand why. There were only two remaining catwalks above him, each with only four ladders. The final one led to what looked like a gantry with a service platform, probably for repairs and maintenance of the shutter. Shedding the jacket, he headed toward the gantry. From there, at least, they could only come at him one at a time, so he could buy as much time as he had bullets. He *snicked* the machine gun into semi-automatic mode, slung it over his shoulder, and made what he expected would be the last climb he would ever make.

From his perch on the gantry platform, the assemblage of guards looked like sailors dressing the deck of a naval vessel. The entire catwalk below him had one guard placed about every ten feet for the entire circumference. No one had attempted to climb toward his outpost, and no one had spoken to him. It was like the natives had surrounded his fort and were waiting to starve him out. The classic impasse—but why? He tried to imagine why they were waiting, and only two scenarios seemed to make any sense. One: They were waiting for someone, perhaps Song Li, or maybe that captain he could barely remember from his drugged stupor; or two: That was the sticker. What was two?

One level below him and about a quarter of the diameter of the room away, a motor sprang to life, and he watched in horror as another gantry, in this case loaded with a boom lift, swung out over the chasm. When it was almost directly below him, two guards who had ridden it out stepped into the bucket and began an ascent toward his position.

What is two? Why am I so important to them? Then it dawned on him. *This machine is the blueprinted device. It must not be complete. And I can't let them finish it.* Now he scanned his surroundings with greater intensity. At their rate of climb, he figured he had less than a minute before he had to do something decisive. Looking at the controls of the platform he occupied, he noted a *LEFT/RIGHT* switch, an *ON/OFF* toggle, and another toggle marked *HOME/ROOF*. He toggled to the *ON* position, and assuming he was already in the home position, he toggled to *ROOF.* Immediately, his gantry slewed to the left. There was an agitated murmur among the guards on the catwalk below, and one of them stepped to a phone in the service wall near him. When the mechanism stopped, he looked up at a panel directly overhead. There were several more switches and buttons, but two caught his eye: *REMOTE CONTROL LOCK-OUT* and *IRIS OPEN.* The second gantry with the guards was only a few dozen feet away, so Felix mashed the *LOCKOUT* button then hit *IRIS OPEN.*

Instantly the roof leafs began to retract away, while the hum and vibrations from below began to intensify. The blue glow became almost unbearably bright. Several floors below, Song Li burst onto the catwalk and shouted to the guards, "Take him! Take him now!"

The nearest troops began crawling up the gantry ladder; the bucket from below was close enough that the riders began to reach out for Fogarty.

This is it—can't wait! Felix fired at the closest man, watching him fizzle away, then slipped back to full-auto and began spraying hot lead downward at anyone unfortunate enough to be in front of the slugs.

"Kill him!" Song Li screamed. "Kill him, kill him, kill him!"

He was protected somewhat by the metal decking of the platform, but as he fired off his last rounds, he caught two himself. He tried to stanch the bleeding from his thigh, but the crackle of electrical circuits and the rending of metal threw him off-balance. He noticed pieces of catwalk whizzing by him—upwards—and through the iris opening. More rending, and a cry from the remaining man in the bucket sounded above the general noise, as it was torn from its mooring and shot upward. To his utter amazement, Felix felt himself falling skyward as well. Shooting past the lip of the roof, along with debris from collapsing equipment and a dozen or so bewildered Silver Star personnel, he looked down in wonder at the developing ruins a thousand feet below. Then the blue light faltered and winked out. He floated weightlessly for a moment, then began slowly drifting. Down, this time. *Alice through the looking glass, indeed.*

A shadow blocked the sun as an airship hove into view. Smaller by two thirds than the Deadalus-class light recon airship, the *Her-*

mes was experimental, and had its landing boom fully extended. Wedged onto the end was Joe Frankels, with what appeared to be a bullwhip in hand. "Hard a-port!" he bellowed to the pilot. He flicked the lash deftly and it wrapped neatly around Fogarty's ankle. Joe pulled hard before his young agent's fall could reach full speed, and dragged his wounded associate onto the boom with him. "Set her down!" he hollered, and though the ship was nose-heavy, the pilot executed a perfect near-ground approach. Before he lost consciousness, Felix noted with wonder swarms of AEGIS personnel already crawling like ants throughout the wreckage of the building.

☙

Song Li and the Black Dog, who had just arrived from the *Silver Shark,* barely escaped with their lives. Neither was confident that they would last beyond their next encounter with Aleister Crowley. With the disastrous loss of the machine, and even worse, the blueprints, "Projekt Abheben" was dead. There would be no liftoff anytime soon. Song Li managed to avoid execution mainly because she had been out of the country when the plans had been lost, and the Black Dog returned to his vessel to nurse his wounds and build a darker grudge against AEGIS in general, and Felix Fogarty in particular.

⌘

From his bed in the HQ infirmary, Felix doodled on a piece of paper. He looked up as his boss entered the ward and headed his way.

"Hi Boss. Listen, my report is this—'anti gravity machine seems to work'."

That elicited a guffaw from the section chief. "Well, the doc says you'll heal up just fine. She said something about 'just a flesh wound', but it was a pretty close shave there, young man." Joe Frankels was glad his young genius was safely ensconced away from the prying eyes of the Silver Star.

"Yep. I was pretty sure my ticket had been punched. I'm sure glad the *Hermes* was operational."

"About that—perhaps we shouldn't mention we used it just yet. Let's just call it a shakedown."

"Okay." Felix raised an eyebrow. "And are we similarly circumspect about your prowess with a bullwhip?"

"Nope. Another life, another time, but not a secret. It's too bad about the blueprints, though. That was quite a show."

"What about the blueprints?"

"Well, before surgery, you did say they were lost."

"Actually, I said I burned them, not that they were lost."

A quizzical look came over Frankels. "What other options are there?"

Felix handed him the doodle he had been scribbling on the paper. Joe studied it for a moment, then a broad smile broke over his face.

"Photographic memory?" Frankels asked. Fogarty nodded. "I had no idea. How much did you get?"

"Every single page, soup to nuts. Plus having been inside their machine, I have most of what they will need to get started on the practical assembly. It's all stored right up here." He tapped his finger to his temple.

"Excellent!" Joe rubbed his hands together gleefully. "We need a better nickname for you than resident genius. How about *wunderkind*?"

"Please, I beg of you, not German!"

"Very well," Frankels considered for a moment, "how about *Miror Hominis*?"

Fogarty grinned, "I'll accept that!"

Three days later, the blueprints in the person of "Wonder Man" were on their way to Menlo Park.

Mind Mists

by Dan Heinrich

It could just be that narrowly escaping an assassin in San Francisco was making him paranoid. Knowing a Shanghai tong sent a hit-man across the ocean just for him had that effect. And the ensuing mix of train and plane travel to cross the country in just under 48 hours had left him exhausted. It was perfectly reasonable that David Li was jumping at shadows.

He reminded himself that particular tong had no established presence here in New York. Still...the Chinese man standing across the street from David's Tribeca brownstone was acting so nonchalant he was actually calling attention to himself. He was only two blocks west of Chinatown, close enough that the occasional Chinese person wasn't remarkable.

David lived here without incident. But the ones who did cross the invisible boundary of Mulberry Street usually had a purpose besides smoking in an alley and looking up and down the street. And at 6 a.m.? Maybe a little paranoia was needed.

David casually unlocked the door and entered his brownstone. As soon as the door closed he moved. His bag went behind the stairs leading up and he strode quickly down the hall to a set of short stairs leading down. The super kept the basement locked, but David had long learned the trick of this deadbolt. He concentrated and his psychic power flared to life. In his mind, he could feel the deadbolt, the tumblers, the knob as if he were touching them. He gave a push with his power, the knob turned, the tumblers fell and the deadbolt slid open. Less time than if he'd used a key. He closed and locked the door and hop stepped across the basement. Small barred windows at street level let enough early morning light to see. Across the room was a door to the street. Another deadbolt, one he re-locked from the outside. He was now catty corner from the watcher, with the building between them.

David jogged two blocks to circle behind his watcher. As he got within half a block of the alley, David slowed and planned his next step. There were several ways to take this mystery man down, but he quickly discarded the flashy ones. For many reasons, David did not like to advertise his abilities, so no showy gimmicks. It was also possible this man was innocent and David was misreading the whole situation. Deniability was needed.

The choice is obvious, he thought. He checked his coat pocket. His bag of fired ceramic marbles was open, in easy reach of his mental powers. *I do love taking down tough guys with a kid's toy.*

He reached the edge of the alley and peeked around the corner. Usual detritus, but nothing of note except for the man lighting another cigarette. David waited a moment for the watcher to take his first drag then turn his attention back to the building. Racing down the alley, David focused on moving quietly. He didn't see the loose pebble he kicked but he heard it as soon as it clanged off one of the metal garbage cans. The watcher heard it too. He turned and started to reach under his coat. Even though David had botched his approach he had the drop on this guy.

David flexed his power and a colorful marble shot out of his pocket, striking the watcher in the temple. The marble was small enough and moving at enough speed that the mystery man literally had no idea what hit him. David blunted the force of impact so the watcher was only stunned. (It was too easy to fling these marbles so hard they did serious damage.) David ran the rest of the way down the alley as the watcher struggled to stay upright with his hand still in his coat.

By the time David got to him, the man had managed to draw a .38 but couldn't hold it steady. A quick surge of mental power and the gun fell to the ground. David came to a stop and picked it up.

"Hey, buddy, you okay? Here, you dropped this." David pressed the business end of the gun in the man's stomach. That got his attention, even through his marble-induced fog. This guy was probably ten years older than David, average height, dark hair. Pretty unremarkable except for the long scar on his right side stretching up from the shirt collar all the way to his ear, ending with a missing lobe. Lovely.

Ear Scar stared back silently. David pushed the gun deeper into his belly. "What are you doing here?"

The man spat a slew of words in Cantonese. Most of the tongs in Chinatown spoke it. David didn't. David replied in Mandarin and got a blank look in return. He really needed to just learn Cantonese already. It was going to get him in trouble one day.

"English." The tough was starting to look defiant instead of dazed or scared. David slowly lowered the gun from the man's gut to his groin. "Why are you here?"

The man slowly looked to where the gun was pointing and took a slow breath. "Stay away from the girl. She's safe. She'll be home soon."

"What girl? Who sent you?"

"Stay away and you'll live a good long life." The man grinned a crooked grin. David felt confused and let his guard down. Ear Scar grabbed the gun and quickly brought it up into David's face. David stretched his power, feeling the barrel, the chamber, the safety. He slid the safety on. Ear Scar pulled the trigger. Nothing happened. Now he looked confused. David smiled sympathetically.

"Oops," David said then kneed Ear Scar in the groin. David grabbed the gun hand and slammed it against the alley wall three times. On the third slam, the man dropped the gun. David used his right hand to grab Ear Scar's throat and slam his head against the wall.

"Who sent you?" The thug shook his head. "Fine." David let go of the man's hand and delivered a left cross to the side of the head. Ear Scar went down. David took a quick look down the street but for the moment, nobody was around. He pulled Ear Scar deeper into the alley and quickly searched his pockets.

Leather wallet. Seventeen bucks in it, no ID. Cocktail napkin with a golden dragon, head surrounded by smoke and gold characters: 心靈迷霧. *Xinling Miwu*—Mind Mists—was an opium den run by the Golden Dragon tong. There was hastily scrawled writing on the napkin. He struggled to decipher the poor penmanship and then realized it was just a grocery list. And one key. Probably for an apartment or boarding house or whatever. Now what?

David thought for a moment then calmly removed the goon's clothes, leaving him in gartered socks, boxers and a dirty undershirt. He emptied the bullets from the gun and pocketed them. He picked up the clothes, left the wallet, gun, key and list, then crossed the street and down the alley of his own building. He dumped everything into separate garbage cans.

He re-entered the building, grabbed his suitcase, and climbed the three floors to his apartment. Did Ear Scar get the wrong building? Did something happen while he was gone? Or was this related to AEGIS? His trip to Shanghai had been his first job for the Allied Enterprise Group for International Security in their secret war against the occultists of the Silver Star. A war he would love to leave behind, but he had the feeling that he was in —for good. Too little information and too tired. Sleep first.

He got to the third floor and froze. His door was ajar. He could hear someone banging around inside. Were they trashing his place? Idiot. The watcher must have been a lookout. Stop using tired as an excuse and think, damn it.

He set his suitcase down and flattened against the wall. He crept slowly towards the door. The frosted glass with DAVID LI INVES-TIGATIONS in black letters was facing away from him so he could see through the opening fairly well. His office was dark but there was a light coming from the kitchen beyond. He could see movement there. He used his power to quietly open the door wider. He sneaked in. Slow, quiet steps to the kitchen door. A large shadow loomed in the doorway.

"Hey!" the shadow shouted. David shot a marble at the shadow's head. It collapsed instantly. David turned toward the bedroom waiting. No one came out. After a minute he checked. No one else here. He went back to the unconscious intruder.

"Oh for the love of..." Irritated, David stepped over the husky body and into a kitchen torn up by someone who couldn't figure out how to make coffee. Might as well make it for when this lunk woke up.

Ten minutes later, David was sipping coffee and looking out his window when he heard a groan.

"David, that you? What happened?"

"Later, Wally. Just get over here."

Wally gingerly stood and came over. David pointed to the alley. Wally asked, "Why are the police arresting a half-naked Chinese man?"

"Because I made a call. You were followed."

"What?" Wally sounded hurt. "No I wasn't. How...? You don't even know why I'm here."

"You only come here when you need help with a case and only when the case involves Chinatown. You're looking for a missing girl, yeah?"

"I... Sorry."

David waved it away and gestured to the second cup of coffee on his desk. Wally grabbed it and asked, "You get anything from him?"

"He said the girl was safe and would be home soon and stay away."

"Bull."

David shrugged. They sat down on either side of the desk. Wally grabbed a file from his briefcase on the floor, dropped it on the desk and jumped right in. "Betsy Schneider. Society girl. She's been gone a few days. Father's a big wig industry type. Only child so Daddy raises her to run the business one day - business school, board meetings. But she got bored. Started hanging out her society girlfriends. She dives into the flapper scene and they hit all the fancy gin mills. Sometimes they stay out all night but nothing too crazy. Then a new girl joins up. Gives the others the willies but not ours. They spend more time away from the group. Then, poof. Betsy doesn't come home." Wally shrugged and sipped the coffee. "I look into it. They've been hitting the opium dens."

"The Mind Mists," David inserted. Wally nodded.

"Where else? And you know I can't get anything out of those guys."

"Think she's still alive?"

Wally shrugged again. "Before this morning, no. Now...?"

"Yeah. Something else is going on. All right, I'm in. For half." Wally started to splutter. "Save it. I'm too tired to argue and you don't have a choice anyway." David took Wally's silence as agreement.

"What do you have on this new girl?"

"Not much. Name's Angela Anderssen. Another heiress. Was engaged to a regular Joe, broke it off recently. Now she's getting hitched to another industry type. Funny time to start hitting speakeasies and dens but rich people, ya know?"

"See what you else you can get. I'll check the Mists. And Wally, this time...be careful."

Wally donned his hat, winked and left the office.

David finished his coffee and flipped through the file. It wasn't just business school. The father taught her golf, tennis, riding, hunting, even had someone in for self-defense. There was a picture of Betsy. Blond bob, pretty smile, a mischievous glint in her eye. He let out a frustrated sigh. Thirty minutes ago all he was looking forward to was a long nap. He pocketed the picture and grabbed his hat. Sleep would have to wait.

David walked the four blocks to the Mind Mists. After the pulps started using opium dens as exotic locales, a gangster named Sheng Lao had a bright idea. Instead of using backrooms of old flop houses, he built a hive of honeycombed rooms exactly like what Americans think China looks like. He used a building close enough to Canal Street that Caucasians would get a thrill coming into Chinatown without having to actually come into Chinatown. It soon catered exclusively to the wealthy and Sheng rose to lead the Golden Dragons. Sheng and David had an uneasy mutual respect. He spent the whole walk trying to find an angle to use on Sheng. He had zilch unless he went in on the up and up.

The Mists wasn't open for business in the morning although it was staffed all day every day. Clients often needed extra time to sober up. So David was surprised that the front door was propped open. Even more surprising, the great room was deserted. Decorated in green and red with a large number of pillars carved with Chinese symbols and coiling golden dragons, the large room took up most of the first of four floors. Velvet reclining couches where clients waited for private rooms were scattered throughout. David knew the mirror high in the wall concealed an office. He looked up and waved. No response. Great. The one time I'm not trying to be sneaky.

"I've got the heebies. Talkin' 'bout the jeebies..." David stopped singing as soon as he realized he was. That Louis Armstrong tune always popped out when he was nervous. Bad habit but his nerves were on to something. This was weird.

David turned slowly in the center of the room. A shadowed stairway led to the upper floors, the rooms for clients and Sheng's office. There was another door opposite. David always assumed it led to a basement. Might be worth checking out. He continued turning. There were stacks of boxes and crates next to the front door that he hadn't noticed when he came in.

Striding quickly over, David looked in the top box. It was filled with small packages of red powder that almost seemed to glow. This wasn't opium. David pocketed one bag and looked at the crates. The top crate was nailed shut. He looked and listened but didn't see or hear anyone. He strained with his power to lift the lid quietly. There was a small squeak of nails on wood but otherwise he succeeded. The crate was filled with packing straw. David moved it aside and saw a microscope and petri dishes. He examined the exterior of the crates but didn't see any shipping labels or markings.

He set the lid back on the crate, and was lining up the nails to the existing holes when he heard voices speaking Cantonese behind him. The voices stopped as soon as he heard them. David turned innocently. He faced Sheng Lao and three Dragons. Sheng took in David, the crates and the open front door. He snapped out what sounded like a sharp rebuke to one of his men. The man stuttered, then hung his head silently. Sheng sighed.

"Sorry, David. Good help and all that." He barked something else in Cantonese and the three mobsters advanced on David. He tried to shoot a marble at the middle one but he was so taken aback by this sudden turn, he sent it wide. It hit a pillar decoration with a *tink*. The middle goon swung hard at David. He had learned—painfully—not to rely solely on his power. He knew how to fight. He blocked the blow high and turned to his right to block a low kick coming from the one on the right. If he could just hold them one moment...

He never saw the blow to the back of his neck that sent him into darkness.

CR

He came to in a fog of pain. His neck and head throbbed in an off-beat staccato. His tired body wanted to sink back down to unconsciousness, into at least a parody of sleep. David squashed the impulse. He was in trouble and he wouldn't get out of it by passing out again.

He took several slow breaths as quietly as he could, listening. The silence that came back told him maybe he was alone. Slowly forcing his eyes open, David looked around. He sat in a metal frame chair, arms and legs tied individually. A quick test demonstrated the knots were ferociously tight. Goons were probably trying to make up for leaving the door open and were working extra hard to make sure he stayed put.

He was in a room with one light directly overhead, that lit only the center of the room. Small room, maybe 10' x 10'. Hard to tell with the shadows. Two feet to his left was a small folding table. He saw his hat, his jacket, his wallet, his bag of marbles with the tie closed up tight, the picture of Betsy and the weird red powder laid out neatly. Great. So Sheng Lao knew everything and David still knew nothing.

All right, this was bad. But if he could clear the pain in his head a little he could work a way out of this. Because while Sheng might know everything about the situation, he didn't know everything about David. Not by a long shot.

He focused on his breath, attempting to breathe through each throb of pain but it was difficult with his head and his neck unsynchronized. Plus, he was really starting to feel the ropes on his arms and legs. And the exhaustion. So it's tough. Do it anyway. He tried again just as the door opened.

Sheng Lao and the remorseful tough from earlier walked in. Sheng wore a sympathetic smile. "I really am sorry about all of this, David." He gestured and the tough opened up a small canvas folding stool and set in front of David. Sheng sat gracefully. "I told my man to kill the fat one before he came to you. The fool got it in his head that he should take both of you out. Your solution was amusing. I was tempted to let him stew like that, but I cannot have my men shamed publicly."

"How you deal with your boys is your business. I just came here to talk."

"I'm sure you did. But you've seen rather too much at this point. I need to determine the extent of your knowledge and if you've spoken to anyone else and then I will have to kill you. Painful or quick is, of course, up to you."

"Damnit, Sheng..." Louis Armstrong's horn started to *braw braw brawp* in his head but David shoved it aside. He couldn't afford to get slapped around. His concentration was suspect already. A few hits from the tough, who was looking eager to atone, and there would be no way he'd be able to use his power effectively. And his power was the only way out of this. So stall, focus, prepare.

"All right, yeah. Wally came to me. He wanted help finding a girl."

"Yes, he was sniffing around the other day. We sent him on his way but it was clear he would go to you next."

"Yeah, good ol' Wally." David kept his breath even. He envisioned what he wanted to do. His power was more than throwing things through the air. He could reach out with his mind and pull forth and manipulate a malleable substance, an ectoplasm.

"And..." Sheng prodded impatiently.

"And nothing. The trail ended here, so I came to talk. You had your thugs grab me."

Sheng shook his head. He picked up the packet of red stuff. "And this?"

"That was a weird thing I saw and I took a quick peak. Sorry I pocketed it but you startled me."

"Come, come, David. There must be more to it than that."

"No. There mustn't." The desperation creeping into his voice was real. He wasn't sure he could keep up the conversation and prepare his escape. "I have no clue what that is. Tell me it's food coloring for a new kind of Gin Fizz and I'll believe you."

Sheng tossed the packet back on the table and cocked his head at David. He was still for several moments which suited David fine. The bastards had to tie all four limbs separately. He had never handled four different flows of ectoplasm before. He exhaled and stretched his mind out into… wherever it was that made this possible. If he survived this he needed to find someone to teach him more about his powers. And Cantonese. Damn it, David, focus.

He almost missed when Sheng said, "Don't breathe a sigh of relief, my friend. I am just trying to determine why you are stalling." David spluttered but Sheng waved it away. "Don't try to deny it. Talking so freely and yet giving nothing away. What else could you be doing? But I truly do not understand why. You can't be expecting help to arrive. My men have already brought the fat one in. He'll be talking soon. You cannot stop that. So what is it?"

David shrugged. "No idea. But if you want to play along and tell me the whole plan, I'll listen attentively."

Sheng's laugh was genuine, deep and long. "Oh, David. I will miss you. I am going to check on your friend. We'll see if you are more honest when I return." He then turned to the tough, said two short words in Cantonese and left the room. The tough advanced pulling a long steel knife from behind his back. Now or never.

David unleashed his ability and the power surged. On each of his limbs, directly below the ropes, silver viscous material appeared. Each stream quickly formed and hardened into razor sharp knives that sliced his ropes effortlessly. David stood. The tough hesitated, not sure what he had just seen. The four knives melted and flowed up his limbs, consolidating in his hands. They melded together into the shape of a curved sword, two and half feet long, solid and sharp. The tough tried to lunge with his knife. David parried and thrust. The tough reacted too late. David ran the sword through the man's chest.

The power ebbed from David as the man collapsed. It had been too complex to hold long. He grabbed his bag of marbles from the table and quickly stepped into the hall. Sheng was two doors down speaking with a goon. They turned at the sound of David's footsteps, eyes widening in surprise. No time to untie the bag. David used his power and hurled the entire bag at Sheng. Sheng ducked. The goon charged silently at David. The goon feinted high with a fist and struck low with a kick. David blocked the kick and thrust a punch at the guy's chest. He blocked easily with his left hand and struck hard at David's face with his right. David dodged, stepping back quickly. The goon followed up with a flurry of blows aimed at keeping David off balance. It worked. David blocked or dodged each but wasn't fast enough to get a counter strike in. He was being pushed back. He couldn't win like this. Fortunately, he didn't have to.

At the next punch, David blocked and stepped forward quickly. He got inside the goon's reach and briefly grappled him. David got the left arm pinned but the right was free. The goon feinted with his right. David flinched. The goon used that distraction to break free. His left arm snaked out of the pin and quickly pinned David's right, bending it at a bad angle. He could snap David's arm in a second. He didn't have a second.

The bag of marbles that had been lying on the floor down the hall was once again flying through the air. It struck the goon in the back of the head. The man's eyes flared and then dulled as he collapsed onto the ground.

David looked up. Sheng gave him a quizzical look then called out loudly. The door the goon was guarding opened and yet another Dragon came out. For the love of... How many guys does Sheng have at the den on a Sunday morning? The Dragon smiled and it highlighted the scar running up his neck and ear. Oh, this guy. He'll be wanting payback.

Ear Scar advanced slowly on David waving a wicked looking knife, dripping blood. Farther back, David saw Sheng hightail it down the narrow hall and up a set of stairs. David slid into a defensive stance. Ear Scar lifted the knife in front of his own face.

"Your friend bleeds really easily." He stuck out his tongue and licked the blood on the knife. What the—? Who licks blood? David didn't hesitate. He slung a glob of ectoplasm right at Ear Scar's mouth. It hit the knife, the hand holding it and the tongue and instantly hardened. Tongue and hand were now stuck to the knife. Ear Scar wailed a confused, scared, stiff-tongued wail.

David quickly stepped to his opponent and grabbed the side of his head. "Never show off in a fight." Then he slammed Ear Scar's head into the wall. It connected with satisfying thunk and Ear Scar collapsed.

Not sure what awaited him behind the open door, David first ducked back into "his" room. He put on his jacket and grabbed his things. He called the bag of marbles to him, untied it and placed it back home in his pocket. Now he was ready for anything. Like rescuing his friend and the missing woman while fighting his way through a building filled with a seemingly endless supply of goons to face down a crime boss and discover the secret plan. David was going to have to rethink taking cases from Wally.

Speaking of whom, David quickly went back out and down to Wally's room. A quick peek around the door showed only Wally, tied like David had been. But Wally had been worked over extensively. He was shirtless which showed off the bruises and cuts all over his chest and arms. His right eye was swollen shut and his lower lip was split. David entered saying, "This is you being careful?"

"Ha ha, Mr. Li. Just get me out of... What the hell is that?" While Wally was talking, David formed an ectoplasm knife to cut the ropes. Wally didn't know David had powers, until now.

"This is me helping." David reached down and sliced the ropes.

Wally stood up and looked at David warily. "You going to explain that later?"

"Later, yeah."

Wally nodded. This room also had a table in the center with Wally's things on it, including a .45 and its clip. Wally started putting on his shirt. "They jumped me right after I left your place. Wanted to know what I knew about some Latin sounding group."

"Latin? Wait. Astrum Argentum?"

"Yeah that's the one."

"Damn it. The Silver Star. We need to find Betsy, get out and get some help. This is bigger than us."

"Guess we're going to have a really long talk later. What's the plan?"

David shot him a pointed look. "You up for a fight?"

Wally snorted. "Please. I've had worse in the ring. You know, I used to spar with John Mabry, when he was a heavyweight contender."

"Really," David deadpanned. "I've never heard you mention that before. We need to grab someone and find out where they're holding Betsy. Move as fast as we can."

Wally loaded his gun, cocked it and released the safety. He nodded ready. They moved fast down the hall, slowing as they went up the stairs. The door to the great room was open wide. They slowed to a stop and David tried to stay hidden in the shadows. There were voices raised in argument.

"And if your drug had worked properly," Sheng loudly proclaimed, "we wouldn't have had to keep her so long. We can go round and round all you like but assigning blame must wait until the situation is resolved."

Two groups were facing off among the pillars. Sheng and three more Dragons, two with pistols, one with a shotgun, were to David's left. Four white men were grouped to the right. All were in conservative business suits, three were holding MP 18 machine guns—probably Silver Star agents. Swaying unsteadily between them was Betsy wearing a rumpled, torn, dirty dress that had probably been fancy before she was taken. She seemed unaware of anything around her. The Dragon with the shotgun held it partially at her back, but David could see even from here the man was more concerned with the armed men across from him than the drugged up girl in front of him.

"We will resolve the situation," the un-armed white man said. "And then we will determine who is at fault and how much damage has been done. You and your men just need to stay out of our way until then."

So outnumbered, outgunned and the one person they needed to protect smack dab in the middle of it. David looked a question at Wally. Wally shrugged back. David nodded towards the closest pillars. Wally gave him a thumbs up. They both moved quickly and settled in behind two columns. The movement must have caught Sheng's eye.

"David, have you finally decided to join us? Is the fat one still alive?" David saw Wally seethe at that and try draw a bead on Sheng. The angle was bad though. Wally turned his gun towards one of the men with a submachine gun. The two groups were still covering each other but each had turned partially towards David and Wally.

"Wally's fine, thanks. Why don't he and I take Betsy out of here and the rest of you can argue without interruption?"

"Generous, but I am afraid our friends would never agree. You can still accept a quick death however."

"Generous, but..." David never finished his quip. Betsy moved like lighting. The tong member's split focus had no room for her. He paid a price. She grabbed the barrel of the shotgun and yanked it out of his hands. He stumbled forward. She drove the butt into his stomach. He dropped to his knees. She raised the gun and fired. An armed Silver Star man went down. Chaos erupted.

Wally fired and his Silver Star agent dropped. David sent a marble flying. Instead of the head shot he was going for, he hit his agent on the hand. Still it hurt enough that the man dropped his gun. Sheng was screaming orders in Cantonese. The head agent was chanting odd words and raising his hands. Betsy was cocking the shotgun and turning to face Sheng.

One of Sheng's men pointed his pistol in Betsy's face. Sheng screamed and grabbed the man's hand. The shot went wide. Betsy aimed at Sheng. Sheng pulled his man in front of him. Betsy fired point blank at the man's chest with devastating results. Sheng shoved the dead man forward, knocking over Betsy who hit the floor and dropped the gun. Sheng's other man fired at Wally but hit only the shielding column. Wally took that moment to run to the next pillar up.

David hurled ectoplasm to cover the gun his target had dropped. The Silver Star agent bent down to pick it up and hit only a hardening silver shell. The bodies of his fellow agents were starting to smoke and dissolve. He turned to grab one of their guns instead. David shot a marble at him but it hit... something a few feet away and dropped.

David looked around in confusion. The lead agent stopped his chant and dropped his hands. Now David could see a faint shimmer between him and them. Damn it. Whatever that shimmer was stopped David's attack. Probably would stop bullets, too. Anyway, Wally had his hands full with the tong.

In fact, Wally was using the lull to advance pillars again. Sheng directed the one Dragon on his feet to drag a struggling Betsy to the back of the room. The one she struck with the shotgun was just standing. The lead agent chanted again and spread his hands in front of him. A wide wave of energy burst forth from his hands. It plowed into the struggling tong member who collapsed. It struck David's pillar and tore pieces off, but David was safe. Wally wasn't. The blast caught him full force between pillars. He dropped hard with a sickening crack, his neck turned the wrong way.

David closed his eyes. Exhaustion struck harder than that energy wave. His friend was dead. He couldn't reach the others through the shield. They could work around his pillar from both sides and trap him. He wanted to lie down and weep. Wally deserves more than surrender.

Nobody was moving. The Silver Star agents weren't advancing. Maybe they would lose the shimmering shield if they did. Maybe they were waiting to see what he would do. Whatever it was, it gave David a moment. And he had one last trick. He couldn't send something through the shield but what about something already behind the shield?

David closed his eyes and focused his power. His last ability let him manipulate small amounts of certain elements, including lead. He just needed a couple moments. Sheng was saying something. David focused and felt the lead bullets in the agent's gun, their shape, their weight. He drew small amounts forth, shaped them into small pellets and excited them. He exhaled and released.

The lead pellets erupted from the magazine. Some went into the agent, some went into his boss and some went into the remaining ammunition which ignited like fireworks at New Year. Sheng and the others were behind the Silver Star agents and largely protected.

The Silver Star agents and the pillars nearest them were shredded.

David stepped out. Sheng had a knife at Betsy's throat. The last tong member held his .45 in unsteady hands. David lashed out with his power and the gun fell. Sheng barked a command and the henchman ran at David. David shot a marble. It punched a small bloody hole in the man's chest and penetrated his heart. He stumbled two more steps then dropped.

Sheng tried to maintain his usual composure. "We seem to be at an impasse, David." He pressed the knife a little into Betsy's neck.

David shook his head. "No. We aren't."

"No, I suppose we aren't," he sighed. "You were wise to keep your skills hidden. I greatly underestimated you."

"Let her go. No cops. I know some people who would like to talk to you about the Silver Star."

Sheng laughed desperately. "You're with AEGIS? Goodness, the gods were against me on this one. No, David, I don't think I would like that. When we started, a most frightening woman told me if I betrayed them she would kill me, resurrect me, and kill me again, repeatedly, for all time. I believe her." He started to slump in resignation, the knife dropping a little. "No, better an—"

Betsy lashed out again. She pushed Sheng's knife hand out from her body. Then she grabbed his arm in both her hands. She angled her hip into his pelvis, knocking him off balance. She used his arm as a lever and flipped him over her hip. He fell on his face. She had his arm twisted behind his back and stepped hard on his shoulder.

"Who is this woman? I'd like to call dibs on one of those deaths." She lifted her foot and struck Sheng in the head. He sagged unconscious. She turned to David. "Thanks for the help. You said you know some people? Can you call them now?"

He called his AEGIS contact. Then he grabbed the rope from downstairs and firmly tied Sheng, Ear Scar and the hallway goon before they came to. He sat down next to Wally. Betsy came over.

"He was your friend?" she asked. He nodded. "I'm sorry. And I'm grateful."

David looked at her sharply.

"No, I mean... You two could have walked away when you saw what you were up against. You didn't and I am deeply grateful."

David smiled wistfully. "If you had known Wally you would know he never would have made any other decision." After a moment he asked, "What was going on here?"

"I'm not certain," she replied. "Angela brought me here and then this guy," she gestures towards Sheng, "shows up and starts ordering her around. She does what he says without hesitation. It was weird. Then he dosed me with a red powder and started ordering me around like Angela. I was groggy with the first dose but otherwise I was myself. They started in on what I should do, how I should behave when I got home. I was confused. They realized it hadn't worked. They kept trying. Apparently these new guys..." she pointed at the dissolving bodies of the Silver Star agents and shuddered. "They were here to examine me and find out what happened. I'm not sure I would have survived that."

They sat in the awkward silence of two people who didn't know each other but had fought a life or death fight together. Soon a horde of AEGIS agents descended on the Mind Mists and started a whirlwind of interviews, investigations and explanations that lasted several days. The agents immediately hustled Betsy away from the scene and David assumed they wouldn't cross paths again. He was wrong.

A few days later, she attended Wally's sparse funeral. David was pleasantly surprised. After the graveside service he approached her.

"Thanks for coming."

"Of course," she replied. They stood next to each in another awkward silence. "Will you walk with me a ways?" she asked. He nodded and they slowly walked down a grassy hill toward the cemetery gate.

"I found out a little more about what happened," he informed her. "The Silver Star was using the Mind Mists to take control of heirs to industrial fortunes. Apparently, a year ago, they had tried assassinating the men who finance AEGIS. This time around they tried taking control of the men and women who will be financing it in a few years. They used Sheng as a front man, promising control of all New York's underworld. AEGIS created an antidote and freed the others, including Angela." Earlier he had wondered if he could ever leave this secret war. Now he wondered if he wanted to.

"How did you resist the mind drugs?" David asked.

"The AEGIS people tell me it was created partly with... with mysticism." A new idea for her that these things were real. "And apparently I have a particularly strong resistance to mystic effects."

David nodded. "I guess you were supposed to be released back to your family the next day. But they couldn't do that until you were under control. Your parents got scared and brought in Wally."

"Yes. I thought my parents would start some kind of search. I figured the best thing was fake a stupor and wait for a chance to escape."

"Very smart, Miss Schneider. So, what's next for you?"

"Actually, I was hoping to talk to you about that."

"Oh?"

"My life..." she took a breath and plunged in. "My life has been ill spent. Dad's business is a bad fit for me. So I turned away and focused almost exclusively on myself. This Silver Star... what they could have done, what they are trying to do, they scare me. I want to do something about it. I want to work with you. I want you to train me."

"I'm sure AEGIS would bring you into the fold."

She shook her head. "My dad is one of their financiers. One day, I will be too. They don't want to risk me, or more accurately, my funding."

"Recent history aside, most of my work isn't for AEGIS or against the Silver Star."

"That's fine. I'm game to help all sorts of people, not just kidnapped for nefarious mystical purposes people."

David smiled at this. He had never thought about a partner before but it had appeal. He knew she could keep her head in a hot situation and more than hold her own in a fight. Plus, he could use a hand. He had picked up several of Wally's open cases, and AEGIS said there was something odd in Atlantic City they wanted him to look into.

"Li and Associate Investigations has a nice ring. All right, Betsy. Let's get to work."

A Valkyrie in Repose

by Colin Fisk

I'm not sure what annoyed me more—the garish display of wealth during a depression, or the fact that I was at a party in a Paris apartment that encompassed half a block and was being thrown by a pair of suspected German spies that I had to be cordial with to keep up appearances.

I could not help but compare the guests to the attendees at the parties my parents hosted. When you grow up in Boston and are a direct descendant of the Dotys who came over on the Mayflower, you're forced into a lot of lavish social engagements with phony people. Even though I rejected cotillion and a coming out party in favor of rock climbing in the Berkshires, or airplane racing at Belmont Park in New York, it wasn't until I was recruited into

AEGIS that my parents understood that their little girl would not be participating in maintaining their genetic heritage anytime soon.

Still, every time I was in the area, they insisted on parading me around to men of equal or higher social strata in the hope I would settle down and give up my "trifling pastime" of helping save the world.

I grabbed a flute of champagne as a server passed me by. I grasped it in my right hand as my left was still slightly incapacitated from an injury sustained in a night drop over Romania two years prior. Though I missed the companionship of the Valkyries as a whole, I'm not sure I would go back if offered, as my friendship with my current partner, Heidi Mueller, was something I valued more than a return to action. Besides, working undercover had its own merits and occasional adrenaline rush, and was usually much safer than dropping in on a group of cultists trying to raise the Vlad Tepes from the dead.

As I approached my hosts, Heinrich and Inga Schmitt, I could not help but notice the man talking to them and how, in profile, he seemed oddly familiar. Well dressed in a tasteful and new black suit, his handlebar mustache twitched in reaction to something Herr Schmitt said.

I drew closer. As he turned to me, I stopped momentarily, surprised to see a friend I'd known since childhood.

"Alyssa Swanson, is that you?"

I moved forward and offered him my cheek, which he gently kissed, his facial hair lightly tickling my skin.

"James Harrington, what are you doing in Paris?"

"I'm here on business, actually." He turned and gestured effusively to the Schmitts, "Have you met our hosts, Heinrich and Inga Schmitt?"

I smiled demurely and shook my head. "I was just on my way over to thank them for their hospitality. Herr and Frau Schmitt, thank you for the invitation to this gathering."

My thanks drew little reaction from my hosts as they quickly turned to speak to another guest who had approached them. I shrugged and turned to James who offered me the crook of his arm. I accepted, sliding my damaged left arm carefully through, and he guided me toward the open doors, which led to the penthouse balcony.

With just the two of us looking over the gardens of the Paris Observatory, I turned to my friend. "What kind of business has brought you to Paris?"

"Would you believe that I work for an insurance company now? The Schmitts are negotiating with my company to finance several property purchases and are offering some of their art as collateral. I've been sent to authenticate the pieces and confirm their value. I only arrived yesterday afternoon and was quickly whisked off to a tailor to buy a suit for this party. I've barely had the tour of the place and have not yet had a chance to view the artwork."

"Art, insurance company, mortgages. What happened to the teenager who dreamed of playing for the Red Sox?"

James laughed heartily. "There was a lack of talent in that area standing between me and my dreams. I got my actuarial training at Harvard and my father made the introduction to Metropolitan Life. With the passage last year of the Housing Act of 1934, we are funding a lot of loans. However, the requirement of tangible assets for securing them has meant that they need more appraisers than adjusters. I minored in Art History and, after the firm discovered that little fact, I've found my-self spending a most of my time looking at art instead of financial tables. But, enough about me. What have you been doing with your life? I heard through the grapevine that you were racing airplanes at one point?"

"That was short lived and mostly done as a lark. I was at Wesleyan studying art and liter-ature and needed an escape from the marital pursuits of various suitors my parents would try and introduce me to. So I picked up a hobby that would scare off the stuffed shirts. You know, the ones that wanted a dutiful wife to stand at their side at social gatherings and not say anything."

James laughed, "That's the young woman I well remember."

"When I graduated, I got a job as an au pair for a lovely couple. A few years ago, they moved here to Paris and brought me along. I left their employ about nine months ago and got a job as a clerk at Shakespeare and Com-pany. These days I live with a roommate and spend my off hours listening to the authors who congregate at the store."

That was my cover story. I actually did take shifts at the store, but spent most of my time in a hidden lab beneath the stockroom helping Heidi test the gadgets that would accompany me into the field when needed.

"So, what you are really saying is, like me, we both are drawn to pretension."

I laughed. "I suppose it would seem that way."

"Would it be inappropriate if I used you as an excuse to tour the apartment to view the artwork? We are probably going to be limited as to what is currently on display. In reality, what they are offering as collateral is being stored in the basement."

Here was my perfect excuse to be seen wandering in areas I should not be. "I would love it. And, in truth, this gown was a hand me down from the mother of the child who was my ward. Since I have no real investment in it, I would not object to taking the full tour, including the pieces not on display."

"Ah, but I'm afraid I would. I did mention this is a new suit. But, if you are truly interested, would you be willing to join me tomorrow? I can even wrangle wages out of my firm if you so desire."

That was something I loved about James. No matter how indelicate your situation, he could bring up a solution in such a way that the person being offered his favor would not see it as a debt.

"That would be lovely. And, I must confess, extra funds would help maintain my extended vacation from true adulthood."

James laughed, and, once again, offered his arm, which I accepted as we wandered toward parts of the house that were off limits for this gathering.

❧

While the previous evening's tour had been educational in the Schmitt's taste in artwork, it had not yielded any fruit in my search for any connection to the Nazis. I was hoping James' offer, which would provide me access to other areas of their residence, might produce a lead.

I arrived at the Schmitt's house promptly at ten in the morning the next day. I had chosen to play the part of the uncouth American and dressed myself in a pair of trousers and work jacket from our storeroom. There was a secondary reason for my fashion choice. Since my wound left me unable to form a complete fist with my left hand, Heidi had created a jacket sheath for my favorite knife. With a specific flick of my wrist, the hilt of a twelve-inch razor sharp steel blade would be an extension of my damaged arm in a matter of seconds.

In addition to the blade, Heidi had packed my jacket and trousers with several other goodies, including multiple miniature cameras, a Farnsworth communicator and a Tesla gun which delivered an electrical charge from a mere spark to a near deadly discharge depending on the setting.

I knocked on the door and James opened it.

"Welcome back, Alyssa."

"Thank you, James. But why are you answering the door?"

He laughed. "It turns out the Schmitts left immediately after the party to their Chateau in the Alps. They handed me the keys as if I were a trusted confidant, rather than a business associate they just met."

"Don't you find that odd?"

"It's certainly unusual. They said something about the propriety of allowing an expert to do their job in a manner that avoids the appearance of outside influence, but it's certainly not the norm."

James ushered me into the house. Instead of taking the stairs up to the third floor where the party was last night, we wandered several corridors before walking into a large kitchen. I'd been in some extravagant houses growing up, all equipped with kitchens designed to be staffed by multiple people, but this was twice the size of any I'd seen. The prep area was larger than the size of the living area and one of the bedrooms in the apartment Heidi and I shared. The stone hearth in the center of the room was over ten feet in diameter.

Much to my surprise, James walked directly to the hearth. When I followed, I saw that instead of a fire pit, there was instead a winding set of stone stairs leading down into the darkness.

"It's a bit disconcerting, but I gather the apartment was built over an old abbey. They used to hide people fleeing the Inquisition in the cellars below. The hearth made a good place to dig out a set of stairs as they could cover the passage with a stone plug that could have a fire built upon it."

"And if the Inquisitors stayed a while?" I asked.

"I'm not sure. Herr Schmitt showed me the staircase last night and showed me to the room where the art is stored. He did mention it was recently wired for electricity, so we won't have to rely on lanterns."

"That's something."

"Indeed" replied James as he pressed a button on a switch that lay on top of the staircase. The comforting glow of electrical bulbs illuminated the stairs.

We proceeded down the surprisingly wide stairs until we reached a stone cellar with three doors. Stacked high along the only wall without a door was plenty of seasoned chopped wood. One of the doors was ajar and I could see empty meat hooks dangling from the ceiling with wood crates lining the far wall. I estimated we were now some thirty feet under the floor of the apartment and the temperature was easily twenty degrees cooler than the house.

"It's this way," indicated James as he crossed over to the large wooden slat door to the north. He clicked another light switch on the wall and pushed open the door.

My first impression was that of a large cave, easily one hundred feet long with some twenty racks full of wine on either side of a central corridor. There were two lines of electrical lights, evenly spaced between the racks.

We strode through the wine until, at the back of the room, there was a sharp right turn into another room about forty feet square. Vertical racks lined this room with a large six foot square table in the center. In each rack were crated objects, presumably the paintings we'd come to view. The table was covered in immaculate white linen and a tool chest lay at the foot of the racks.

The rest of the morning was spent uncrating paintings and removing the giant sponges that helped preserve the art. James then studied each piece for ten minutes or so, and we crated them back up.

Though I had studied art in various museums during the last year, most of the artists were unfamiliar to me, though there was a particularly stunning harvest painting I suspected was a Reubens. The other two that stood out were a painting of a mermaid and one of a female resting against a rock as she knitted a fishing net. James seemed in his element and was making copious notes, but left me no time to investigate.

We broke for luncheon around one o'clock and went back upstairs. James produced an impressive array of meats, cheeses and bread, along with various spreads and several beers from the icebox. The food was excellent and our conversation was mostly reminiscing from our school days.

Finally, as we strode back down the stairs, I casually asked, "What's behind the other door?"

"I'm not sure. I tested it when I came down early this morning so I wouldn't look the fool when I led you to the art, but it was locked."

"Pity."

James laughed. "You always were the snoop. Remember when you found those South American statues in Katherine DeQuincy's mom's closet?"

I joined in the laughter and helped fill in the blanks of his memory about that particular incident, leaving out the part where they were an altar to an obscure Mayan god, less I break cover.

CR

James and I had parted amicably in the late afternoon with ambiguous promises to meet for dinner over the weekend. It was well into the night when Heidi and I returned to the apartment.

Unlike the laborer's outfit I had worn this morning, I was now clad in black, though similarly equipped as before. Heidi carried her black carpet bag which housed even more gadgets and weapons, though I knew she had a Tesla within easy reach in one of her pockets. In addition, the thick cane she held in her right hand had both a blade as well as a long bore shotgun concealed as part of the walking stick.

We got to the front door. I inserted the custom pick Heidi had designed for me into the lock. I pulled the trigger several times and could feel the cylinder twist in my hand, then was quickly rewarded with a "click" indicating the lock had been sprung.

We entered through the door quickly, but casually, as if we were supposed to be there, and closed it behind us.

I guided Heidi to the moonlit kitchen and, as we entered, I heard a muffled thump and a cry of pain from the bottom of the well lit staircase.

I looked at Heidi and she nodded; she had heard it as well.

Heidi raised her cane into a more offensive position and I pulled out my Tesla.

We started down the steps methodically, with me craning my head to take in as much as I could without exposing myself. About halfway down, I swore I could hear the sound of scrabbling footsteps. We finally reached the bottom of the steps and the room was empty, though all three doors were ajar.

There, in front of the previously locked door on the west wall, was the prone form of James, a small pool of blood oozing from a wound on the back of his head.

Protocol demanded we sweep the room before checking on my friend. Heidi and I shifted so our backs were to each other, and we slowly turned in a circle.

We cleared the meat locker first and I closed the door behind us. I could see nothing in the wine cellar and had no inclination to enter that large a room with only two of us, so I shut that door as well.

I finally moved to James, saw that he was still breathing and stepped over his prone form, Heidi now at my side.

The room in front of us was not what I expected.

I'd hoped to find a cache of maps, communications from Germany and maybe weapons that implicated the Schmitts in spying activities.

Instead, what I saw was a twenty by twenty room with a central altar that had large bloody ropes connected to it by metal loops augured into the stone. There were more red stains spattered around the base of the four foot high rock formation. The single light bulb centered over the altar shed enough illumination to show the walls were blank save for what appeared to be arterial blood spray in eight different patterns. Oddly, there were no candles, incense or ritual knives in the room, nor an effigy, though it was clear sacrifices were being made, presumably animal.

Heidi looked ill, which wasn't that surprising. Though she was field qualified, she did so to understand the conditions I would be operating under. In reality, this was only the second time she had accompanied me and the previous was on an overnight stakeout.

I motioned for her to attend to James and I stepped forward into the room. Upon closer examination, the position of the ropes and the size of the altar was not for an animal, as I had expected, but to my disgust, a human. The presence of multiple strands of human hair, in different lengths and colors, confirmed my suspicions.

I turned to speak to Heidi when something detached itself from shadows in the corner to the west of the door and came silently running at me. I had the impression of a large, humanoid, black figure, claws glistening with some type of viscous fluid and deep red eyes before I leaped into action.

"Heidi!" I yelled as I twisted out of its path and snapped my left arm out, flicking my wrist at the same time. The comforting feel of my knife's hilt settled into my hand and I grasped it as tight as the damage would allow, though it wasn't necessary as the support structure was actually in the sheath.

I narrowly dodged a slash from its claws and returned the favor with a backhand riposte to its center mass. I could feel the impact shudder down my arm as the knife struck home. The creature did not make a sound as the blade tore through its midsection and it went down in a heap. My Tesla clattered to the floor.

I took two steps back and, was wise to do so, as it turned and leaped for me again with such force that I was showered with dark red blood from the abdominal wound. I spun the opposite way, nearly making contact with the altar in the process, and scored another hit; this time cleanly lopping off its arm just below the elbow.

Before it could turn to attack again, there was a loud concussive *bang* and its head exploded, spattering the wall instead of me.

I turned to the sound of the noise, my ears ringing, and there was Heidi, her shotgun cane socketed against her shoulder. She advanced into room and racked another round into the chamber all the while keeping it pointed at the unmoving form.

"*Der schwartze Mann,*" she exclaimed at an exaggerated level.

"What?"

"*Die Butzemann.*" She shook her head. "Sorry, in English it would be the Bogeyman. The creature from the shadows that steals children, but the Bogeyman is just a myth, right?"

"Evidence would suggest to the contrary."

"What in tarnation is going on," James demanded groggily as he came up from behind Heidi, rubbing his head. He pointed at the corpse on the floor and looked at Heidi's shotgun, then at the knife in my left hand. "What on earth is that thing? When did you get here, Alyssa? I came back to check on one of the paintings, which I think was stolen. Who is your companion? And why do you have a knife covered in blood?"

"That's going to take some explaining, but not here. Heidi, we need to get him out of here."

Heidi nodded and brought the cane down slightly. She turned and took the three steps to where her open bag lay. She knelt down and glanced at its contents for a moment before reaching in, grabbing a rag and throwing it in my direction in a smooth motion. She didn't bother to look back to see if I'd caught it, instead swiveling her head to keep scanning the room.

I snatched the cloth out of the air and quickly cleaned off my blade. I then bundled the rag and pushed the tip of the knife against it gently, releasing my grip on the hilt. It retracted back into my coat sleeve clicking into its ready position and I dropped the bloody towel into my pocket.

I picked up the Tesla and said, "Let's go, and quickly. James, follow me and Heidi will cover your rear flank." I held up my hand to

cut off his next question. "I'll answer everything, but not here."

◯℞

We covered the walk back to Shakespeare
and Company in less than fifteen minutes.
James had started to wobble by the end of our
jaunt, and Heidi held him upright as I unlocked the door.

We entered the store, and I was hit by the
lovely waft of must and old paper, which
slowed my heart rate down to normal. Heidi
locked the door behind us, and I pocketed the
Tesla. I grabbed James' hand with my right
and pulled him toward the back of the store,
comfortable in my element even without the
lights on.

We pushed past the curtain to the storeroom and I reached for the false light switch.
Letting go of his hand, I quickly depressed the
buttons in the proper sequence and then
crossed the large storeroom to the back wall. I
grabbed the bust of Shakespeare that sat on a
pedestal and turned the head counter-clock-
wise ninety degrees. The hidden panel slid
open and the stairs leading down to our base
lit up.

"What on earth is going on?" asked James.

"Follow me, and I will explain."

I descended the stairs carved into the limestone quickly, walked into the common room and turned, my arms outstretched in welcome.

James came down the stairs cautiously and stopped at the base.

"Welcome to AEGIS," I stated, a smile on my face.

"AEGIS? You mean..? You're with AEGIS? How did that happen?"

I walked forward and grabbed his arm, gently pulling him to the sofa which faced the door.

"Have a seat, and we can talk about it."

James slumped into the couch and rubbed the back of his head.

Heidi crossed over to the door on the west wall and reemerged a minute later with an ice pack that she handed to James. He thanked her, held it in place where he'd been hit, and looked at me expectantly.

"This is my partner, Heidi Mueller. Heidi, this is James Harrington, an old friend."

He looked at her and smiled, then turned his gaze back to me.

"I've been with AEGIS for five years now."

"Five years? How did that happen?"

"It was the airplane racing that first caught their attention, but my degrees in folklore and archaeology didn't hurt either. I was recruited and, after a lot of hard training, was accepted into the Valkyrie squadron."

"You're a Valkyrie?"

"I used to be. About two years ago I was injured in an operation in Romania. When I recovered, they moved me into an operational role here in Paris with Heidi. She's an amazing gadget and weapons designer. I do actually take shifts here at the bookstore, gathering social intelligence in my spare time, when I'm not down here helping Heidi test out her latest creations."

"Who else knows?"

"From back home? My parents, that's it."

"Why the secrecy?"

"To maintain my cover. Within my parent's social set, trips to Paris are common. Before that, I was too busy going out on missions or training to see anyone from Boston. Most of the action I saw was nowhere near where someone from the Back Bay would ever consider visiting, so there was never any chance I would run into someone I knew.”

“Then how did you wind up at the Schmitts’ party? Were you following me?”

I laughed. “You were a happy circumstance. The Schmitts came on my radar about a month ago when a patron at the store casually mentioned to another about their new-found wealth. The Nazis have started expatriating party members and setting them up with money to spy on the social elite here in Paris and other major cities. We assume there’s a longer game in play here, but we don’t know what the goal is. I figured they were worth checking out and you gave me the perfect excuse to snoop.”

“And that thing on the floor?”

Heidi started rapidly speaking in German.

When she came to AEGIS three years ago, she only spoke her native language. When she was stressed, she tended to revert back to her upbringing. Fortunately, I’m good with languages and picked up conversational German within the first months of our partnership.

I waited until she finished and turned back to James.

"Truthfully, I don't know. Heidi is pretty serious in insisting it was a bogeyman."

"*Die Butzmann, ja.*"

James looked at me incredulously. "You aren't serious?"

"Why not? It's a legend that spawns across most cultures. My experience has been that a tale like that, one that doesn't know borders or gaps between continents, has some basis in truth. The specifics change, but the root story stays pretty consistent."

"I'm still trying to wrap my head around... wait, you said your experience?"

"The Valkyries may look great on the news reels, battling the forces of dictators and despots, but a lot of our missions involved the occult and the unexplained. Let's just says that my studies didn't stop after Wesleyan and proved to be more practical than I would have ever imagined. So yes, I'm willing to entertain the possibility that was a bogeyman."

"I don't know what to say. It's a little over-whelming and I'm not sure if it's the knot on the back of my head that's causing my head to ache or this little revelation."

"I understand. I do have a favor to ask. Can you tell me what you remember?"

James shrugged and winced. "Honestly, I remember coming down the stairs. I was determined to check on that Ruebens which I think went missing in the Great War. I saw the locked door from this morning was open and went to investigate. Then nothing."

"That's fine." I turned to Heidi "It's probably safe to presume that thing came from some passage to the house cellar. It would be consistent with the myths. Sticking to the shadows."

Heidi nodded. "That makes sense."

"Can you grab my copy of Swenson's and a map of Paris? Maybe we can figure out where it came from."

Heidi strode to the eastern door which contained our research library and her workbenches. While her part of the library focused on Physics, Chemistry and Mechanical Engineering, mine was filled with folklore and language texts. During the few minutes she was gone, I spent the time reassuring James that the worst of it was over for him. Finally, she came back with a rolled map of the city and the large, leather bound book I had asked for.

"What's that?"

"It's my copy of Gustav Swenson's tome from the eighteenth century on subterranean creatures. I remember an entry on the bogey-man."

I opened the book to the index and ran my finger down the parchment until I found the entry I was looking for. I turned the pages quickly and found the passage. I scanned it quickly, and then looked up. Both Heidi and James were staring at me expectantly.

"Well, the descriptions are vague in just about all cultures but they could match."

"Then what was it doing down there?" demanded James.

"That's the part you're not going to like. While most of the legends are about a creature that steals children away once a month, usually to eat them, there's not a lot about other motivations. Except for the Ottomans, where the name they use, *Ocu,* is essentially a corruption of the Arabic word for genie. Swenson advanced a theory that people would sacrifice their neighbors, adults and children alike, to the Ocu for wealth and power and that's where the wish granting powers of the *djinn* came about."

James turned pale. "You mean?"

I nodded. "It's possible you were meant to be an offering in exchange for wealth. There was clear evidence of multiple people having been tied to that altar. So, it's possible the source of the Schmitts' money has nothing to do with Germany."

"But, how can they get away with something like that?"

"Like what? You finished your job and mentioned to them about exploring Paris. That's the last they saw of you."

James stammered out objections for a few more minutes, growing more pensive as I countered each one with an explanation I'd heard before. Finally, he slumped back on the couch, closed his eyes and let out a soft moan.

I turned to Heidi, who had unrolled the map on the low table in front of the sofa.

"You know the city better than I," she said.

I nodded and sat down next to James who was now muttering a diatribe about the circumstances that had led him here. I studied the map, considering the layout of the Schmitts' domicile and rotated it ninety degrees so I was now looking at it from the direction where I was standing in the altar room. I traced an imaginary route with my finger, first north, then south along the boulevard.

"*Merde*," I shouted. "It's too obvious. The street runs south directly into the old limestone mines."

"Mines" asked Heidi.

"Better known as the Catacombs. And what better way to hide the bones of your victims than in a maze of skeletons?"

"So, if they are down there, does the book say anything about how many we might be looking at?"

I shook my head. "No. But the legends are always about a solitary creature for each village or region."

"Paris is not a village. There are almost 3 million people living here. There could be hundreds of those things."

"I don't think so. I saw less than ten blood patterns on the wall back in that room. If you figure the Schmitts have been here about two years and, say they somehow made contact with the bogeyman almost immediately, that's still, maybe, a victim every three months. Given the average adult is, for argument's sake maybe five times the weight of an average child, you're looking at meat for two."

James went pale. "I can't believe we are having this conversation."

Heidi nodded. "It makes sense. At least for this nest. We know that bullets can kill them. I should get more guns."

"And lights. They appear to blend very well into the shadows. I figure we should start by looking for a passage into the altar room." I turned to James as Heidi left the room. "You are staying here."

"You will get no argument from me, though, promise me this; if you arrest the Schmitts, I want to be there."

"Deal."

ℭ

Back at the house, we entered quickly, then stopped in the foyer. Heidi handed me a white overcoat from her carpet bag. I looked it over and carefully ran my hands along the armored cloth. There were translucent ropes running the length of the garment every six inches, as well as coils of the same running down the sleeves.

"Put it on and hold mine up."

I shrugged the jacket on over my knife sheath and did as she said. She pulled a bottle from the bag. After unscrewing the cap, I saw it had a dropper built into the lid. She carefully squeezed a single drop into holes in each of the strands on my garments as well as her own. As the liquid entered the rope, a bright light began to emit from each strand, growing as the chemical spread throughout.

"Very nice."

"It's a simple reaction, really. But it's also very stable, so it won't explode like the earlier prototypes."

I chuckled nervously, "That's good to know."

Heidi put the dropper away and handed me a Colt .45 pistol and a Thompson submachine gun with a fifty-round drum.

"You're not messing around, are you?"

She put on her own glowing coat and then armed herself with another pistol as well as two shotguns from the carpet bag. She slung one of the long guns over her left shoulder, the carpet bag over her right, then then stood up.

"Your math about the feeding needs is sound. But we still know very little about these creatures. I would rather be overprepared than under."

"Fair enough."

As we headed down the halls toward the kitchen, I swung my arms, experimenting to see if my range of motion would be limited. I was pleased it was not. It was then that I realized that, despite the glow, I could still see well ahead of me. I asked Heidi about it.

"The chemicals are balanced to provide enough light to illuminate your way, but not so much that the structures in your eyes adjust to the light radiating from you."

"That must have taken some time to get it right."

"I started working on the idea when I was still in Germany. It's only in the last year that I've been able to get the reaction close to where I want it to be."

"It's working just fine."

"Yes. But it's not yet perfected."

We descended the stairs side by side, weapons at the ready. As we reached the base of the stairs, I could see the creature's body was still in the same place.

I pointed to it with my left hand. Heidi nodded.

We entered the altar room. With the additional illumination, I could now see the area where the first attack came from. Where there should have been a corner to the room, a new entrance had been created from a two-cinder-block-wide section of the wall had been pushed into the room.

Heidi handed me some of her special noise canceling earplugs. I would be able to hear normal sounds, but as soon as noise reached a certain level, such as a weapon firing, the plugs would dampen the sound. I gratefully put them in my ears.

With the opening only wide enough for us to move single file, I went first, grateful for the lights on my coat to illuminate my way.

I stepped into a rough stone passage, the walls reinforced with old timber. Clearly, this had been part of the old mine, but not so far as to yet be part of the burial storage. I looked around, taking in my surroundings before moving forward. The air was cool and dry and nothing was moving within my sight. I glanced down and could see footprints, drag marks and blood trails heading west. I moved to one side to allow Heidi into the area and pointed at the mess on the floor.

She nodded grimly and we followed the marks through nearly a half mile of tunnels before coming to an open cavern.

What I noticed with my initial scan of the area was the cave ran about sixty feet deep and maybe twenty wide. There were several tunnels that intersected along all sides. Against the wall to my right was a series of stalactites with curved metal hooks dangling from several of the larger. On two of the hooks were bodies that had clearly been partially consumed. And then there were the bogey-man.

I counted at least eleven, all initially shrinking back from the lights on our coats, then exploding into action, racing at us in complete silence.

My mind registered the concussive explosion of Heidi's shotgun and then I was swinging my Tommy gun into play. I targeted the closest to me, and pulled the trigger. The machine gun stock hammered against my shoulder and the creature went down. I shifted targets and fired again.

It was over in less than five minutes, but as it always was with extended combat and my mind, time seemed to slow down into a series of jumpy movie scenes: Heidi exhausting the ammunition of her first shotgun and swinging the second into action in a perfect ballet of motion. The pair of bogeymen that tried to flank us. Heidi and me moving back to back to guard each other. The final attack coming from the ceiling as the creature grabbed stalactites like playground rungs to reach us. Heidi's shot shattering the formation causing the bogeyman to drop to the floor and my final shots from the Tommy finishing it off.

After the last rounds were fired, and nothing was moving in our vicinity, Heidi and I reloaded, still with our backs to each other, rotating slowly to confirm we were alone.

"I stand corrected. My math was right, but clearly they had other patrons," I said.

"If this was the only den," Heidi offered.

"I know. But clearing the Catacombs will be a job for the Valkyries."

"Of course," Heidi agreed. "Maybe they can also discern who else was providing them with victims."

"That's a problem for a later day. Right now, I have a solution for the Schmitts."

03

I heard the sound of the key scratching at the lock, then the tumblers dropping into place. The door opened without a sound and I could hear the voices of the Schmitts talking excitedly in German.

They walked into the house, expectant smiles on their faces.

"I wonder what they have left us in reward this time," exclaimed Frau Schmitt. "I hope it's..." Her voice trailed off as she saw James, myself and the AEGIS security agents standing in the front hallway.

"Handcuffs, I should think," I replied.

The Veiled Lady

by Trish Heinrich

Spring had come to Los Angeles in a glory of heat that made the city limp along during the day, but revive at night when a cool breeze settled on the parched landscape.

At this time of night, most children were being tucked into warm beds, ready to dream of fame, fortune or the next day's baseball game. But one child, small for her age and impossibly brave, crept out of her window and down the fire escape. Her mission was desperate and secret, especially since no one would believe tiny Ada Mesmer when she insisted that her brother wouldn't just run away. In her gut, Ada knew something terrible had happened to her beloved brother, as well as the dozens of other young men and boys who had gone missing in the last six months.

She couldn't take the way her mother tried to hide her tears, or the empty place at the dinner table, one more day. If the police wouldn't do anything to find her brother, Ada decided, she'd just have to.

The trouble was of course that being a sickly child of ten, she hadn't much experience with the world outside her small apartment. Beside the school and the park at the end of the block where she lived, Ada had hardly been anywhere, the risk to her health generally too great.

But sometimes, you have to risk much to gain much.

So, with a coat over her thin body, a thick pair of socks and boots still a bit too large, Ada went to the one place most of the missing boys had seemed to frequent: the Abandoned District.

No one knew why the small, square block had been abandoned, or why it was terrifying to so many people. It was something that most people just accepted after a while, not caring about prime real estate left to rot. But the boys of her neighborhood and a few others had made it a place to test their bravery and escape families that didn't understand them for a few hours.

The problem was, of course, that some boys had not come back from the Abandoned District.

The shadows felt deeper the moment Ada stepped over the invisible line that demarcated the Abandoned District, a chill creeping down her spine that had nothing to do with the cool night air. The wind stirred her newly straightened hair, making Ada jump in fear of someone that wasn't there. She reached a trembling brown hand up to smooth it back, dark eyes boring into the shadows in search of hidden threats.

When she was fairly certain no one was around, Ada took a deep breath and felt in her left pocket for the small mechanical bird she'd made from the scraps of metal her brother brought home from shop class. It was cool and hard in her pocket, a reminder of the love her brother felt for a little sister who was stuck at home more often than not.

"If you can't exercise your body," her brother had once told Ada, "then make sure your mind is strong."

So she had. Reading every book her mother could get from the library, discovering a talent for invention along the way. Fiction never interested her, not as much as cold, hard facts that she could count on and use to create things.

"There's nothing here," she told herself, standing up straight. "Nothing but empty buildings and my brother."

The fear built until it was a herculean effort to lift one foot in front of the other. Still, little Ada kept going, sweat trickling down her body.

Then, just as suddenly as it came upon her, the fear simply left.

Ada looked around, expecting something to explain the sudden calm that had come upon her. But there was nothing aside from abandoned buildings and—

"A light..."

One of the buildings, far to the end and half-hidden behind another, had a faint light in one of the windows. If Ada could have run, she would have. Instead, she walked as swiftly as her legs could carry her to the building. As she drew closer, the sound of faint humming reached her ears, like electricity through a machine. The sound built and then dissipated, only to build again, like a wave of energy.

The building spilled weak light through its windows; those on the bottom floor were grimy. It took Ada a few tries to climb on top of some crates under a window and looked inside, legs shaking.

It was a large space, with lamps burning around the perimeter that sputtered with the hum of energy. A large, upright rectangular machine sat to Ada's left, coils at each of the four top corners that had golden wires leading to a crown with a twining serpent. The machine had knobs and pressure valves that were being checked and adjusted by someone in all black, thick rubber gloves on their hands, goggles on their eyes. Across from the machine sat what looked like a metal wheelchair, clamps holding the ankles, wrists and forehead of a young man in place as the machine gave out a loud hum of power.

The lamps inside sputtered out completely as the power built, and as they did, the serpent in the crown began to glow bright and brighter until—

"You don't want to look at that kid," said someone behind her, clamping hands over her eyes.

The hum was almost unbearable, the sound punctuated by a scream from inside.

Those large hands left her eyes, the light from inside back to a normal, dull glow. Ada turned around to see a tall man with a pair of goggles over his eyes, clad in a white homburg hat, dark suit and duster. He grinned, showing white straight teeth as he pulled her off the crates.

"You shouldn't be here," he said with a grin. "Let me handle this and go home."

Ada stared, mouth gaping. She'd heard of the legendary Vigil Corps, everyone in California had. Her brother had been obsessed with Domino Lady and the Laughing Mask before sports had supplanted them. But Ada had never forgotten, indulging in stories about the heroes since, after all, it was fact—not fiction.

"You're... You're..."

He swept a bow. "The Laughing Mask. Nice to meet you. Now, go home."

With those words, Ada shook off the hero worship that had temporarily rendered her mute.

"No."

"This isn't the place—"

"My brother is in there, and I'm not leaving until I find him."

The Laughing Mask crossed his arms. "Brother, huh? And what would he say if he knew you were here?"

"He'd tell me to use my mind and get him out."

"Mind, huh? You're smart, are ya?"

Ada nodded.

"Then go home."

With that he jumped on top of the crates, shimmied up the drain pipe and swung up onto the flat roof of the building, disappearing into the night.

Ada clenched her jaw. "Not likely."

She crept along the sides of the building until she found a small window, up high near the roof. There were many more crates, these looking fairly new with an address from Egypt on one. Something tickled the back of her mind between that and the crown she'd seen with the coiled serpent but she didn't want to waste time trying to figure it out. Whatever they were doing in there to those boys wasn't good.

I just hope I'm in time to save Donny.

She climbed on top of the crates with clumsy movements that nearly toppled the stack. When she reached the top, Ada was panting, her arms and legs shaking. After a few minutes, she was able to stand on her tip-toes and reach the window. It was small, too small for any full sized person to climb through and for that reason the people in the building had left it unlocked. Ada's thin arms shook once again as she pulled herself up to the window. The crates under her teetered as the toes of her boots scraped along the top of one. She grunted with the effort of pulling herself up just a little more so she could get her torso through the window. It took three tries, and she ended up knocking over the crates in the process. Scrambling to get through the window, she fell into a dark room, hitting her elbow on the cold floor.

Tears leaped to her eyes and Ada forced them back. If she could endure countless allergy shots every year, she could endure a few scrapes.

Footsteps shuffled along the concrete outside the window. Ada froze, heart pounding in her chest. After a few moments, the footsteps retreated and she could breathe again. Looking around, she realized she'd fallen into a kind of broom closet with cleaning supplies stacked on the shelves in neat rows. She walked to the door and peeked out. There was a long, gray hallway with dim lights that just barely managed to keep the gloom away. She heard a door slam to her right and closed the door to the closet, leaving a little space to hear what was said.

There was the sound of something being dragged, but nothing else. When Ada was sure they'd passed by, she opened the door enough to look out. A young man, probably the one that had been in the chair, hung limp between two other men, both dressed in black like the one operating the machine. The young man's clothes were strange, and Ada realized, just before they turned a corner to the right at the end of the hall, that it was a uniform that someone working at a Hollywood cafeteria would wear.

Donny's best friend worked at one of those, and he disappeared the same night as Donny!

It was evidence enough for Ada that her brother was here.

Taking a deep breath, she eased herself out of the closet and down the hall. Her boots, though soft-soled, felt far too loud in the bare hallway. She reached the end and was about to turn the same direction Donny's friend had been dragged when large hands clamped down on her mouth and pulled her in the opposite direction. She flailed and scratched but it was no use.

"Cut it out!" whispered a now-familiar voice.

Ada huffed an irritated breath and stopped struggling.

"Kids never listen," he whispered, turning her around. "You want to get killed? Or worse?"

"I want to find my brother!"

The Laughing Mask sighed, bending down to look her in the eye. Ada crossed her arms this time, knowing that with her slight frame and short stature she was anything but intimidating and decided that stubborn would have to do.

"You're not going to leave, are you?" he said after a moment.

"Nope."

Ada had to bite back a smile when she heard him swear under his breath.

"Alright," he finally said. "You run when I tell you and you stay out of sight, understand?"

Ada nodded, not able to hide her wide grin this time.

The Laughing Mask turned away, but not before Ada caught a hint of a smile under his beard.

After checking to make sure no one was coming, Laughing Mask and Ada crept down the hall. It sloped a little towards the end and curved to the right where a set of stairs appeared descending into a dark corridor.

Laughing Mask opened his mouth as if to say something then stopped. He pushed Ada down at the same time that he drew his pistol from an unseen holster and fired behind them.

Bullets ricocheted around them, and Ada crawled behind Laughing Mask. He drew another pistol and fired, standing with legs spread, his duster hiding Ada from sight.

After a few moments the bullets stopped, replaced by the echo of booted feet on the concrete floor, rushing toward them.

Laughing Mask threw punches at lightning speed, but Ada could see as he shifted his stance that they were outnumbered. Looking around for a weapon or some way to help, she saw something odd peeking out of the pocket of one of the men Laughing Mask had shot. Yanking on the small packet, she grinned and dug around in the same front pocket for a lighter.

The packet of fire crackers she was now trying to light was from an illegal shop just outside the city. She knew because her brother got in trouble last year for bringing them to school. The guard, or whatever he was, must've taken them off of one of the boys when they'd captured him.

Once the fuse caught, Ada threw it toward the guards who were beginning to overwhelm Laughing Mask.

The sharp staccato of the fire crackers pierced the air, and the men danced their way back, unsure of what was making that noise.

Ada yanked on Laughing Masks duster and ran down the stairs.

"Good thinking kid," he said. "But if you haven't noticed we're now trapped."

"We can get the boys out, that's what we came here for. One of them has to know a way out."

"Single minded, I admire that. Even if it might get us killed."

They ran down the stairs and faced a broad, metal door, the sound of muffled crying reaching them. Ada felt her heart pound in her chest, dark spots appearing in her vision. This was usually when she laid down, trying her best to avoid the tightness in her chest that was starting to build.

Hold it together, just a little longer, you can do this.

"Stay behind me," the Laughing Mask said.

She took some deep, slow breaths and moved behind him, a little relieved that she wouldn't have to see what was behind that door, making someone cry.

The door opened on soundless hinges, the sound of crying intensifying along with something else: a soft, deep female voice crooning something to someone. They didn't go inside, hanging back instead to hear what was happening.

The crying stopped, cut off as if someone had simply turned off a radio. It chilled Ada to her core with how wrong it was.

"Another is prepared," the female said. "Get him upstairs and into the chair."

"The machine was never designed to convert this many this quickly, you will overwhelm it," said a nasally male voice.

"Do not question me," she said, tone becoming cold. "I know what is necessary. Now go."

Laughing Mask jerked back and picked Ada up, desperately scanning the small room they were in for a place to hide.

He finally ducked under the stairs, the space barely big enough for the two of them as the door they'd just been at opened and footsteps sounded up the the stairs.

Laughing Mask waited a few moments and then nodded at Ada, who was the first to crawl out of their hiding spot...

Standing there was an impossibly tall woman in a long, red dress and white hood with a veil, flanked by two more guards, all in black.

"Well," she said, folding elegant arms across her chest. "It seems we have visitors."

Two more dragged Laughing Mask from under the stairs and he grinned at the woman.

"Veiled Lady," he said. "How nice to finally meet you."

"And you, Laughing Mask. Though it won't be for long, I'm afraid."

"Pity. You starting a charity? What do you need all those boys for?"

"Ah yes, this is where I start to tell you my plan and you try to stop me."

"I was hoping."

The Veiled Lady laughed, a low, throaty sound. "I'm afraid you will have to live with disappointment. Though not for long."

She flicked her long fingers and the guards punched Laughing Mask in the stomach, then proceeded to pummel him with their fists.

"No! Stop, you'll kill him!" Ada said, turning to the Veiled Lady. "What kind of person are you? Stealing boys and then killing someone! And for what? Why did you take my brother!?"

The Veiled Lady angled her head as if she were looking down at Ada, who swore she could feel the woman's eyes boring into her soul.

No matter how much Ada might have wanted to look away, she held her ground.

"Fascinating," Veiled Lady said. "Such a strong mind in such a frail body. If only I knew how to relieve you of it."

Ada recoiled at those words despite her best efforts.

"No matter," Veiled Lady continued as Laughing Mask collapsed to the ground. "Soon your mind will be in service to my masters. We will try to do something about your body later.

Take them inside, and make sure to put the Laughing Mask into a separate cell."

One of the guards plucked Ada up, while two others lugged a bloodied Laughing Mask through the door. Once inside, Ada gaped at what she saw.

A long surgical table, surrounded by lamps straight out of an Egyptian palace. Incense tickled her nose from the various pots where its smoke curled in lazy circles. A tapestry hung on one wall, covered in Egyptian hieroglyphs, a few that Ada recognized as symbols for intense devotion and love, the kind that bordered on obsession. In the center of all the hieroglyphs was one large picture of a king, tall and beautiful. At one end was a stand with a large Pharaoh's crown, very similar to but larger than the one being used in the machine upstairs.

And that's when something clicked into place for Ada.

Ramses the Second! They're using the crowns of Ramses to...do what? How are they using them? And why?

Before she could figure it all out, they'd been taken through another door and to an adjoining room where cells that were little more than cages stood all along the walls of the room in a giant U-shape.

And, in one of those cages—

"Donny! Donny!"

"Ada?" her brother said, brown eyes large in his face. "What are you doing here?"

"I had to find you."

"Shut it!" the guard said, shoving her into a cell across the room from Donny.

The space was empty, save for three boys staring at the walls as if they were aware of nothing else.

Laughing Mask was thrown into the one empty cell in the room, and the guards left without a backward glance.

"I knew you were here," Ada said, smiling at her brother.

His clothes were torn and dirty, and his face was streaked with filth, but he was the best thing Ada had ever seen.

"You shouldn't be here, Ada," he said, tears shining in his eyes. "They'll hurt you and I can't stop them."

"We'll get out, I know it," Ada nodded toward the Laughing Mask. "Don't you recognize him?"

Donny really looked at the cell this time, his eyes growing large. "Is that—?"

"Yep! No one defeats the Laughing Mask!" she said.

Some of the other boys were roused out of their melancholy by this news and stood, gaping at the unconscious hero.

"He doesn't look too good," one of them said.

"He'll rouse, don't you worry," Ada said with far more confidence than she actually felt.

Glancing at the three young men in the cell with her, she frowned. They were still staring out into nothing, their faces slack, eyes vacant.

"Hey, didn't you hear me? We'll be getting out soon."

"They don't talk," said Donny.

"Why not?"

"Whatever it is they're doing to us, it went wrong with the three of them."

A jolt of fear lanced through Ada's small body.

"You don't know what's going on?" she asked.

"Not exactly. But I think it has something to do with mind control. A few other guys came back and were like puppets, doing whatever the creepy lady told them to."

Ada frowned.

The crowns... Ramses the Second's crowns... The machine... I've seen a machine like that before, a picture of it in—that's it!

"It is mind control, though I can't believe it."

"What I can't figure is how she's doing it," Donny said.

"The crown belonged to Ramses the Second, one of the most influential kings in all Egypt. That machine is something used in hypnosis therapy. It must be amplifying any power in Ramses' crowns, brainwashing you all. But why?"

"Whatever the reason is," the Laughing Mask said, sitting up and wincing. "It's not good."

"You're awake!" Ada cried.

"Yep, though I wish like hell I wasn't."

"You have any way to get out of here?" Donny asked, his dark eyes shining as he gazed at his hero.

The Laughing Mask wiped some dried blood off his lips and nodded. "The trouble isn't getting these locks open, it's getting away when I do. Though...damn...I think I might have a way."

The Laughing Mask dug around in one of the pockets of his duster and produced a small, black and red object, no bigger than a small brooch. He held it to his lips, whispered something, and then returned it to his pocket.

"What was that?" Donny asked.

"I'm calling in a favor. Now, to get these locks—"

The door opened, and in walked two guards. Laughing Mask slumped against the bars, as if he were still knocked out, and the boys in the cells crouched down to make themselves smaller and not draw attention.

"She said the girl and..."

Ada's heart leaped to her throat. She knew who the guard would choose.

"That one," the guard finished, pointing at Donny.

"No!" he screamed. "You don't need her—she's little, weak! Just take me and leave her!"

One of the guards produced what looked like a baton and jabbed Donny with it, the telltale *zing* of an electrical current reaching Ada's ears. Once the baton made contact, Donny's body jerked and he cried out.

"Stop!" Ada yelled.

Her brother fell to the cold concrete floor, moaning. One guard opened the cell door and flung Donny over his shoulder, while the other one went to Ada. She glared at him, infusing it with all the angry malice she could muster.

The guard just chuckled.

"Spirited little thing, aren't ya," he said, jerking her out of the cell by her arm. "The Lady has a special mission for you, I think."

She wanted to hit him, spit in his face, but where would that get her? Instead, Ada held her head up high and forced her trembling legs to move forward.

Out the door and up the stairs, down several hallways, until they reached the large main room Ada had seen earlier that night. The Veiled Lady was looking over the machine, which hummed like a great animal. Hieroglyphs were painted on the floor around the machine and the metal chair, toward which the guard now pulled Ada.

She struggled as he slammed her down into the seat. Two others forced her head and hands into place, as another closed the clamps to hold her where the Veiled Lady wanted her.

What they didn't notice was that Ada's head and wrists were simply too small to be held tightly in place.

At last there's a benefit to being sick all the time!

An idea formed at lightning speed in her mind, and Ada hoped no one would notice what she was about to do until it was too late.

And a diversion wouldn't be amiss right about now either! What is Laughing Mask doing? Waiting for an invitation?

"You are a smart girl, much like I was at your age," the Veiled Lady said, positioning herself on one side of the machine.

At first Ada thought the Veiled Lady had put a different top on, but then she realized the villain's arms were actually bare, the pale skin covered in tattoos.

"You like them?" the Veiled Lady asked, gesturing to her arms. "I could teach you all about them, what they mean, the power they give. You'd never be sick again, never be at the mercy of your body's limitations. Can you imagine that? Playing outside, running with the other children? Never having another shot?"

Ada frowned. "How do you know all of this?"

The Veiled Lady laughed. "My dear child, I know more about you than you think. I know more about Donny and the rest of the rubbish downstairs than anyone would ever believe. And I know these things because I chose strength over the weaknesses others call morality."

"It's not strength, it's cowardice."

The Veiled Lady hissed, and Ada swore she saw eyes of fire glaring at her for a moment under the thick, white veil that hid the Lady's true face.

"Begin!" she yelled, her voice cracking like thunder in the room.

The low hum of the machine started to build, as did the light illuminating the crown. Within moments, that machine would make Ada a mindless drone if she didn't act fast enough.

The Veiled Lady raised her arms above her head, body swaying as she spoke what must've been an ancient Egyptian tongue.

It was now or never.

Ada shimmied her left hand out of the clamp, gasping as the skin of her thumb scraped the metal, air stinging the cut. Ignoring the pain, she reached into her left coat pocket and found the little mechanical bird. She'd made a modification that morning, in the hopes of finding Donny and impressing him. Now, since he was still unconscious, she'd have to settle for saving him.

Winding the bird with the nimble fingers of one hand, and flicking the tiny lever on its back, Ada aimed as best she could toward the machine and let it go. The bird zoomed out of her hand so fast Ada jerked back. In a shower of sparks, the bird became lodged between the crown and one of the wires that held it in place. The machine's humming became a high-pitched whine, smoke spilling from the top.

"*What did you do?!*" the Veiled Lady shrieked.

Sparks flew and the machine groaned. Ada scrambled to free her head and other hand, jumping out of the chair as the Veiled Lady lunged for her.

"I'll kill you!" she growled, grabbing for Ada.

"Leave my sister alone!" Donny slammed his body into the Veiled Lady from behind, sending them both sprawling to the ground.

The machine gave a loud *pop*, then flames erupted, enveloping the crown of Ramses the Second.

"No!" The Veiled Lady ran for the crown, but the flames were too plentiful.

Once again, Ada swore she could see eyes of flame glowing as the Veiled Lady turned toward her. Raising her hand, the Lady began to speak that same language as before, only this time Ada could feel the threat oozing from every sound.

She ran to her brother, smoke now generously spilling out of the machine. "We have to get out of here!"

"Right you are!" the Laughing Mask called, pulling them both up. "Donny, get your sister out of here."

"What about you?" Ada worried.

He grinned at her. "Kid, this is what I do."

Donny scooped Ada up like she weighed nothing, and ran for the small door to their left. Ada looked over Donny's shoulder and saw the Laughing Mask dodging what looked like a bolt of light from the Veiled Lady's hand. Bullets pinged from the Laughing Mask's gun.

At that close range, he should've hit her. But she's just standing there like it was nothing! Who is this woman?

The machine trembled and exploded, metal flying everywhere. Ramses' crown flew across the room right behind Donny.

"Wait!" Ada cried. "Get the crown! She can't be allowed to keep it!"

Donny stopped, glancing from the door to the crown before releasing Ada and diving for the object, barely missing a bolt of lightning.

"I told you to go!" the Laughing Mask said, firing the last of his bullets at the Veiled Lady.

"You fools!" the Veiled Lady shrieked, her voice manic and high. "This is not the end! You have just made a powerful enemy!"

The lightning around the Veiled Lady built until she was surrounded with its harsh light. Laughing Mask stood in place, transfixed. Ada coughed and fell to her knees. It was so hard to breathe that she wondered if she'd pass out.

"I think we're done here," Laughing Mask said, plucking Ada from the ground and pulling Donny along.

The three of them ran to the door, which burst apart in an explosion of light and fell at their feet. Ada and Donny stared at the open doorway in fear. Just as Donny was starting to turn away, a woman appeared. She wore a form-fitting white shirt and black pants, black boots, and a yellow sash. Her raven hair was swept back from her face, a pair of aviator goggles atop her head.

"Someone call for a rescue?" she asked, grinning. Then she looked behind them, her eyes widening. "Holy—!"

The Laughing Mask shoved Donny ahead and raced out the door, the woman following close on their heels. As soon as they were a few feet from the building, strange *zing* and *pop* sounds hurt Ada's ears. Then the light from the warehouse was gone.

"Who the hell was that?" the woman asked.

"Tell ya later," the Laughing Mask said. "I have a theory."

Ada looked over at Donny, who stood there, staring at the woman, mouth open.

The Laughing Mask chuckled. "Donny, Madame Strange. Madame Strange, Donny and his sister, Ada. Now, let's get out of here."

"Wait, what about the other boys?" Donny asked.

"Already out, and hopefully half way home. Now let's get!"

"This way," Madame Strange said, leading them to the middle of the street where a ladder hung down.

Ada looked up and gasped, awestruck for the first time that night.

Flying overhead, barely illuminated by the moonlight, was the strangest, most amazing aircraft she'd ever seen. Wide body with wings protruding out and a cockpit up front, twin propellers sat on top of either wing with blades whirring.

"I don't think I can climb with Ada," Donny said.

The Laughing Mask took her out of Donny's arms. "Climb on my back kid."

She nodded, still looking up at the aircraft.

"What is it?" she whispered.

Madame Strange laughed, a sound like bells of pure pleasure.

"That, my dear girl, is a Gyro-Jet."

"Not your usual conveyance," the Laughing Mask said as they ascended the ladder.

"I was testing new modifications on this baby when you called. Besides, you said you had passengers."

In no time they were inside the Gyro-Jet, buckling themselves into their seats.

"I win the bet," Madame Strange said. "You called in the boon in less than three months. Pay up."

The Laughing Mask sighed. "Yeah, yeah."

Madame Strange laughed again and disappeared into the cockpit. Within moments, they were flying through the air.

Ada looked out her window, marveling at the sight of Los Angeles so far away, the lights twinkling below. From up above, it all looked so beautiful.

Donny groaned beside her.

"Don't worry kid," the Laughing Mask said. "It'll be a short trip to...hey, where do you live anyway?"

❧

Ada had expected her mother to demand a lengthy explanation. But the moment they stepped inside, Mom began to cry, hugging them both tight. It took a few days for her to question where her children had been, and by then Ada and Donny had come up with a pretty good story: a sweat shop kidnapped Donny, Ada went to look for him and found Donny had escaped on his own. Ada's recent cough was a product of being out in the wet, spring night air.

"The truth is too good to tell her," Donny had insisted. "She'll never believe it."

Perhaps it was because she was so happy to have her children back that their mother swallowed the lie—hook, line, and sinker.

Life fell back into its usual routine. Ada missed the next week of school because of her cough, which the doctors gave her a series of shots to help cure. It was irritating to know what had caused it and not be able to tell them. Still, the shots did ease some of the discomfort in her lungs.

Two weeks after the adventure, a certified letter came just before dinner time. Their mother looked at it and frowned.

"What is it?" Donny asked.

"It's for Ada."

Ada and Donny glanced at each other.

"Is there something you two aren't telling me?" Mom asked.

"Nope," Donny said.

"Nothing," Ada confirmed.

Mom studied them both for a moment and gave Ada the letter, not taking her eyes off her daughter.

Ada opened it and read the contents, her mouth falling open.

"Well?" her mother asked.

"It's... I..."

Her mother took the letter, her own eyes bulging once she'd read it.

Donny snatched it up and laughed.

"You're..." Mom said. "An invitation to the most prestigious private school in California. Fully paid."

"Not just any school," Donny said, bouncing on the balls of his feet in excitement. "Half their graduates go on to work for places like AEGIS. Ada! This is the opportunity of a lifetime!"

Ada felt tears sting her eyes and she shook her head. "But...my health. I can't go."

"Yes you can, look," Donny said, squatting down to meet his sister's eyes. "They have doctors there. Good ones. The best, probably. Maybe they can figure out more than these others have been able to."

"He's right," Mom said, smiling, her eyes shining with tears. "This...sweetheart, this is your chance to learn so much more than you ever could here. You could be whatever you wanted after this."

"But," Ada felt tears slide down her cheeks. "What about you?"

Her mother's arms encircled her, holding her tight. "Oh, my precious girl! I'll miss you every day, but what kind of mother would I be if I denied you something like this?"

Ada cried on her mother's shoulder, knowing she was right.

"Well," her mother said, wiping her own eyes. "I think this calls for something special. Donny, run down to the bakery on the corner, see if they have anything for dessert."

Donny grinned at them and ran out.

"I'll get the meatloaf out of the oven," her mother said, kissing Ada's cheek before going to the kitchen.

Ada stared out the window, watching the sunset light up the buildings and hills. She thought of the Gyro-Jet, of the Laughing Mask and Madame Strange. She thought of her mother and brother, and the threats she now knew existed in the world.

I can help defend this world against people like the Veiled Lady, especially if I do this.

Ada grinned.

Look out world! Here comes Ada Mesmer, the Whiz Kid!

Ukungu

by Todd Downing

Doctor Maria Caruso woke with a start, sitting bolt upright. The warm, tropical rain continued its sporadic assault, drumming a hollow cadence on the twisted aluminum gondola frame. The deflated silk envelope of the powered balloon lay draped across a small grove of large mahogany trees, one untethered corner snapping in the breeze. Shaking the cobwebs from her head, she slowly rose to a standing position, feeling twice her actual thirty-five years.

Blood seeped from a deep cut on her right arm, staining her khaki shirt. She winced, looking over the rest of her body for any other injuries. Some bumps, bruises and minor abrasions—she'd be colorful for awhile, but no significant harm.

The sun hung low in the African sky, barely a red glow through the thick cloud layer that lay over the valley. Caruso glanced at her watch: 6:27 PM. Even in springtime, valleys situated between high mountain ranges like this tended to lose light earlier than true sunset. It would be dark soon. She blinked hazel eyes in the evening mist, smoothing a lock of bobbed chestnut hair back behind her ear.

The old map lay trapped under a metal first aid box near the wrecked gondola, the free half fluttering in the wet breeze. She bent down and retrieved it, grimacing at its condition: soaked with rain, stained in what she presumed to be her own blood, and torn down a fair portion of the center. She gingerly folded it into a manageable rectangle and noted the gondola's open door—which had apparently opened on impact, sending her out into the muddy grass.

She approached cautiously and entered, and immediately recoiled in shock. Lt. Brand lay slumped forward over the console, the back of his head caved in. The likely culprit—a large fire extinguisher—was embedded in the windscreen to the right of the panel the tree had obliterated.

The German geologist, Dr. Muir, was up and attending to the American botanist, Leigh Taggart, who still lay unconscious in her safety belt. "Good to see you made it, Doktor," he said, keeping his attention on the blond scientist. "Brand was not so lucky."

"I know," Caruso answered, scanning the interior as best she could in the waning light. She found a flashlight on the floor and flicked it on. "How is Taggart?"

The young botanist began to stir. Muir stepped back and smiled. "Good, I think."

"Wh-what happened?" Taggart asked. "Did we crash?"

Caruso busied herself checking over the control panel. She hauled Brand's body away from the console and noted the navigation compass was still spinning. "It would appear so," she explained. "But I think we made it to our objective." She began to search the nose of the gondola for any trace of the field radio.

Of course her first expedition would end up like this.

The map had turned up a month ago on a black market saturated with valuable artifacts in the wake of the Great War. It was purchased by one of her father's academic contacts and authenticated as late 16th century Portuguese by her father, a respected university historian.

Her father, who had shown up at her home in Livorno, on the Tuscany coast, gut-shot and bleeding out on her doorstep. Her father, who had managed to stammer out the words, "*Astrum Argentum. Loro sanno. Prendete questo a AEGIS,*" before collapsing dead in her arms.

Silver Star. They know. Take this to AEGIS.

Her father, who smuggled a three-hundred-year-old map from the black market and was murdered for his trouble. Already scrutinized as a potential dissident by Mussolini's fascist government due to her status as an academic, Maria Caruso wasted no time in putting the family horse farm up for sale and fleeing via tramp steamer to France. There, she made contact with the Allied Enterprise Group for International Security.

She met with a group of serious men in pinstriped suits in a back room at the Louvre. They were somewhat interested in her academic credentials and experience working with her father's archaeological digs around the world. They were extremely interested in the 16th century map depicting part of the remote Congo valley, down to the quaint warnings of aqui tem dragões scrawled in Portuguese.

The men in suits also had intelligence that the Silver Star knew about the place and were already trying to find a route overland. So they sent her to Africa, assigned her an international team, a local guide and a powered balloon, and put her in command of the expedition. Congratulations and welcome to the organization. Depending on the team's findings, she could expect more help and personnel in a month or so.

She knew Razi from before the war. Even as a youth of seven or eight, he'd been incredibly useful to her father's archaeological expedition to several sites along the Congo River. She remembered he used to call her *Maua* —"flower"—due to a misreading of "Maria" in her handwriting. Now a grown man, he was slender but well-muscled, full of intense, barely-contained energy (and even more knowledgeable about the region than he'd been a decade ago).

They'd spent days going over the map and the potential dangers in the place Razi called *Bonde la Ukungu*—literally "Valley of the Mist" in Swahili. He said the valley was taboo to the tribes living adjacent to it, due to the monsters and dark magic that protected the place. He said compasses didn't work there, radios were almost as useless, and the thick cloud layer kept aerial surveillance to a minimum. But Razi didn't see any of those as reasons against going.

They took a German geologist from Tanganyika, an American botanist from Nairobi, and the Canadian pilot who came with the powered balloon via Cairo. They packed for a deep African expedition, including jungle camping equipment, weapons and extra rations.

They set out from Bunia at dawn, sailing over the mountains and vast, green expanse of the African interior for most of the day. Then the compasses began to spin and they suddenly found themselves on a trampoline of strange air currents and thermals that sent them on a vomit-inducing thrill ride for a solid hour.

The rain started, and Caruso had ordered Lieutenant Brand, the pilot, to make a slow, controlled descent. And that's when a tree branch from the canopy shot out of the misty sunset and shattered the windscreen. The force of impact wrenched the nose of the gondola down, ripping cables as the balloon twisted away. One of the electric engine fans snapped as the gondola pulled off the tree limb.

Down they went, the gondola spinning nose-down beneath a rapidly deflating balloon. The remaining outboard fan continued to spin, forcing the balloon down in a corkscrew. The primeval African jungle loomed out of the darkness and fog below. They were crashing. Down, through the endless trees. Down, through the tropical rain and mist. Down, to the valley floor.

Muir noticed her poking through a pile of debris in the smashed nose of the gondola. "The radio was destroyed. I believe it is beyond repair," he noted.

Taggart freed herself from the safety harness and stood with a groan. "And the one guy who could fix it is dead."

Suddenly Caruso looked up, worried. "Has anyone seen Razi?"

Taggart shook her head. "He wasn't strapped in."

"Could he have been thrown clear, like you?" Muir asked.

A dim flash of lightning in the distance led to a quiet roll of thunder. Razi's silhouette appeared in the hatchway. "This is the valley," he said with authority. "We have made it to Ukungu." His tone suddenly tuned dark. "And we cannot stay here."

Muir squinted through the dim light of the gondola. "Why?"

Caruso knew Razi well enough not to question a situation of life and death. He was young, but incredibly wise beyond his years. And this was his area of expertise. He knew the jungles and back country of the Congo like no other local guide she'd encountered. "Grab what you can," she ordered. "Food, first aid and weapons. We're getting out of here."

Muir and Taggart sprang into action, gathering various canvas duffel bags and satchels of field rations and medical supplies. Caruso stashed the wet map into her satchel and holstered a Mauser M1921 pistol while Razi shouldered a Beretta carbine and shoved a half dozen spare magazines into his bag. Thus, laden with basic supplies and two flashlights among the group, they stepped out into the rapidly darkening African night.

That's when Razi froze in his tracks, listening to the sky, feeling the vibrations in the ground. "Run," he instructed quietly.

Then the jungle trees burst aside and the monsters were behind them.

"Joka!" huffed Razi as he dashed to the front of the group, blazing the trail for everyone.

Maria Caruso caught the briefest glimpse of two reptilian heads plow through the tree line, and nearly tripped over herself as her feet seemed to depart on their own. Muir and Taggart followed suit without a single word.

Caruso huffed to keep up with her guide, but the wet, grassy mud sucked at her boots, doubling the effort required. She flipped a quick glance over her shoulder and could make out a pair of bipedal saurian predators. Theropods. Large, forward-thrust heads were counterbalanced by long, muscular tails. Joka, she thought. That's 'serpent'—or 'dragon'—in Swahili. Then her university instruction in paleontology took over and she realized she was looking at a pair of living dinosaurs— allosaurs, by what she could make out. Specifically, *Allosaurus fragilis*. Close to nine meters long from nose to tail, powerfully-muscled, with oversize heads full of dagger-sharp teeth. Faster than the larger Tyrannosaur, with larger and more effective forelimbs for grasping prey. Truly the apex predator of its day. Somehow alive in 1927.

The group struggled at a fast jog along the tree line, hidden somewhat by the growing shadows and rainy mist. Caruso glanced back again and saw the pair of creatures nosing around the balloon wreckage. She estimated they were perhaps 200 meters away, with no clear destination.

"Razi," Caruso hailed, "slow down!"

The Congolese man slowed and turned back to monitor the group. Muir and Taggart limped along at the rear. Caruso sloshed to a halt beside Razi. She looked back again to see that the crash site was now vacant and still— and absent one pair of allosaurs.

"Where are we heading?" she asked finally.

Razi turned and pointed ahead into the mist, which was beginning to thin and dissipate. "Up there. Rocks and high ground."

Caruso squinted into the dark, shining her flashlight in the direction Razi was pointing. "How do you know there is high ground?"

"See," he said, nodding at the valley floor. The wetlands they'd been trudging through from the wreck gradually gave way to rockier, sandier soil. Still moist from the dampness in the air, but easier to traverse on foot. "I think we will have rocks and high ground within a kilometer."

Muir agreed. "It would follow what we know of African topography."

Caruso looked back and squinted into the distance at the wreck. No sign of the allosaurs. She ran the toe of her boot through the drier soil and nodded. "Alright. Let's keep going. We'll be away from the trees soon. Out in the open."

As if on cue, the jungle suddenly erupted in an explosion of tree branches and sundry vegetation. The allosaurs had rediscovered their scent, and had closed the gap. Huge, sinewy coils of muscle powered piston-like legs, propelling the monsters forward. The group turned away collectively and shot into a dead run, following Razi toward the promise of high ground.

Caruso reached for her pistol and winced in pain as she realized she had yet to tend to the open wound on her arm. The ground thundered beneath them as the loping reptiles grew closer. Making sure Muir and Taggart were out of her way, she fired three shots over her shoulder toward the predators, but didn't stop to check her work. She continued at her labored sprint, canvas satchel pounding against her bruised hip.

The two flashlights pierced the lifting fog ahead of them, and the ground became gradually rockier and more solid.

Two hundred meters.

Somewhere in the distance, lightning flashed. The group ran on, the thunder of the sprinting allosaurs mingling with the thunder in the evening sky. Razi was well out in front of the group. Caruso couldn't blame him. She remembered her childhood helping her uncle saddle train dressage horses on his Tuscan farm, and she wished she had one now.

Three hundred meters.

The air hung thick and heavy in their lungs, tinged with a hint of sulfur. They kept running.

Caruso scanned the night behind them, flashlight in her left hand. Muir huffed under the weight of his years and several added kilos in the survival bags he carried. Taggart wasn't next to him.

Four hundred meters.

Caruso adjusted to make sure she wouldn't trip and fall, casting a quick glance over her shoulder toward the rear of her party. Muir kept at his clip and passed her. Taggart shone visible in the beam of Caruso's flashlight as she straggled along. Then she disappeared as a giant pair of jaws snapped down over her head and torso. Without so much as a scream, Leigh Taggart was gone—the only sound was the horrible rending of flesh and the growls of the dinosaurs as they fought over her carcass.

Dr. Caruso turned and bolted away, her heart pounding in terror. As terrible as the loss was, she was adamant that it would not be in vain if it bought the others a few extra moments to escape. She passed Muir, who had turned back to see where Taggart had gone. His flashlight beam was met by the bloody faces of the marauding pair of allosaurs, and he instantly turned and followed Caruso at top speed. Razi had disappeared into the misty darkness ahead. The terrified scientists sprinted as best they could, packs of supplies jostling and bouncing as they ran.

Five hundred meters.

Caruso could feel the hot breath of the predators behind her. Then Razi shouted something from the dark ahead of them, and she was aware of looking down. The ground became rockier and more solid, despite the spitting rain. Her boots finally found purchase. The heavy satchel pounded and smacked against her leg, bruising it more and more with each contact.

Then a stone ridge loomed up out of the dark and suddenly someone was pulling her behind an outcropping of boulders and up a steep incline. It was Razi, wiry muscles straining from the rolled-up sleeves of his khaki safari shirt. "This way, *Maua!*" As he hauled her up to the crest of the rock, she could see one of the allosaurs impact the first of the scattered boulders, momentarily dazed as the other slowed and stalked away from her flashlight's beam.

Muir came bounding up the incline with seemingly renewed vigor, but he lost his footing at the top and fell down the opposite side, catching his boot in a crevice. His leg snapped at a 45-degree angle with a horrible *crack!*, and he cried out in agony.

The allosaurs growled and gnashed their teeth and continued to stalk the perimeter of large boulders, frustrated at their inability to reach as high as the outcropping.

Caruso ran the flashlight beam down the other incline and into what she could make out as the mouth of a cavern of some kind. Muir writhed at the bottom of the opening, his left leg caught in a hole and bent grotesquely.

"Dr. Muir!" Caruso hailed. "We're coming!"

Razi un-shouldered his rifle and Caruso used it as a hand-hold on her way down the incline, the young Congolese bracing her from his place at the top. When at last she could stretch no further, she let go the rifle and half-skipped, half-ran to the floor of the cave mouth. Razi was close on her tail.

"I seem to have taken a bad step," Muir quipped, attempting something between stoicism and nonchalance. Then a wave a pain hit him and he went pale. *"Mein Gott,"* he shivered.

Caruso set her satchel down and knelt by his side. "Primary wound shock," she muttered. "Razi, find one of the blankets from that big survival bag."

Razi produced a wool army blanket from the large duffel and wrapped it around Muir. Together they extracted the German scientist's leg from the hole in the rock and, each taking a corner of the blanket, pulled him into the cavern, just as violent lightning filled the sky and the rain came down in torrents.

The cavern floor was packed sand and gravel, stretching seventy meters through a basalt lava tube into a wider chamber. Caruso noted crudely-chiseled petroglyphs covering the walls of the entry, from floor to ceiling. Vaguely human stick figures locked in deadly combat with giant, toothy dragons—*joka*, as Razi had called the allosaurs. This meant the valley had been—or still was—inhabited by humans... or humanoid beings. And they'd been in contact with saurian predators which had escaped mass extinction tens of millions of years ago. From what they'd experienced already, Dr. Maria Caruso was willing to lay money on who'd won, and why this place was off limits to natives of the region.

Her flashlight beam criss crossed with Razi's, illuminating the vast cavern interior. The entire chamber was perhaps a hundred meters deep and half as wide. Stalactites clung to the cavern ceiling fifteen or twenty meters above the floor. A small hole at the top let a steady flow of rainwater into the cave, cascading delicately down a single stalagmite that protruded from a shallow lagoon at the center. The floor around the small lake was a soft layer of white sand over solid rock, and to their initial observations, it looked long undisturbed.

They staked out a resting spot to the side of the entry passage along the west wall of the main cavern, and Razi set to work unloading the necessary gear to set Muir's broken leg. Caruso tore along the seam in his trouser leg and examined the break—his calf and shin were swollen in shades of dark yellow and purple, and she could see where the tibia had snapped. Fortunately, the bone hadn't penetrated flesh. She felt a bit more optimistic that they wouldn't lose a third member of the expedition. Not from this, anyway.

Razi prepared a splint and bandages, while Caruso took firm hold of Muir's left foot. Razi put the canvas strap of one of the duffel bags in Muir's teeth and the German scientist bit down. Caruso nodded to Razi, who gripped Muir under his arms. Muir nodded back, teeth clenched on the canvas strap.

It was over quickly. She pulled his foot toward her, and felt the bone snap into its proper place—more or less. Muir grunted and growled against the strap, and finally passed out.

Razi gently wrapped Muir's upper body in the blanket, then scurried over to employ the splint. Caruso leaned back against the cave wall and closed her eyes. She let herself exchange a few deep breaths for the first time since they'd arrived. Then she felt a twinge of pain and remembered her own arm.

Her shirt was caked in partially dried blood and sand from the cavern floor. She deftly ripped the torn sleeve at the shoulder, revealing a deep but fairly clean puncture wound about three inches long, traveling north-south along her triceps. She swabbed some tincture of iodine over the area and dressed it in a combination of adhesive bandages and cotton gauze.

By the time she'd finished tending herself, Caruso noted Razi had completed the splint on Muir's leg, while the German scientist slept, cocooned in the army blanket. "Well done, Razi," she complimented, sliding down the cavern wall to lay propped on her elbows.

"Thank you, *Maua*," the young man smiled at her, then picked up Muir's flashlight. "I will take a quick look around."

She watched him roam to the far end of the cave, flashlight playing over the ancient volcanic rock. Then she unrolled her own blanket and reclined on it, using her satchel as a pillow. As she settled in, she kept catching glimpses of Razi's wandering flashlight beam, and wondering how long it had been since another human being had occupied this natural shelter. She wondered how the saurian predators could have survived the mass extinction of their kind millions of years in the past. She wondered how they'd ever be able to get out of here. She took a deep breath, and fell instantly asleep.

The warm, golden light of morning crept down the entry to the cave. Caruso woke with a start and had to take a moment to remember where she was. She squinted as her tired eyes roamed the cave interior. All was quiet, save Muir's rhythmic breathing as he continued to sleep.

There was no sign of Razi, and the rifle was missing.

She found the young guide standing lookout atop the stone ridge outside the lava tube entry. He was scanning the valley through a pair of field glasses, rifle slung on his shoulder. Caruso noticed he'd rigged up a climbing aid with a length of knotted rope secured to a steel piton at the top. Her safari boots gripped the incline and she hauled herself up on the rope.

The storm from the night before had blown itself out; only the low cloud layer remained, trapping the heat in the valley like a thermal blanket. Caruso erupted immediately in beads of sweat. She gazed out over her small corner of the valley. Plutonic ridges rose from the veldt of the valley floor, encrusted with quartz formations like salt on a pretzel.

"No sign of the joka," Razi reported, "or Taggart." He handed the field glasses to Caruso, who peered out toward the jungle where they'd crashed.

"We'll find her. Or her remains. Eventually." She turned her gaze south, searching for signs of the allosaurs. But she caught a plume of dust several kilometers distant, and nudged Razi. "Look there," she said, handing him the binoculars. "Is that from an engine?"

Razi took the glasses and stared at the dust cloud for a few moments before letting a quiet gasp escape his lips. The blurry silhouette of a motorcycle and sidecar was visible through the haze and distance. Someone else was in the valley.

"Motor scouts," Razi offered.

Caruso frowned. "Then they are already here."

Razi nodded. "The Silver Star? Yes, it would appear so."

Caruso scuffed her boot on the rough stone as Razi continued staring through the binoculars.

"They are heading north, across the plain," Razi observed, swiveling in a 90-degree turn. "There is another ridge a kilometer to the west of us. If we hurry, we can be there when they arrive."

While Razi threw together a small field survival bag, Caruso woke Muir to tell him of their plan. He had plenty of fresh water and a week's worth of dry rations, if he was careful. He had his Luger pistol for protection, and the rest of the camp gear for comfort. Caruso and Razi would head to the next ridge to make contact with the unknown party and—depending on their identities—get help, or try to eliminate them and take their motorcycle. If they didn't return by nightfall, it was a good bet Muir would be stuck in relative safety but with a broken leg and a limited food supply. If need be, he could keep a bullet in reserve for a more dignified end than starving to death.

With time at a premium, Caruso and Razi said a quick farewell and clambered out of the cave and down into the flatlands. To the north, a craggy range of granite mountains ran east-west, with what appeared to be a large river snaking its way toward the ridge formation to the west—the very hills they were headed for.

They set off at a decent clip, Caruso struggling to keep up with the athletic Razi. They jogged across a savanna of dry grasses and scrub brush punctuated by the occasional thorny acacia tree or giant clump of pampas. They hugged the rocks as best they could, and Caruso found herself checking over her shoulder every now and again, just to be sure the allosaurs weren't stalking them from the east.

The target ridge was much like the one in which they'd camped; a collection of boulders and basalt tubes and crags, creating a perfectly defensible hiding place. Razi scampered atop the highest rock shelf and was immediately assaulted by an irate puff adder whose sunning spot he'd disturbed. Without much but a secondhand regard, Razi angled his boot to catch the serpent's bite, then stepped down hard, trapping its neck. In one fluid motion, he unslung his rifle, popped the butt on the ground, severing the adder's head from its body, and slung the rifle back onto his shoulder.

"Impressive," Caruso complimented.

Razi shrugged, his attention on the approaching dust cloud. "You grow up in the Congo, you learn to deal with snakes." He put the field glasses to his eyes and peered through them. "Two riders," he reported, "Maxim gun on the sidecar."

He passed the binoculars to Caruso, who noted gray poplin safari shirts with matching pocket trousers, black field boots and gray patrol caps with a four-pointed star pinned to the front. "Those uniforms are Silver Star." She nervously shifted her weight back and forth, passing the field glasses to Razi, who stashed them in the field bag. "We're going to have to do this carefully," she warned.

The motorcycle pulled to a dusty stop a dozen meters away from Caruso's vantage point. Razi was positioned at the other end of the ridge, creating a crossfire zone. The driver raised his goggles to rest on the bill of his cap, dismounting the 1923 British-built Douglas RA cycle and squinting along the ridge. Suddenly he dropped his gaze to the ground under the basalt lava tubes, and that's when Caruso noticed what had seized his attention: strewn along the base of the ridge were thousands of glimmering quartz-like stones, just like those she'd seen all over her own ridge camp. She stifled a gasp.

The valley was lousy with raw diamonds. They were just lying there, on the ground.

The driver stooped to pick one up and held it aloft for his partner to see. "Crowley should be quite happy with this discovery," he offered in an East London accent. "These formations along the central plateau are ripe for the picking."

Just then, Caruso's foot scraped the rock on which she lay, causing a small avalanche of sandy pebbles to slide down the back. She pressed her body tight against the warm stone, making as low a profile as she could. After a couple seconds, she ventured to raise her head to look.

The gunner in the sidecar saw her, and opened fire with the Maxim machine gun.

She ducked back down just as the rock in front of her was pulverized by a volley of incoming .303 bullets that popped and whizzed by her head.

She saw Razi pop up from his position, aim his Beretta OVP, and fire a short burst into the occupant of the sidecar. She heard the driver swear and answer Razi's fire with his own MP-18 trench sweeper, but she couldn't see where he was. The scout and her own guide traded shots a few times, then Caruso popped up from her own vantage point and fired two shots into her target's center of mass.

The driver fell, still clutching his MP-18 in one hand, the raw diamond in the other.

After several deep breaths, Caruso slid anxiously down the rock to examine the scene with Razi. The bodies were already beginning to sizzle and smolder. AEGIS field agents had been reporting this phenomenon since the spring of 1925—the siphoning of a dead or captured Silver Star agent's life force, presumably to the benefit of supreme leader Aleister Crowley or one of his select lieutenants. Most importantly, it left no one to interrogate.

Within a minute, the two soldiers were empty uniforms and a few random bone fragments. The lingering odor was like cured ham with a tinge of sulfur.

Razi stood agape. "Have you ever...?"

"Never," she answered. Maria Caruso had been in ancient temples, had encountered ley line nexus points and dimensional portals, had held mystical artifacts from the dawn of human existence in her hands, but she'd never watched a person dissolve before her eyes, drained of all living essence.

She suddenly remembered why they were there. "I don't know how to drive this," she confessed.

But Razi had already loaded the guns and was shrugging into the scout's uniform shirt. "I learned on a Douglas," he smiled. "Can you work the Maxim gun?"

She returned his toothy grin. "That I can do." Then she tucked her bobbed hair into a Silver Star field cap and prepared to swap out her khaki shirt for the remaining scout's uniform. "Don't peek."

Within minutes, they were speeding across the arid grassland of the valley, heading south, from whence the scouts had come. Caruso looked over the cramped sidecar and discovered four stick grenades secured to the right exterior panel, adding them to her mental inventory. They noted the active volcanoes that dotted the perimeter, contributing to the cloud layer above. They saw herds of grazing stegosaurs and giant sauropods, and flocks of primitive pterosaurs—possibly *Rhamphorhynchus*—circling overhead.

At the opposite edge of the valley rose another mountain ridge. They turned east and followed the rocks and hills along their dusty border. The greenhouse of trapped heat was oppressive. Finally they hit a small greenbelt and turned again, heading north. Caruso unfolded the map and saw where the Portuguese explorer had made note of the landmarks.

They crossed another self-contained island of jungle trees sprouting from the grassland before they arrived at a massive tree line.

Caruso nodded at the map. "This must be the opposite side of the jungle where we crashed."

Razi agreed. He took out the field glasses and scanned a three-hundred-sixty-degree perimeter. Caruso saw his double-take when he looked eastward, past the pockets of jungle in the open veldt.

"What is it?"

The young guide nodded in the direction of his discovery. "I think their base must be there, just shy of the ridge. I saw a truck headed south along the rocks. And a guard tower."

Maria Caruso sighed. This was a larger Silver Star presence than she was hoping for, by a factor of many degrees. They could bypass the camp, which would of course lead to an investigation into their missing motorcycle scouts, and an eventual direct conflict which her expedition of three couldn't hope to win. Or they could take stock of their assets and put them to the best possible use in taking the fight to the Silver Star. She gazed away in thought, then her face darkened with a mischievous grin. "I have an idea," she announced.

They bounced and rocked along a path clearly laid by the predators of the area, probably the very allosaurs which had given them chase the previous night. Suddenly Razi slowed the bike and Caruso raised her goggles to her cap. In the center of a slight indent at the base of a giant tree trunk lay a tidy nest full of reptilian eggs. The jigsaw-piece remains of a female human were scattered about the vicinity.

Leigh Taggart.

They hadn't stopped more than the few seconds it took to realize what they'd stumbled on before the thunder started, and the same pair of allosaurs appeared from the darkness of the jungle.

"There they are!" Caruso shouted excitedly. She fired a single shot from her Mauser, hitting the first predator in the chest. It had the desired effect—the allosaur shrieked, almost birdlike, and gave chase.

Razi didn't wait for instruction. He twisted hard on the throttle and the Douglas took off along the path, coiled reptilian leg muscles pounding the earth behind them.

They raced for almost three kilometers, as fast as Razi dared take the uneven ground and dense jungle to each side of the primitive road. Caruso fired the occasional gunshot over her shoulder to keep them interested.

When they burst from the tree line, they were within a short sprint to the Silver Star base camp. They knew the lookout in the guard tower would see them. This was the pivotal part of the hastily devised plan—one that could easily end in their destruction. Caruso hoped the guards would buy their disguise, and would choose to focus on the pair of rampaging dinosaurs behind them.

Which is precisely what happened.

As Razi steered the motorcycle through the open stockade hewn from native trees, another machine gun erupted in fury from the guard tower, tearing into the allosaurs, which in fact only made them angrier. As the bike sped past the tower, Caruso grabbed one of the stick grenades and tossed it casually under one of the struts.

The guard tower crumpled over with the resulting explosion, the sundered leg flipping end-over-end and impaling a troop truck. The allosaurs, undaunted, held course, and Razi took them on a tour of the Silver Star camp. Soldiers spilled from canvas tents, guns spitting fire and lead every which way. The mounted Maxim gun on the sidecar answered in kind. Then Caruso saw a stack of propane canisters and dropped another stick grenade at its base as they passed.

Razi throttled the bike to full speed, and Caruso smiled through clenched teeth. They were agents of chaos, bringing death to acolytes of darkness. As they passed scattering groups of men and women in paramilitary uniforms, she felt a righteous anger well up in her. Perhaps these were not the actual perpetrators of her father's murder, but they served the same madman, and wouldn't have hesitated to kill her if their positions were reversed. So neither did Caruso hesitate on her trigger. The mounted Maxim gun spat death into the masses. One of the officers saw through the deception and fired his C-96 pistol at the side-car and the bullet ricocheted away. A second shot grazed Caruso's right arm, drawing blood.

Then the Douglas was past the officer and the two allosaurs stormed through the crowd, flinging bodies left and right like rag dolls. One of the creatures diverted behind a row of canvas military tents, the other keeping pace behind the motorcycle.

The propane canisters exploded in an or-ange-tinged ball of heat and flame, igniting the nearby tents and several Silver Star agents, who flailed blindly and fell over one another in an almost-comical ballet of death. The al-losaur chasing the motorcycle burst through the flaming wreckage of tents and supplies and personnel. It too was on fire, and clearly not pleased at the fact.

Caruso nudged Razi and gestured ahead to a tent at the highest point in the camp. "Up there! The radio tent!" She dumped the Maus-er in the floor of the sidecar and grabbed the MP-18, wrenching back the bolt to cock it.

Razi sped forward and skidded to a halt outside the opening.

"Keep driving! Don't wait for me!" Caruso was out of the sidecar and rolling into the tent before the bike came to a complete stop. Razi looked over his shoulder just in time to pull out of the path of the rampaging, flaming dinosaur.

Caruso rolled to her feet inside the radio tent, prepared to fire the submachine gun into whomever stood in her way, but the structure was empty. She took a step toward the large, older model radio console, but realized they'd never be able to carry it out with them. Peering out through the open tent flap, she spied the fiery allosaur thundering in her direction.

Firing full-auto out the back of the tent, Caruso created a neat perforation that split in half as she dove through. The tent crumpled and ignited as the dinosaur stomped over it like a stampede of elephants. Radio parts and fragments of burning canvas were flung everywhere as the wounded allosaur tumbled down the opposite hill, snout over tail, clipping Caruso's leg and sending her rolling into the dust.

She lost her grip on the submachine gun, but grabbed it again as she scrambled away from the wounded dinosaur. A giant tail thrashed, almost flattening her. She scurried down the hill toward the monster's head, emptying the contents of the magazine into its burning body. The creature flicked its tail again, and Caruso hit the ground with a thud and lost her breath.

Razi pulled the motorcycle into the shadow of one of the infantry tents and began to open fire on every enemy agent who ran into his line of sight. But some of them were already starting to smolder and dissolve on their own. It was not uncommon for the masterminds of the Silver Star to preemptively pull the plug on a failed operation, gathering the life force of the agents home to be used another day. Razi shrugged to himself—at least it made his job easier.

Then he saw the row of tents begin to flip into the air and crumple to the ground as the second allosaur sprinted up the path toward him. Flinging his gun into the sidecar, Razi jumped back onto the saddle and departed at full throttle.

The allosaur pursued, but its feet and body had become entangled in tent rope. It staggered and limped along after the speeding motorcycle. Razi noticed, and slid to a stop. The dinosaur stomped closer. Razi stepped from the bike and released the third stick grenade from the sidecar, gripping the handle tightly.

The giant creature stepped within a half-dozen meters in front of Razi, lowered its head and bellowed its horrible, angry animal cry. Razi could have frozen in terror—most rational people would have. But at that moment he hurled the grenade into the open mouth of the beast, and ran diving to the ground with his arms flung across his face.

The grenade exploded, sending a macabre spray of reptile meat, bone and brain matter in an impressive radius. The allosaur, virtually headless, stood twitching for a good ten seconds before collapsing to the ground. Razi finally let himself look up, expecting an armed squad of Silver Star agents to take him prisoner, but none came.

Maria Caruso staggered to her feet, watching the first allosaur roast and crackle in a giant heap of flesh and tent canvas. A cloud of dust gradually revealed Razi astride the Douglas.

"You okay, *Maua*?" he asked.

"I think so," she replied, groaning as she slowly ambled toward the vehicle. "What about you?"

Razi gestured and made an "explosion" noise. "See any more agents?"

Caruso shouldered the MP-18 and leaned against the sidecar. "By the smell of things and lack of enemy gunfire, I'd say we're clear."

"What about the radio?"

"It was too big to carry, and now it's in pieces." Caruso ripped the Silver Star cap from her head and rubbed her aching temples. "But we might be able to salvage parts."

Razi nodded, removed the cap from his own head and tossed it onto the burning allosaur carcass, then pulled his driving goggles down over his eyes. "Where do we go now?"

Caruso took a deep breath and gazed up at the hot blanket of clouds that hung over the valley. "We should go back and check on Dr. Muir," she instructed. "But first, we've got some work to do."

⁂

They found the second troop truck abandoned outside the Silver Star camp, smoldering uniforms scattered inside and out. Caruso took the truck, and Razi stayed on the Douglas. They cleaned out the non-burned supplies from the camp, then retrieved the remains of their compatriots from the jungle clearing and the balloon crash site.

They made the central cavern encampment as the sun fell behind the western mountains. Muir was already in good spirits, but they improved even more when the two entered the cave, packs laden with more rations, weapons and radio components.

Caruso tasked Muir with taking stock of their haul, while she and Razi returned outside the lava tube to bury the remains of John Brand and Leigh Taggart.

Muir assembled a Sterno-Inferno camp stove and started water to boil, then busied himself with the packs. A good week's worth of rations, some tools, and radio parts. He looked them over for some time, until Caruso and Razi reappeared from outside, soaked in the sweat from their physical labor.

"What do you think?" she asked the German scientist.

"I think we cannot build a two-way radio with this," he answered. "Maybe a weak receiver."

Caruso's face furrowed into a mask of worry. "Then we should settle in, and figure out how to survive. It may take AEGIS a month or more to send help, and we should assume the Silver Star would not willingly give up the valley."

"We need to be ready to fight," added Razi.

Muir nodded. "The valley has fresh water, shelter and seemingly plenty of wild game. And the diamonds and other minerals... this will be a prize for AEGIS, if we can hold onto it."

Caruso nodded to the stockpile of weapons next to the cave wall. "At least we we'll have a fighting chance. And then there are these..." She picked up her canvas satchel and opened the flap, producing a fist-sized object and handing it to Muir.

He peered over his glasses and beheld a pale sand-colored dinosaur egg with light purple mottling. This couldn't be part of her plan.

Caruso looked at the floor. "You know my family back in Tuscany raised saddle horses..."

Muir looked at her in astonishment. She smiled, winking at him.

The egg began to twitch in his hand, a small crack beginning to form.

ABOUT THE AUTHORS

TRISH HEINRICH was one of the co-creators of the superhero comedy webseries *The Collectibles.* Her first novel, *Serpent's Sacrifice,* was published in 2017 and is the first book in an urban fantasy superhero series, "The Vigilantes". She currently lives in Washington State with her writer/editor/producer husband, and their two geeky children. You can connect with her at *www.trishheinrich.com* or on Facebook: *www.facebook.com/Trish.Heinrich.Author.*

R.L. PACE has had a widely diversified career ranging from circus ringmaster and radio broadcaster to financial planner and rocket fuel researcher. That rich background has served as a springboard and catalyst for his writing, which in addition to this contribution, includes the novels of the *Rising Son* trilogy, essays, short stories, and political commentary. He lives with his wife, two cats, and a dog in the Puget Sound area of Washington State.

DAVE CLELLAND took up writing at an early age, but only recently began putting serious words to pages. Airships and antique airplanes hold a special place in his heart, and he loves a good adventure, so he is excited to contribute to the *Airship Daedalus* canon. When not wordsmithing, he can be found counting fish and traveling the world.

COLIN FISK has been publishing stories and games for more than thirty years. Though best known as one of the writers and designers of the original *Cyberpunk* RPG, he's worked on more than ten published games as well as various supplements. When he's not writing or working at his day job in the technology world, he can be found speaking at conventions, watching movies, taking photos, or cooking with ingredients from his garden. Colin lives in Reno, Nevada, with his wife and fellow author, Margaret McGaffey Fisk, and their four cats.

DAN HEINRICH is the co-creator of the critically acclaimed web series *The Collectibles*. He has also served as story editor for the full length *Airship Daedalus* novels and "The Vigilantes" novel series from his wife, Trish Heinrich. Although he is a veteran screenwriter and voracious bookworm, this is his first published short story.

JAMES STUBBS is a longtime game designer and author of fiction under various pseudonyms. He served as line producer on the popular 1PG roleplaying games from Deep7 Press, authoring many supplements in addition to publishing original and licensed material under his own Heyoka Studios imprint. He also contributed to material to the *Airship Daedalus* roleplaying game. A die-hard pulp fan and aficionado, James lives in Darlington, South Carolina.

RON DUGDALE was born in Iowa and moved to Washington State at a young age. A former Navy man, Ron came back from the Gulf War and opened a "geek boutique" called The Gamut in Seattle. He was a founding partner of Deep7, and in recent years has moved on to other endeavors which includes his own photographic studio. He currently lives in Everett, Washington.

TODD DOWNING has written extensively for stage, screen and tabletop adventure games over the past thirty years. He is the author of the Airship Daedalus series, as well as *Calico Kids, The Parish,* and *Sakuru.* He is the original creator of the AEGISverse, having written the comics and radio dramas that everything in the setting is based on. You can connect with him at *todddowning.com,* and keep up to date with *Airship Daedalus* and the AEGISverse at *airshipdaedalus.com.*

Also available:

A Shield Against the Darkness

Assassins of the Lost Kingdom
(by E.J. Blaine)

The Golden City

Legend of the Savage Isle

The Arctic Menace

Raiders of the Red Storm